Found With You

A MOUNTAIN TOWN ROMANCE

WITH YOU SERIES
BOOK ONE

LYNSEY HARPER

Copy Editing: Ramona Mihai, bookeditoronline.com
Cover Design: Acacia at Ever After Cover Design, everaftercoverdesign.com

1st Edition 2025

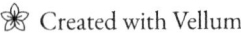 Created with Vellum

Content Warning

This is a book about love, but with that comes a whole lot of trauma, heartbreak, abuse and grief. Please look after yourself while reading, and feel free to step away if something is too hard to read. Looking after yourself is the most important thing.

I promise to make you laugh around the sad parts.

Note To The Reader

Thank you for picking up my book - there are not enough words to describe how grateful I feel to be sharing this story with you. As a first-time indie author, this is truly the stuff of dreams.

This journey has been all consuming, I have put my heart and soul into creating a world that I've come to love. I hope you love it too, but if you find that it's not your cup of tea, that's totally okay... I just ask that you don't reach out to me or tag me in your reviews.

On the flipside, even the tiniest sprinklings of positivity will make this all feel worthwhile. If you find yourself falling in love with the characters, story or setting, my DMs are always open – I'm a true praise girly at heart, what can I say?

Once again, thank you for choosing to read Found With You.

Lots of Love, Lynsey x

I had not intended to love him.
— Charlotte Brontë

To the girls waiting for someone who sees all of our broken parts and chooses to love us anyway.
This one is for us.

Prologue - Millie

Seven Years Earlier

In Memory of Richard Justin Adams.

I run a finger across the photograph on the front page of the order of service. He looks nothing like the man I knew. He's much younger and full of life, something I never had the chance to see in him.

I fold the pamphlet in half, sliding it behind the radio on the kitchen counter. I'm not sure why I'm keeping it. It'd be better placed in the trash, but even after everything he's done, I can't bring myself to throw away his memory so carelessly.

"So," Mom huffs out, "where do we go from here?" There's a humorous lilt to her voice, but I don't miss the quiet fatigue that's resting underneath it. She's tired, not just from the chaos of the past few weeks but from the entirety of the life we've lived.

I don't have the right words. I'm not sure there's ever a

right thing to say when it comes to death, but a situation like ours is even more awkward to navigate.

I load up our dinner plates with roast chicken, glancing over to the living area where Maddie lies curled up in a blanket on the sofa, absorbed in her favourite show. "Maybe we should wait until Mads is asleep before we get into it."

Mom nods her agreement, passing me the gravy bowl as she shifts her attention back to the stove.

There's three plates and three place settings, yet the empty chair to my right serves as a reminder that we were once four. I half expect to see his drunken figure stumbling through the door. He'd collapse at the table, popping a beer open with his teeth and we'd all sit a little straighter, waiting for the first stone to be thrown. Assuming our parts in the dance we know all too well.

I don't know what I expected this day to feel like. I thought it would all feel more final – that everything would be different, but we're doing the same things we've always done.

He's gone, but we're still here in the mess he's left behind.

I watch Maddie as she moves her fork around her plate, shifting food from one side to the other. It'd be hypocritical to ask her to finish her dinner while I sit here with a full plate and similarly missing appetite.

She's dressed in the same cow print pyjamas and matching pink dressing gown she's been wearing all day, a stark contrast to the dark formal wear Mom and I are still wearing. Yet she wears a sober look not so different from ours.

I want to believe that at eight years old this won't be something that sticks with her.

She's still so young.

But I know that's just wishful thinking, she'll hold onto the memories in the same way I do – a childhood like ours isn't something that comes with the luxury of forgetting.

No matter how hard my brain tries to push all of this to the back of my mind, I know that with every raised voice, shattered glass, or forced smile, my body will still remember.

I gulp down the thought and force a small forkful of potato across the threshold of my lips by way of example. Deafening silence forms the soundtrack to the rest of our meal.

"Time for bed, little darling." Mom pushes up from her chair, scraping our untouched dinners onto her own plate.

"Sweet dreams, Moo." Maddie's tiny body rests in mine as I pull her into a hug, kissing her forehead.

I wish I could hold her like this forever.

I let a single tear slip down my cheek, my thoughts heavy with grief for the life we were meant to have.

10.35 p.m.

Twelve hours ago, we stood around the grave site that is now the keeper of my father's broken bones and torn flesh. A handful of his colleagues donned suits to pay their respects to Dr Richard Adams, a man they only knew on the surface.

It felt strange to accept their muttered condolences – hand-shakes and acknowledgments that he was a good man.

Good man, my ass.

I'm not sure I can say I knew him for who he really was either, but he certainly wasn't as honourable as his public persona would make it seem. The bruises have faded, but the damage he's done on the inside remains testament to his true character.

Funerals are awful.

We're expected to do all of the right things – cry, remi-nisce, and mourn. We show up dressed in black and go through the motions of every exchange – the poems, the flowers, and lengthy silences. There's an allotted time for grieving and then once the day is over, we're supposed to go back to normality and move on with our lives.

Move on.

I'm not sure I can do that.

I'm not so much mourning the death of my father, as I am the loss of everything that could've been, twenty years of my life that I won't get back. There are so many greyed-out moments in my memory, ones I wish I could go back to and paint over with the right colours, or with the right kind of man.

Most people leave behind some sort of pain in their wake. Sometimes it's nothing but love, other times, it's wounds or scars. But then there are those who tear you apart so badly that you're left unrecognizable against the person you could've become without them.

That's what he's done to us. That's what he's left behind.

A soft hand on my shoulder pulls me back to the present

and I glance up to find Mom holding out a fresh pair of cotton pyjamas and a damp face cloth.

"What's going on in that head of yours, Mills?"

I wish I knew.

My damp cheeks and tight chest are a clear indicator that I've slipped into the corner of my head that I usually try to stay away from. I let my breathing settle as I slip into the soft bottoms and pull my hair up into a loose bun.

Mom busies herself in delicate movements as she begins cleaning the kitchen. She's still so good, even after the world dealt her a shit hand of cards.

She eases her sun-spotted skin into the soapy water, a gentle sigh of relief escaping her lips. The creases and purple shadows under her eyes are still there, but there's a subtle change in her. She appears lighter, as if a new lease on life has whispered to her, letting her know it's waiting in the wings whenever she is ready.

"I feel some kind of way, Mom." I sigh, grabbing a dish towel and picking up the bowl she just placed on the rack. "I don't know what to think or how to feel."

"I get that," she muses.

"I think I'm supposed to feel sadness, or loss, or regret." I puff out a short laugh. "But I don't know if I feel any of that – or not in the way I should."

Her eyes find me as she releases the plate she was holding into the sink with a splash. "Millie..." Her soft lips plant a kiss on my forehead as she pulls me into her arms. "Stop beating yourself up. You don't need to feel anything. Especially not guilt about how you think you *should* be feeling. None of this was ever going to be easy, and there's no guidebook to walk us through this."

"Mmm," is the only reply I can manage as my throat closes up and roils with emotion.

The silence sits between us for a while, as though neither of us can find the right words.

"You know," she pauses, waiting for my eyes to meet hers, "I watched my husband's coffin lower into the ground this morning, knowing everyone was looking at me with pity, wondering how I'd go on after this. But inside? I was saying my silent thank yous. Thinking, *'Thank God. Thank God that my girls now have a chance at the life I didn't give them with their father. Thank God fate finally made the decision to take him away when I couldn't find it in me to leave. Just... Thank God.'* And I'm feeling lots of things right now, but I don't feel guilty for thinking those thoughts, not one bit. So if you're going to feel anything in the wake of this, Millie, let it be hope or relief or the want for something better... because we didn't go through all of this for nothing. The worst of this life is behind us."

CHAPTER 1
Millie
PRESENT DAY

I don't know why they call them goodbyes, not one part of leaving behind the ones you love feels good. In fact, this particular instance happens to hurt like hell.

I bite back my tears as I take in the last moments here with Mom and Maddie. Braggan Valley is a mere twelve-hour bus ride away, and I'm only leaving for six months, but there's still a tightness around my lungs that I can't seem to shift.

This shouldn't be a big deal.

It's just one summer. Most people my age have already done this ten times over, backpacking across Europe for months or moving across the country to take high-flying corporate jobs – but I'm the one who always stayed. Always too scared to push myself beyond my comfort zone, paralyzed by the fear that something bad could happen if I switched up my routine. I've let those thoughts stand in my way for most of my twenties, convinced that any sort of change would hurt more than staying the same ever could.

But I'm ready now and, at the ripe old age of twenty-seven, I'm finally leaving Rowenbridge behind for the first time.

Mom gives me a tight nod, as if she's currently caught up in the same dance as I am, saving her sadness for the drive home. I've watched her hold in her tears enough times over the years to know she'll fall apart as soon as she pulls her car door closed.

Guilt clogs in my throat at the thought.

"You'll be back to them soon, love." A stout man with a thick white head of hair approaches and gestures towards my cases.

His light blue button-down, thick navy sweater, and matching pants suggest he's the one who'll be driving me across the province to Alberta tonight. I squint my eyes to read the embroidered stitching across his chest. *Gus – Westway Coaches.*

"You bet," I nod, trying to convince myself as much as anyone else. I push my luggage towards him, digging my booking documents out of the canvas tote slung over my shoulder.

"Off to Braggan Valley, are ya?" he asks, scribbling down my details on the baggage tag. I squint at his chicken scratchings, not able to identify a single legible word.

"That's the plan." I try on an upbeat tone for size, but it comes off shaky. I'll be having a word with my vocal chords later for not supporting my attempts to sound sure of myself.

"The Lodge, nonetheless." He throws my suitcases into the bed of the coach.

I wince.

There's an entire collection of skincare essentials inside and I hate to think what state those glass bottles will be in in twelve hours' time.

"You'll be grand there, love. I've been dropping off in that town since '85. I know Bill and Maura from way back. Hearts of gold. They really care about their people, even if you're just passing through."

His words are just the salve I need.

I catch his knowing smile as he heads back to the front of the bus. If he's been doing this route since before I was born, I'm sure this isn't his first rodeo with travelers who are homesick before they've even left.

"Coach leaves in ten," he calls back, glancing at his clipboard as he prepares to check in the next group. It feels as though time is slipping through my fingers at twice the speed tonight as I scramble to hold onto it.

I throw my arms around Mom, knowing if I open my mouth to utter a single word my tears will spill over. Maddie joins in on our tight squeeze, letting her unbothered-teenager facade slip for just a second.

It's just six months.

Yet somehow, with those six months laid out in front of me – and no idea of what is going to come, or who I'm going to be when it's done – it feels like an eternity.

"Get on the bus, Millie." Mom releases me and pats at her cheeks, erasing the tears she'd promised herself she wouldn't let escape just yet. "A love like this—" she gestures between the three of us, "—doesn't ever change, we'll be right here when you get back."

Shit, that'll do it.

I turn on my heels, lifting my right arm to wave goodbye

as an involuntary sob racks around my hollow chest. I've always been a crier. I cry when I'm happy, when I'm sad, when I'm angry, or when I'm tired, but the tears that are falling now seem to hurt a little bit more than usual.

Gus pats my shoulder, offering a shred of comfort as I climb the coach stairs and search for a vacant spot to crumble into.

Training my eyes on the seat in front of me, I avoid the worst of the goodbye. The coach pulls off from the bay, leaving Mom and Maddie behind in the only place we've ever known, as I go in search of the parts of myself I couldn't seem to find here.

The setting sun offers the perfect excuse to hide my puffy eyes behind oversized sunnies, staring out of the window at the city as the sky starts to paint day into night.

Booking a ticket for the night bus seemed like the perfect plan. I thought I'd be able to sleep on the drive and let my nerves float away into dreaming. But of course, I didn't take into account the multitude of variables that might be hell-bent on disrupting said plan. Like the rough polyester scratching at the side of my face as I twist and turn trying to find a comfortable spot, or the way the fixed armrest digs into my thighs as they splay across the seat.

Not only am I sad, but now I'm sad *and* uncomfortable, and the two together don't bode well for the sleepy escapism I so desperately crave.

I pull my journal from my bag, adjusting the reading light above me to face my seat. I'd like to say I planned this trip spontaneously, that I just quit my job, grabbed my things, and headed off on an unknown adventure at the drop of a hat. But I'm not that type of girl. I've been planning this for months, and yet – even with every detail mapped out, and plans A through D at my disposal – my anxiety is still tapping away like a woodpecker inside my skull.

In an attempt to unfurl the ball of chaos in my mind, I let words flow out through my pen as shaky handwriting fills the page in front of me.

> *Dear Universe,*
>
> *I think I might be losing my damn mind. Just left Mom & Mads behind in Rowenbridge – immeasurably painful, would not recommend to my worst enemy, let alone a friend. Desperately want this all to work out, but right now it feels like someone is dragging a knife right through my gut.*
>
> *This bus stinks, and my heart hurts.*
>
> *Please send me a sign that I'm doing the right thing.*
>
> *Millie x*

I'm not sure if I'm awoken by Gus's deep voice coming across the PA system, or the thick trail of drool rolling down my chin, but judging by the tight crick in my neck, I must have fallen asleep after all.

Not for long enough.

I have another eleven hours ahead of me in this hell-coach, and the thought depresses me. It took no more than five minutes to realize this would be anything but a luxurious journey, especially when every bump in the road sends a metallic screech through the luggage bins above me.

Every. Damn. Time.

I guess you get what you pay for, and I should have known that filtering my search by lowest price first would have had this exact outcome.

"Evening folks, Gus here," he booms across the speakers, far too jovial for this time of night. "We'll be stopping in at the services in the next ten minutes. Stop's an hour, so plenty of time to grab something to eat and stretch your legs."

We roll around a few bends before coming to an abrupt halt in front of a line of gas pumps. Across the parking lot, a horseshoe mall with a small collection of eateries beckons me.

My anxiety dissipates slightly to make way for my appetite.

I lose my sleepy amble, picking up the pace at the thought of a hot plate of food. I've never been all that enamored by gas station cuisine, but I'm too hungry to care at this point.

It seems like everyone else driving the highway tonight has decided to stop for food at the same time, and the shortest line-up still looks like it's going to suck. I let any hope of a hot meal crumble away, planting my feet in the queue for the bakery with an accompanying grumble.

I'm almost at the front of the line when a deafening crash fills the space around me, reverberating through my skull in a tinny echo. Time seems to slow as my heart rate picks up. It takes a second too long for my brain to catch up with what my eyes are telling it and, by the time the scene in front of me starts making sense, my lungs are already heaving.

A handful of smashed plates litter the ground to the right of me, butter chicken seeping into the grouted tiles as a red-faced woman tries to mop up the mess with a stack of napkins.

It's okay, Millie, you're safe.

My heart continues its off-beat tango in my chest as I try to convince myself to move my weighted feet towards the counter.

"What can I get for you, Miss?" A freckled teen hovers over the till expectantly. I take him in, inspecting his gingham shirt and cropped auburn hair. My mouth betrays me, lips tingling at the corners, as I try to find the words to pick something from the selection of sweet and savory bakes lining the glass display.

Another employee jostles past me, pushing a cleaning cart in the direction of the heaped chicken and ceramic on the floor. I watch as he slows and bends to pick up the larger chunks, before dirtying his spot-sweep with thick orange sludge.

"Miss," Freckles groans with frustration, tapping his pen on the counter. "There are people behind you... *waiting.*"

"Yes... Of course." I nod, taking in the world moving in

slow motion around me as I wrestle with my stilted breaths. "Can you just pick for me? Sweet... I'd like something sweet."

"Sure," he huffs, wasting no time throwing a muffin into a brown paper bag and gesturing to the price on the card machine, waving the next customer forward with an apologetic scowl while I pay.

Beady eyes seem to hone in on me from around the food-court, their gazes mocking as bodies move around me, bustling through my personal space like it doesn't exist.

I don't know if anyone's really paying any attention to me at all, or if my mind just went into overdrive the minute I falsely flicked the panic button. Regardless, I do know that I'm mere seconds from a grade A meltdown, and I need to get out of here, fast.

I tumble out into the fresh evening air, planting my shaky hands on the railing to steady myself.

Deep breaths, darling girl.

It's Mom's voice I hear, which is as comforting as it is embarrassing. I'm nearing my thirties, and I still can't seem to make it through the onset of a panic attack without the help of a better functioning adult to ground me.

I tear open the brown paper bag, managing to stomach one bite of a stale raisin muffin before throwing it into the nearest trash can and taking unsteady steps in the direction of the bus.

I knew I shouldn't have trusted Freckles with my bakery choice.

CHAPTER 2

Caden

I came home for all of the right reasons, but it's been one of those days where I wonder why I ever moved back to Braggan Valley in the first place. It was only supposed to be temporary, yet here I am still working at the lodge three years on.

Stagnant.

I'm a trained Wildland Firefighter. I shouldn't be stuck here, wasting my time doing shit like this. I should be over in BC, getting ready for another season out on the job, doing something that actually matters.

Fighting fires was my life for ten years. Throwing myself into danger gave me a certain thrill that I couldn't seem to find anywhere else. I loved the chaos of it all, and I knew I was doing a good thing. I knew that one day I might be the person that would save someone from having to lose the places or the people that they love. I knew how important that was, and it kept me going, day in, day out.

But I gave it all up to come back here.

I had no intention of ever slowing down or dipping out early, I had a good few years left in me before I thought I'd be hanging up my boots. But when I got the call about Uncle Bill's injury, I had no choice but to come home. Aunt Maura couldn't look after everything here on her own – she'd already faced so much loss and hurt in her lifetime, I couldn't let her lose the lodge too.

I hate to think how quickly this place would have run itself into the ground if I hadn't stepped in. I wasn't much of a numbers person back then, but I quickly learned how to stay on top of everything.

Orders, invoices, maintenance.

The lodge was the closest thing I had to a home, and I'd be damned if I let it fall to shit.

I did what had to be done, and now business is better than ever. We've got the funds to build five new cabins on the opposite side of the river, and people love coming back to Braggan Valley Lodge, year after year.

Yet, despite my best attempts to be a loving, doting nephew and save this place from ruin, Maura seems to have some sort of vendetta against me these days. When she's not handing me a list of jobs the length of the province, she's sending me out on activity trips with the most intolerable guests known to man. Usually, city slickers who've never stepped foot out of suburbia let alone into the backcountry, the ones who think they know everything or that the rules don't apply to them.

They're morons.

But unfortunately, they're the same morons who keep the paychecks hitting my bank account each month. And Maura loves to remind me of that.

Today's batch of certified annoyances were sent straight from the depths of hell – Bridezilla and her entourage of sixteen equally rotten bridesmaids.

They showed up at the front desk, brochures in hand, demanding to head out on a fishing trip. Of course, once we got out to the river, it quickly became apparent that they had no intention of catching anything other than a suntan. They took their obligatory photos in the gear, discarded their rods without mercy, and then spent the rest of the day lounging by the water – dressed in way less than might be considered acceptable for a family-friendly fishing spot.

I did contemplate getting in some fishing of my own, but that desire quickly died when I couldn't work out a way to drown out the frenzied screeches of the bridal mob. Not without drowning them, and that might have been considered a tad too far. Even for me.

Instead, I spent the afternoon in the sweltering heat of the lodge minibus, willing time to go faster so I could cart the demons back to their cabins and finally have some peace.

I thought the day would never end.

Leaning back into my deck chair, I let the cool fizz of my beer roll down my throat, hoping it'll do its job of taking away any lingering agitation from the day.

Doug nuzzles his head into my knee, as if he's picking up on my mood and doing whatever he can to soothe it.

People are a fucking nightmare. But dogs? Best thing on earth – they just seem to get it.

I'm not ashamed to say that he's the best friend I've ever had.

I found him abandoned on the side of the highway two years ago, limp and emaciated with thick mats throughout his coat, and raw, infected wounds around his nose. Every inch of life in his eyes had been stolen and replaced with the cold acceptance of his reality. As though he knew that he was loved once, but not anymore.

I bundled him up into my truck and took him to the nearest shelter, made sure the attendant had filled a bowl for him, and wrapped him in a blanket before I left. She promised to look after him and try to get those mats out of his coat once he was more at ease in his kennel.

I put my trust in her that the shelter would find him a good owner – someone who had the time to look after him, to give him the life he deserved.

But I quickly realized I couldn't rely on trust alone, not when I couldn't get his broken eyes out of my mind.

Within an hour, I was back in Aspen Ridge, bursting through the shelter doors and searching the kennels for him. They were closing up, but I begged the attendant to let me fill out the paperwork to take him home. I would have signed my life away, paid any amount of money to take him with me. I knew what it was like to be the one left behind, and I couldn't with good conscience do that to him.

It's been just us ever since, and I couldn't imagine life without him now.

One man, and his dog.

Caden and Doug.

I give him a scratch between his ears before pulling a bone-shaped treat from my pocket, extending my palm, and asking him for a paw.

I don't get the paw, but I give him the treat anyway.

I've heard you can't teach an old dog new tricks, and this

guy is old as hell. Training him to be less of a lazy grump is probably out of the question at this point.

Movement catches the corner of my eye. *Aunt Maura.* She strides across the bridge over the creek towards the main house, sashaying her hips in that tell-tale way that suggests she's up to something.

"Looks like our peace is about to be interrupted, Dougster," I sigh, necking the rest of my beer.

"Caden, darling." Maura slumps down in the chair to my left. "How was your day?"

I let the silence sit between us, my eyes closed in a fake slumber. This won't work, but it's worth a try.

"I know you're awake." She prods my shoulder. "You haven't been able to sleep before midnight since you were a toddler and I need your help."

Reluctantly, I open my eyes and turn to face her. "You sent me out with a gaggle of morons for the day. Is that not helpful enough?"

"They were lovely girls, darling. Most of them are single," she smirks. I should have known she was trying to play cupid again, finding me a wife seems to have become her passion project since I moved back to Alberta. "At your age, you should be thankful I'm sending you out with pretty girls for the day. Time is ticking for you to find a nice lady, put a ring on a finger."

"I'm thirty-three," I point out.

"Exactly," she jabs back.

I shake my head. I'm hardly at the age where I need to be stressing out about finding a wife. Hell, I'm not even sure I want one *ever*, let alone right now.

I'm quite happy getting my dick wet with no strings attached.

A wife sounds like something you might worry about losing, and I have no interest in growing attached to something that could easily be taken away in the blink of an eye.

"Looks like we're in for a good sunset tonight." I point towards the clouds as they move across the sky against the setting sun. Diverting the conversation away from the topic of my relationship status is easier than getting into a debate about why I'm better off alone.

I know she just longs for me to be happy, to have something like the love she found with Bill. But it's not in the cards for me, and even if it was, I wouldn't want it.

I'm not the relationship type, and she'd do well to accept that.

"What did you need help with?" I ask.

"Bill's stuck in Jasper and I need you to run into town tomorrow for a pick-up." She clasps her hands together. "We have a new hire joining us for the summer."

My eyes search over her face suspiciously, waiting for an explanation. We filled the team in April. If anything, we're over-hired until the guest numbers pick up for the summer and activity bookings start coming in.

"A new hire?"

"Yes." She pushes up from her chair and begins ambling back towards the lodge. "7.30 a.m. pick-up, at the town visitor centre. Don't be late, Caden!"

I count through the team on my fingers, we're a small operation and even though we hire double the staff in the summer, we still only need a handful for each department.

Maura is *definitely* up to something.

CHAPTER 3
Millie

It's not often my prayers are answered but today we seem to have stumbled across success. Bright light streams in through the bus window, alerting me to the fact that I've somehow managed to make it through the night without the screams of the luggage bins stealing my sanity.

Pawing at my eyes, I rub sleep away and begin to take in the views as we pick up speed along the highway. I pinch myself, nails clawing into my skin as I try to wake up from whatever dream I've been dropped into. I expect the scenery in front of me to blend back into the greys and browns of downtown Rowenbridge. I wait for it all to fall away, but it doesn't.

This place might actually be real. I've never seen anything so vivid, so full of life. It's like I'm watching it unfold in high definition.

Jagged granite mountains rise up in every direction, hints of snow still dusting their towering peaks. The valley floor is a mosaic of fir trees, aspens, and marshland grasses, with thick rivers and tributaries snaking through in romantic curves. I pull myself closer to the window, my nose squashed against the glass as I try to capture this moment for my memories.

I think I might be in heaven.

I was eager to make it through this journey as soon as possible, but now it's all moving too fast. I want to capture every second of it, slow it down and replay it over and over again. I pull my phone from my pocket, ignoring the 4% battery life remaining, and begin recording another video.

Nervous excitement pools in my stomach as the scenery continues to move past my window frame by frame.

This is going to be my life.

I feel soft warmth pooling in the corner of my eyes. I can't look away, as if I'm somehow tethered to the untouched beauty of the landscape revealing itself before me with each mile.

A quiet gasp escapes me as the forest gives way to a series of small lakes, reflecting the rising sun in muted tones of pink and orange. The engine kicks down a gear as the bus slows slightly, pulling my attention towards the road signs populating the grassy verge to the right.

Braggan Valley, 10km.

My heart thunders in my chest as the coach veers off the highway and makes tracks towards my new home.

We weave through a stretch of alpine forest, gaining slight elevation before arriving in the centre of Braggan Valley. The main street extends before us as we drive towards the far end of town, single-story shop fronts lining either side of the narrow road. There's coffee shops, and book-stores, and specialty confectioners, each boasting log framing and complimentary signage in muted tones. It feels like I've been transported into the midst of a Hallmark movie set.

"This is you, Millie." Gus shuts off the engine and hops down the steps, cranking open the luggage compartment to confirm that my suitcases have already been on an adventure of their own.

"Thanks, Gus." My voice shakes as my nerves make their way back to me.

"Bill usually picks up just outside the visitor centre." He guides me towards an empty bench. "He shouldn't be too long."

"Right... yes," I nod, following him as he drags my cases across the sidewalk. "I'll just... wait here."

"Don't look so terrified. You'll be alright, kiddo." He leaves me with his signature warm smile as he heads back to the coach.

I laugh. I'm not sure I can still class myself as a *kiddo* at twenty-seven. That being said, I don't feel that different from a lost seven-year-old right now. I'm alone in a new place, and I really have no idea what I'm doing. If somebody were to show up right now and ask if I needed a hand to hold as I cross this road into the next season of my life, I'd probably say yes.

I don't know if anyone ever really feels like they've mastered this whole adulting thing, but I sure as hell do not.

CHAPTER 4
Caden

I've made many mistakes in my life, but letting a dog sleep in my bed has to be up there with one of the worst. I make the meals, clean our space, and pay the bills. And yet here's Doug, living rent-free, sprawled out on my bed and leaving me less than a quarter of the mattress for my scheduled rest. He stirs, casting a stink-eye in my direction as if he knows I've been shit-talking him in my head.

"Move over, Doug." I pull at the comforter, trying to create enough space to lie down without my limbs hanging off the edge of the bed.

The sun is starting to peek under the blinds as the shrill cries of my morning alarm break the silence.

Fuck this.

If you were to tell me I'd been used as a human pinata in my sleep, I wouldn't be at all surprised.

My body aches.

I throw my phone back in the general direction of the

bedside table, pulling a pillow over my head and plunging the room into perfect darkness.

Less than five minutes later, I'm disturbed again.

A fist that I can only imagine belongs to Maura bangs against my door in rhythmic thumps. She's got to be fucking kidding. Rage fills my lungs as I throw on the first pair of jeans I can find and pull a hoodie over my head.

I crank the door open, ready to unleash a torrent of abuse on the five-foot woman in front of me, but her palm is already raised in front of my face as if she knew what was coming and has already decided she has no time for it today.

My jaw twitches as I cross my arms, leaning against the door jamb, waiting for her explanation. I'd love to know what inspired her to drag me out of bed with such aggression this morning.

"This better be worth it," I grunt.

"You're late, Caden!"

"For wh—" The words fall off as I remember agreeing to a morning pick-up in town – the new staff member that we definitely don't need. A colossal waste of my time for no good reason. "I thought we were fully hired," I grumble.

"Put this on!" She ignores me, throwing a fading black ball cap adorned with the Braggan Valley Lodge logo in my direction. "That way she'll know you work for us, and that you're not the serial killer that you look like right now."

She.

This girl better come with a background in the trades and arms fit for chopping logs, or she's no use to me.

"Maybe I am a serial killer." I pull the cap down over my hair, covering up my unwashed bed head, save for the few strands peeking out at the nape of my neck. "You checked in the basement recently?"

"Don't test me!" Maura scorns, pushing me out of the main house door towards my truck. "I don't condone speeding, but you better put your foot down, Caden. First impressions matter."

I couldn't give two shits about first impressions.

I skulk towards my truck with Maura's eyes like cattle prods in my back as I help Doug up into the cab.

My arm stretches out behind the passenger seat as I reverse. I've driven this highway since I was a teen, so I know I could make good on my promise to get there on time if I wanted to. But alas, I've zero interest in good timekeeping today. Dirt kicks up from the back wheels as I accelerate out onto the winding road towards town, before dropping down to a slow crawl once I'm out of Maura's view.

I'd enjoy this Saturday morning drive much more if I wasn't painfully aware of the gormless new recruit waiting for me at the end of it.

I say gormless with confidence.

I reckon a good fifty percent of the people who arrive in Braggan Valley for the summer leave before the season has even begun. Apparently, it comes as a shock to some people that the reality of living in the mountains is a little different from the aesthetic videos they've seen online.

One sighting of a coyote or bear scat, and they've packed their bags ready to head back to the city. It's a basic life out here, and most people aren't cut out for it. I've got no reason to believe this girl will be any different.

The rising sun is just kissing the tips of the mountains, a cool breeze meeting my hand as I hang my arm out of the driver's window. I crank the volume and let rich, velvety country music fill the cab as I adjust my jeans to sit more comfortably. The road curves through the forest, light pouring in through the blank spaces in the trees intermittently. Letting my thoughts wander, I gently pump the brakes, inviting my truck to slow down as I attempt to reclaim some alone time.

Despite my best efforts to turn this thirty-minute drive into an hour, the truck has eaten up the best part of the journey and the lodge is long gone from my rear-view mirror.

I can probably get away with stalling the inevitable a little longer with a few spins round main street. Newbie has no idea what my truck looks like, and I doubt she has any other options for transportation. There's only one taxi rank in Braggan Valley, and Dusty is probably still half cut from last night.

If she wants to make it to the lodge today, she can wait.

I stop off at The Coffee Pot, picking up a breakfast bagel before heading a block over to Frank's hardware store where I'm bound to find him behind the counter. Frank can yap, and a yapper is exactly what I need if I want to waste some time right now.

The door jingles as I step into the open space of the hardware store reception area. Yes, the store has a reception. I'm pretty sure it's Frank's way of making sure he gets in his daily quota of small talk.

Could never be me.

"Caden, my boy!" Frank coughs, moving out from behind his till and patting me on the back with a beefy paw. "What's brought you into town?"

My eyes land on the leftover breakfast decorating his rusty grey beard. *Nice.*

"Maura has me on a staff pickup." I throw a few lengths of rope into a basket as I continue to peruse the shelves for things I don't need. "Thought I'd grab some supplies for the lodge while I'm here."

"Right you are." He hooks his thumbs inside his overall straps and rests on a stool, his round belly folding over the denim. "Some spring we had this year. I've not seen the lake melt that early since the nineties."

"True. I'm holding out for some rain."

The last thing we need is an early wildfire season in the Rockies.

"Wouldn't do us no harm," he agrees. "I'll get the blame if my wife's grass ain't the greenest in the Valley."

"She'll murder you," I add.

Frank seems to shudder.

There's no denying that Stella wears the trousers in that relationship, and there's a very real chance that he'll come to harm if her garden isn't up to scratch by June.

I let him ramble about the weather, the trials of the junior hockey team over in Aspen Ridge, and the recipe Stella's planning on using for his birthday pie. I agree that the addition of mayonnaise to the pie crust seems strange, but that it most definitely could be the magic ingredient.

I've never met a pastry from Stella's bakery that I didn't like.

My phone vibrates in my pocket. It's no surprise that it's Maura calling, checking up on my whereabouts – no doubt gunning to give me an earful for being late.

"Good morning, Caden's Taxi Service," I answer, sliding

my finger across the screen to accept the call as I settle up for the rope and curtain hooks. "How may I help you?"

"Caden Thompson!"

Oh, she's livid.

"Where are you?!" she roars. "You should have been at the visitor centre twenty minutes ago. Stella just called from the bakery, the poor girl is stranded."

Stranded seems like a stretch. She's in one of the most beautiful mountain towns in the world, right next to a bakery. Could be a hell of a lot worse.

"I think I'm lost," I say, trying to keep my voice steady as I goad Maura, playing with fire. "Can you remind me how to get to the bakery?"

Frank raises his brow across the counter, his expression somewhere between concern and amusement.

"The only thing you'll be losing is your job, Caden!" Her voice seems to go up an octave with each sentence. "Stop with... whatever this is... and get your ass to that parking lot. Now!"

"Yes, Ma'am," I reply, hanging up and sliding my phone into my pocket. "Gotta go, Frank."

He shakes his head, waving me off as I head out the door and back to my truck.

CHAPTER 5
Millie

Motherfucker.

It died on me. I tap repeatedly at the blank phone screen, hoping it'll miraculously burst into colour and present me with the time. Pacing back and forth across the sidewalk, I let out a pathetic whimper that feels dangerously close to the start of a temper tantrum.

The bakery on the corner seems to be the only store with any signs of life, the rest lie dormant, waiting for their respective humans to arrive for the day. Apparently, things are a little more lax in the mountains. Businesses tend to open later in the morning and being on time is more of a guideline than a rule. *Mountain Time*, they call it. Which sounds about right, given that my driver is nowhere to be seen, and I'm currently stranded in an empty parking lot.

I contemplate leaving my luggage against the bike shelter by the visitor centre, but quickly think better of it. Abandoning all of my worldly possessions in a strange place I've never been before hardly seems like one of my smarter choices. I did read that the crime rate is much lower out here, but I'm not going to take my chances. I humph, dragging each of my suitcases to the stoop of the bakery door, one at a time. My forehead is beaded with thick sweat by the time I'm done.

There's still a chill to the wind despite it being early May. Stepping out of the cold into the bakery feels like a warm hug, goosebumps rise and fall across my arms as my body adjusts to the temperature inside.

I packed a jacket, of course. I just packed it in the very same suitcase that I'm refusing to open until I reach my final destination, for fear of a clothes explosion. I exerted myself so thoroughly trying to zip it shut that I wouldn't dare risk a second try. For now, I'm stuck with the same sweatpants and cropped half-zip I wore on the journey over, and I'm not quite sure they're a match for this weather.

I drool as I take in the selection of freshly baked pastries and scones laid out in front of me, hoping one of them might make me feel a little better. Nothing soothes the anxious soul quite like a sweet treat, and there's plenty to choose from. It's quite the spread for a town that is apparently void of life this morning.

"Morning!" The words startle me, coming from somewhere beyond the counter.

I push up on my tiptoes looking for their owner. "Hello?"

"Sorry, honey." An older woman rises, dusting her hands on a flour-covered apron. "I was just finishing up the bun orders for today. We keep them down below so they're easy to grab."

I smile and nod. I'm not sure why this information has

anything to do with me, but the last thing I want is to appear rude.

"New in town, or passing through?" she quizzes, shifting her attention to decanting a tray of rocky-road slices into a glass serving dome.

"New," I confirm, then realize I should probably offer something more. If I'm going to live in a close-knit town like this, I'll need to get used to participating in all of the small talk that goes with it – the thought fills me with dread. "I'm going to be working at Braggan Valley Lodge, I'm just waiting for someone to pick me up."

She frowns, running her fingers through her short white curls. "Bill's never late for the bus drop-off." She glances at the clock with confusion. "Wait here... I'll give Maura a call."

I guess it's true what they say about small towns – everyone really does know everyone.

I listen to the snippets of one half of the conversation unfolding from the back.

"... yes, I was shocked when she said she was waiting... of course, I'll let her know... not to worry... Frank and I will be up to the lodge when he's back down... rhubarb pie... give Doug a big kiss for me, bye for now."

Pushing through the beaded curtain with another baking tray filled with hot croissants, the woman returns. "On route," she nods. "Now, let's get you some treats for the road. I'm Stella, by the way."

"Millie," I say, returning a tired smile.

"Welcome to the Valley, Millie." Her voice is raspy, but soft. "You ever need anything while you're in town just let us know. My husband, Frank, has the hardware store a few blocks over. We know everyone around here, and everyone knows something about something. You're never alone out here. Sure, we're rural, but it's a close-knit community, and we help each other out."

"That's good to know," I reply politely, knowing full well that I hate to ask for help and will likely never take her up on that offer.

"I know that look," she laughs. "You'll have to get used to accepting the kindness of strangers. This isn't the big city anymore."

"Oh, I..." I didn't know I was that easy to read. "Well, yes. I guess I will."

By the time I step back out into the morning, I've been loaded up with so many pastries I feel like a pack mule, one arm laden with raspberry donuts and cinnamon bear-claws for the drive, the other balancing a fresh rhubarb pie for Maura & Bill.

It all smells *so* good.

I eyeball the drop from the bakery to the sidewalk, taking a calculated step down to ground level. Not one of these pastries deserves to spend its day face down on the pavement. I take it slow, not breathing until both of my feet are firmly planted on the ground again.

Phew.

I'm so caught up in my cake-protecting mission that I completely fail to notice the truck that pulled up outside the bakery, or the imposing man leaning against it, until I'm right upon them.

Dark blue eyes rake over me, but not in a way that anyone could find flattering. It's like he's sizing me up, taking inventory of each of my flaws. I can't pinpoint the exact energy he's giving off, but it's definitely in the same family as disgust.

I'm sizing him up too, but in a more literal sense. I've never been good at judging height, but he's *tall...* I close one eye, trying to work out how many footlong subs I could stack up alongside his body from head to toe. At least six, and definitely a few more inches on top of that.

A faded Braggan Valley Lodge logo is etched into his cap. I'm sure Maura said Bill was her husband. I'd imagined an older man, but this guy can't be much older than me. Aside from the murderous look on his face, he's objectively attractive. Strong features, a seriously chiselled jaw with just the right amount of stubble, and thighs that fill out his denim jeans perfectly.

Get it, Maura.

I gulp down the attraction, realizing now is not an appropriate time for my ovaries to kick into action.

Plus, this is the *husband* of my new boss.

I scuttle towards the closest bench, carefully setting down my collection of pastries. With my arms now free to introduce myself, I take a deep breath and turn back towards him.

I expect him to speak first, to introduce himself or ask for my name – but he gives me nothing.

Nothing.

"Hi, I'm Millie Adams." I extend my hand, trying to break up the awkwardness and reroute my first impression. "You must be Bill?"

His nostrils flare as he makes strides towards my luggage. Taking a suitcase in each hand, he throws them into the bed of the truck as if they weigh nothing at all.

Closing the tailgate, he looks down at my hand with

disdain. My arm is stupidly still extended in his direction, words lost on my tongue as he glares at me.

Embarrassment crawls up my skin as his next words prompt hot tears to prick at the back of my eyes.

"Get in the fucking truck, Princess."

CHAPTER 6
Caden

I know I'm being an asshole, but I can't help it.

The minute I saw her walk out of Stella's bakery, it all made sense. Maura didn't give me any information about this new girl, because she knew I'd connect the dots and refuse to come.

If I'd known, I would have called up *Westway Coaches* myself and ordered them to take her right back to whichever god-forsaken city she came from.

But she's here and she's in *my* truck.

Sitting less than two feet from me, staring out the window with her body angled away, no doubt holding back tears from my bitter introduction.

It's abundantly clear that sending me to pick up *Millie Adams* has nothing to do with Bill being out of town, and everything to do with Maura's sick plan to get me hitched before my 35th birthday.

If I'd given her a brief for finding someone who's just my type, she would have nailed it with this one. But I didn't give her a brief, because my love life, or lack thereof, is none of her fucking business.

This meddling has to stop.

I screech out of the parking lot, checking my gas tank gauge as I merge onto the highway. I've got close to a full tank and should be able to cut ten minutes off the drive with a little bit of foot-down.

Silence fills the cab.

I glance in the rear-view mirror. Doug is sprawled across the back seat, his mouth wide open, catching flies without a single sound to break the tension. It's interesting that he snores like a freight train through the night when I'm trying to sleep, but can't help me out with a few grunts right about now.

I shouldn't look at her, but my mind is begging me to steal a glance. She showed up in beige sweatpants and a matching cropped fleece, scoring zero points for common fucking sense. Those bottoms aren't going to last five seconds in the murky slush that's currently forming a moat around the staff house.

I didn't miss the fact that she didn't seem to have a jacket either.

In fact, I didn't miss a thing about her as she walked towards me, protecting those cakes like her life depended on it.

My cock twitches in my jeans as I think about the contrast between her tiny waist and the abundant curves of her chest and hips.

And those freckles across the bridge of her nose.

Fuck me.

This is going to be one long ass summer if she defeats the

odds and ends up sticking around.

I can't let that happen.

I need to make sure she's running back to the city before she even has time to unpack.

I've still got a first-class view of the back of her head. She seems to have twisted even further towards the open passenger window, her cheek resting on the sill as her wavy brown hair flows with the wind.

I push the dial to turn the radio on, cranking the volume up so high that country music spills out onto the highway and into the trees. Millie bats her hand at the dial before the first song even has the chance to make it through the intro. The truck is plunged back into a thick smog of silence.

"What do you think you're doing?" I demand.

She unfurls from her pretzel position, turning to face me dead on. "Turning the music off, clearly."

"For what reason, exactly?" I blurt. This girl has got some nerve.

"Because I don't want to listen to it," she says, as if that's reason enough.

"And?" I seethe. "This is *my* truck, I make the rules. You don't like it? You can walk the rest of the way."

There's a click as I flick the button on my arm rest, unlocking the doors and giving her full permission to get the fuck out.

She opens her mouth, closing it again before she lets any words fall out.

Just as well.

I can't imagine she would have anything to say that would make me want to do anything other than kick her out on the side of the road.

I turn the music back on.

I'm in a race with the clock on the dash. If I can make it to the crossing in the next ten minutes, we'll miss the trains. Being stuck on this side of the railway while the Monday morning freights make their way through the valley is not on my agenda for today.

Especially not while I'm confined here with *her*.

The music cuts again and fury gurgles in my gut. I turn to face her, but the anger dies on my tongue as I clock the tears pooling in the corners of her eyes.

"You know," she gasps, as though sadness has stolen the air from her lungs. "You were kind of an asshole back there, and you're *definitely* being an asshole now."

I pin my eyes on the road in front of me. I don't like seeing people cry, but I refuse to let her emotions run roughshod over me.

I need to stay focused.

Need to find a way to make her leave.

"I *am* an asshole, honey," I grunt. It's not the closest thing to the truth, but I'll do whatever I can to make her believe it.

"I can see that," she blurts. "I... I've come all this way, and all I want to do is start over and find a place where people aren't total shitheads. I'm terrified, and anxious, and out of my bloody mind hoping this works out. And you can't even find it within yourself to show me the tiniest bit of kindness. You couldn't even tell me your name before you started barking at me and trying to burst my eardrums with your country trash. So yeah, I think asshole is about right."

Country trash?!

I wasn't that fond of her to start with, but she's just

made it a whole lot worse with that statement.

I've only just met this girl yet, somehow, we've already fallen into quarreling territory with the startling ease of ready-made enemies.

Releasing whatever dam she's managed to keep up for the first part of the journey, she folds into painful sobs across from me, hyperventilating as she tries to catch her breath.

For fuck's sake.

I reach over her towards the glove compartment, releasing it with a click and dropping a box of tissues onto the dash.

It's not out of kindness. I just want to make sure she's got the means to keep her city germs to herself.

Doug stirs, clambering over the central console and straight into her lap, forgetting any bro code I've tried to instill in him.

Wiping at her eyes with the corner of her fleece, she looks down at the traitor resting on her legs, letting out stilted breaths as she strokes a palm over his greying coat.

"Hi, baby," she murmurs softly in between whimpers, ruffling his fur as he laps up her attention. "Aren't you the most handsome pup?"

Interesting.

It seems like she does have some reserved softness left within her, just not for me.

My jaw ticks as I stew over her outburst, wincing as I remember the quiet hurt resting in between each word. I don't want her here, but I'm not sure I can stand to see her crying like that again either.

"Caden," I say, swallowing my pride and offering her my name as a temporary truce. "I'm Caden. And that's Doug."

CHAPTER 7
Millie

Caden.

He gave me his name. Which is about as much of a peace offering or apology as I think I'm going to get today.

He's not Bill, and *Thank God*. I couldn't imagine a woman as lovely as Maura being married to such a grumpy bastard. I can't wait to meet her in person, she'll no doubt be a tonic after enduring this man for a seven-hundred-hour drive.

I stumbled across the Lodge – and, in turn, Maura – by chance last fall. Up until that point, my life had always been meticulously planned out. It made me feel in control in some kind of way. I had always felt like I was keeping myself safe from all of the things that could go wrong, all of the people who could throw my world off its axis if I let them in. But moving into my late twenties, I'd started to feel a yearning for more. The walls that had once kept me safe were now starting to feel more like a cage, and I was looking for a sign to take me out of my comfort zone and away from the life I'd always known in Rowenbridge.

That sign came to me in the form of a discarded brochure on the bench next to me at the park one frosty afternoon. *Discover Alberta.* I flicked through the pages, paying little attention to the ostentatious golf courses, Nordic spas, and $1000 per night hotels. But I was instantly pulled in by a quaint lodge nestled in the Canadian Rockies surrounded by trees, spread across page seventeen. *Braggan Valley Lodge.*

Between all of the greens and blues of the advertisement it would've been easy to miss the tiny white text box in the right-hand corner, but my eyes were drawn there, and I instantly knew that this was my sign. *Now Hiring for Summer!* I pocketed the brochure and, after a few too many margaritas for courage, sent off my resume alongside a pleading cover letter.

A few days later, I sat in front of a computer screen, sweat glistening across my forehead as I waited for the interview that could uproot my life. Nervous, and feeling like I should just hang up before she had the chance to reject me.

There's something weird about sitting in the same box room that's seen all of your one-night stands and failed situationships, with a dress shirt on top and pyjamas on bottom, hoping to appeal to a potential employer. I wasn't entirely sure that the four walls around me weren't cursed, just waiting to witness another 'it's not you, it's me' scenario, but this one employment related.

When it was time for the call, an older woman with blonde-grey waves falling loosely from a scrunchie on the top of her head popped up on the screen. There was something about her that instantly put my nerves at ease. I let my muscles soften and it didn't take long for me to share a bit of myself, to let her see some of the parts that I so often keep hidden from the world. Maura seemed like the closest thing to warm honey in human form, a soft-spoken accent with hints of Irish and Canadian mixed together. We chatted at length about why I wanted to get away from Rowenbridge, about the lodge, and the ins and outs of working the summer season in Braggan Valley. And without paying any attention to the time, a call I had expected to last fifteen minutes stretched on for over an hour.

I'd already scoured the internet for more information on the lodge and its surroundings in the early hours, so I didn't need much convincing of its ever-changing beauty. But as she told me of the landscape, with its towering fir trees, hidden waterfalls, and pristine lakes, largely unchanged by mankind, I was drawn to the magic of this place.

It felt like it was meant for me.

I needed something to run towards, the chance to start over, and Braggan Valley Lodge felt like that place.

The only upside of being subjected to this man and his pig-shit mood is the lump of fur currently curled up at my hips. There's something soothing about the gentle rise and fall of his sleepy breaths. Mom would be happy to know I've found something to keep me calm.

I should text her to let her know I've *almost* arrived safely.

Using up all of my phone battery to take photos and videos, without even thinking about the potential of an emergency, wasn't my smartest move.

This feels like an emergency.

I'm stuck here with a clear sociopath, who could be kidnapping me and driving me to a cabin in the woods for all I know.

"*Fuck*!" His thick voice pulls me from my spiraling thoughts.

We've just veered off the highway and run into a line of slow moving cars ahead. A white gate complete with flashing red lights falls across the road, signalling the arrival of a train.

"Rail crossing," Caden grunts, pointing towards the railway. "We'll be stuck here for at least ten minutes while the freights pass."

Great.

Stella must have a sixth sense, because now I'm certainly hungry and in need of an edible distraction to get me through this wait. I rest a paper bag on Doug's sleeping body, pulling out a braided pastry covered in sticky cream cheese topping.

My desire to impress my driver evaporated somewhere between the bakery and now, which is a blessing because there is no attractive way to eat this. I tear off a hunk with my teeth, flaky pastry falling all around me.

Caden shakes his head in my periphery, resting his forehead on his palm as he taps his opposite hand against the steering wheel.

I make a concerted effort to make more of a mess with my next bite.

He reaches across the central console, grabbing the paper bag.

"Excuse me," I protest, mouth filled with pastry. "Those are *mine.*"

He doesn't seem to register my words as he dives a large hand inside the bag, claiming the cinnamon bear-claw I'd earmarked for later.

"Didn't they teach you to share in kindergarten?" He scoffs as he shoves half of the bear-claw into his mouth.

I narrow my eyes into slits, wondering if I'd manage to drive this big ass truck back to the lodge by myself if he somehow came to harm.

It's a stick shift, and I've only ever driven automatic, but how hard could it be?

The first train trundles over the rails ahead of us, a loud horn sounding every few seconds. Caden cranks his chair back until it's almost horizontal, letting his thick thighs spread out into a V as he reclines.

Now I'm the one that can't stand the silence.

I turn the radio back on, searching through the channels for something other than country music. To set the record straight, I have nothing against country, and I'll repent later for calling it trash. I just do not need to be listening to anything that might make me think about this man in *those* jeans.

He might be an asshole, but he's an asshole built like a lumberjack.

I settle on classical music, satisfied that it'll help me drift into a fantasy realm far away from this truck and its driver.

"No," Caden barks, sitting upright and starting another tug-of-war over our music choices.

"Yes," I retort, moving my hand back towards the dial, but before I have the chance to flood the cab with more Stravinsky, his calloused fingers wrap tightly around my wrist.

Deep blue eyes pin me in place.

"Country FM, or nothing."

"Uch, whatever," I huff, crossing my arms over my chest as he fidgets with the radio controls. He's firmly back on his side of the truck, but reminders of his hot touch still linger around my wrist like a handcuff.

Somehow, this short car journey has already felt longer than the twelve hours it took to make it across the province on the bus.

"Why Braggan Valley?" Caden's accusatory tone adds to the tension between us.

"I needed a fresh start," I answer, even though I don't owe him an explanation. "I've been in the city all my life. I wanted to try something different."

He rolls his eyes, pushing the truck back into gear as the gate lifts ahead of us. "What are you running from?"

"Excuse me?"

"Anybody who says they need a fresh start is running from something," he points out. "Nobody just packs up their shit and leaves their life behind without good reason."

I don't reply.

He's right, but I won't give him the satisfaction of knowing he's worked me out right off the bat.

CHAPTER 8
Millie

I make a concerted effort to memorize my steps as I trail behind Caden, trying to keep up but failing miserably. He's taking two stairs at a time, a suitcase in each hand, without so much as breaking a sweat. I think I might have to call in the emergency services if my heart doesn't stop walloping against the walls of my chest. If I'd known I was going to be on the third floor of the staff house, I might have rethought my plans and whether this move was really worth it.

This house feels like it was built in the stone ages, the sixties at best. One glance at the crumbling paint on the walls has any hope of a functioning elevator disintegrating.

"Room 14." Caden drops a key into my palm. "Maura will be at the lodge reception when you're ready." He wastes no time leaving, jogging down the stairs as if he can't get away from me fast enough.

The feeling is mutual.

I knock softly three times before turning my key in the

lock and pushing the door open. I expect a musty smell similar to the hallway, but instead I'm met with the soft scent of amber incense and moss. One half of the room is decorated in a vibrant display of oranges and yellows, with throw blankets and Aztec pillows scattered across the bed. Macrame plant hangers line the walls, while a collection of photographs in colourful hand-made frames occupy the left side of the dresser. The other side of the room is completely bare, as though an invisible line separates the two halves. Save for a single beat-up pillow and a rolled-up twin duvet at the bottom of the bed, the space is a blank canvas.

I guess this is me.

I haul my suitcases across the faded carpet and into the dorm, wondering how on earth Caden managed to carry one of these with such ease, let alone two.

I'm exhausted after the journey, weighed down by lack of sleep and nervous anticipation of what's to come. I'm going to have to repeat days like this several times over in the coming weeks. Meeting new people, hoping to make a good impression, and then quickly realizing that I don't fit in with them either.

The thought clogs in my gut like tar.

I step over the invisible border into my roommate's half. It's easy to pick her out from the photos, she's the only one in every picture. Braided blonde hair, tall and thin, with an affinity for patterned sweaters. I run my finger along one of the frames. Her arms are wrapped around a sequoia tree, one leg cocked up behind her as she looks up at the sun filtering through the branches above. Laughter dances across her face.

She looks so free.

A pang of jealousy moves through my veins like barbed wire.

I'd imagined how this moment would feel a hundred times over. I thought I'd arrive and feel like a weight had been lifted from my shoulders, that the hardest part would be leaving. I'd get here and just know that this was the right decision. That I'd instantly feel at home and like this is the place for me. Instead, I'm alone in the dull half of a shared room, with no one to talk to and no idea where to go from here.

The one person I've met today seems to hate me already, and instead of showing my softer side and winning him over, I instantly put up my walls. My bratty attitude and outbursts gave him the perfect evidence to back up whatever story he's told himself about me.

I really thought this would be easier, but the reality is already overwhelming me.

Disappointment pulls at my cheeks, a frown developing where I thought there would only be smile lines from now on as I slump down on my bed.

The frame creaks beneath my weight, reminding me that any luxuries I had at home are now gone.

I'd gone shopping for new bed linen the day after Maura offered me the job. She explained the staff house at length, highlighting the shared kitchen on the main floor and the reality of sharing a single shower block with fourteen other girls. None of that had bothered me, but I'd felt myself recoil when she noted that I'd have to sleep in a twin bed.

Leaving behind my queen-sized bed was up there with the hardest of my goodbyes.

The only twin sheets I could find in the apartment were a relic from Maddie's childhood, and I wasn't going to be the twenty-seven-year-old sleeping under a glittery princess duvet in the staff quarters. So I splurged on gingham linen sheets in pastel green, paired with a hand-knitted cream blanket and matching silk pillowcases.

That Millie was hopeful, but this one just feels utterly defeated.

I don't bother to unpack the bedding from my suitcase, instead pulling the bare, pilled duvet up over my shoulders and closing my eyes tightly to hold in all of the emotions begging for release.

"Hey... hey." The words are distant, dripping in an accent I can't quite make out. I feel two hands moving my shoulders back and forth. "Hey... Wake up."

Suddenly aware of the person standing over me, I sit bolt upright. I throw her arms away from me and scamper back against the wall, gasping as my lungs grapple for air.

It's the girl from the dresser photographs – my roommate.

"Sorry," she mouths apologetically, taking a step back with both hands raised. "You were writhing like some kind of wild animal. I thought I'd do you a favour and wake you up from whatever nightmare you were stuck in."

I nod, trying to re-calibrate my mind and bring myself

back to the present. I have no idea what time it is, or how long I've been asleep for. Rifling through my tote bag, I pull out my phone and plug the charger into an outlet.

Her eyes rake over me, filled with something in between sympathy and curiosity. "Let me get you some water."

A drawn-out croak leaves the door's hinges as she yanks it open and steps out into the hallway.

I'm drenched in cold sweat, a stark contrast to the wave of searing embarrassment that washes over me as I realize I've butchered yet another first impression here in Braggan Valley.

My new roommate is probably down there in the kitchen, wondering what the hell she did to deserve Little Miss Unhinged as her summer roommate.

I drag a wet wipe over my face in an attempt to soothe my flushed skin, removing remnants of cracked foundation and smeared mascara from my cheeks.

The girl returns, passing me a pint glass filled with water and dropping a granola bar on to the bed next to me. She falls back into her own bed, letting out a deep sigh coated in fatigue.

"It's nice to finally meet you, Millie," she says, taking a bite out of a banana before continuing with a full mouth, "I'm Elodie."

"Hi," I murmur back, raising my hand in a half-hearted wave. She knew my name already. This small-town thing really is going to take some getting used to.

I take her in as she leans back against her headboard. She's wearing high-waisted black dress pants with a polo shirt tucked in at the waist, the Braggan Valley Lodge logo embroidered into the chest. She looks just like the pictures, with thick blonde hair falling down her back in a Dutch braid and spirited green eyes that catch the light differently at each angle. Even dressed in her work uniform, and clearly worn-out from the day, she still seems abundantly free and full of life.

We exist in companionable silence as I slowly begin unpacking shirts from my suitcase and placing them into drawers while she lounges with her arm flopped over her eyes, blocking out the afternoon sun.

I'm running the last five minutes over in my head, trying to erase all of my awkward moments and replace them with something objectively cooler when her voice breaks through the quiet.

"Shall we just cut the bullshit?" she asks, rolling on to her side to face me. She must catch the confusion on my face. "You know, instead of the boring getting to know you questions, and trying to work out if we're coming on too strong, or giving the right impression. Can we just fast forward to the part where we're friends and tell each other about all the dumb shit that goes on around here?"

Laughter bubbles up through me. I drink in her kindness, it's exactly what I need after my rough start this morning. Somehow, she seems unphased by the generous dose of crazy she witnessed when she woke me up.

"I'll drink to that," I affirm, taking a gulp of my water in the absence of vodka and extending my pinky in her direction. Wrapping her finger around mine, she shakes on our promise.

"I've gotta head back." Elodie jumps up from the bed,

smoothing her hands down her polo and checking herself over in the mirror. "See you later, Mills."

She blows herself a kiss and then darts out into the hallway before I have a chance to offer my own goodbye.

Mills.

Warmth fills my cheeks at the light relief of hearing my nickname on the lips of someone new.

CHAPTER 9
Caden

Maura stabs at a slice of pork.

"You're more stupid than you look if you think I'd waste my labour budget *just* to bring in a woman to raise your heart rate," she spits, pointing her fork, which looks suspiciously like a weapon, in my direction.

"That's what paying guests are for," Bill chortles by her side.

He's quickly met with a swat to the arm. Something has pissed Maura off today, that much is clear.

"Why did you hire her then?" I counter. "It's not like we're short on staff for the season."

Bill shakes his head next to me, throwing a slab of meat under the table for Doug. He's already learned a valuable lesson that I'm yet to master - never start an argument with Maura McCullough, unless you're ready to lose.

"You really ought to learn to keep your nose in your own business, Caden." Her words are pointed.

I raise my eyebrow in her direction. This woman hasn't kept her nose in her own business a day in her life.

"If you must know, I hired her because her email... rambling as it might have been... broke my heart." Pain moves across her face as she gestures with her hands. "And once I spoke to her, I could see that the girl needs a fresh start, a chance to heal wounds that she's been living with for far too long. *You,* of all people, should understand that."

I grind my teeth, stone-faced as she tries to pull at the heartstrings I've spent the best part of adulthood trying to sever ties with.

"When your parents died, this place saved me. I showed up with you two kids and all of my broken bits in a back-pack. Starting over here helped me to piece myself back together. I met Bill, and I fell in love with the land, and suddenly I had something to live for again." She bites her lip. "God forbid I want to give that to someone else. That girl is broken, but I see the fire in her. I know it, because it's the same fire that was in me all those years ago."

At that, I've lost all of the fight in me.

"Millie stays," she affirms. "We'll find the work."

I spend the rest of the evening trying to push down memories of my parents. I've gotten pretty good at rele-gating thoughts of them to the back of my mind, but that's a little harder when someone spreads their memory out in front of you at the kitchen table.

I don't have it in me to deal with missing them right now.

I take another swig of my beer.

Whether unfairly or not, I hadn't pinned Millie as the type of person who had any real-life problems. When I accused her of running from something, I'd expected it to be a fling with her boss or some other trivial personal crisis. Something that might hurt on the surface but wouldn't cause enough pain to grow deeper roots.

Maura's admission has me doubting myself.

One half of me is caught up in a dance with guilt, wondering if I was too much of an asshole to her earlier. The other half is still secretly hoping she has one foot out the door, ready to run back home.

Nothing good could come from the way my body reacted to seeing her for the first time.

If Maura won't send Millie packing, then my only other option is to avoid her at all costs.

I'll do whatever it takes to make sure I avoid coming in contact with those freckles and that button nose again any time soon.

CHAPTER 10
Millie

Who knew cleaning shit stains off the inside of a toilet bowl could be so truly therapeutic? When I handed in my notice at the factory, Ackermann looked at me like I had horns coming out of my head. That man really thought I had it made being his Executive Assistant. If he could see me now, he'd revel in the opportunity to tell me I had proved him right.

My hands, thankfully gloved up to my elbows, have spent the best part of the morning scrubbing at all kinds of human excrement and clawing hairballs out of shower drains. I've somehow drawn the short straw Tuesday, Wednesday, *and* Thursday this week, landing me on bathroom duty for the third day in a row.

I shouldn't complain. Maura has given me an opportunity to work in this beautiful place with much cheaper rent than I could ever hope for this far West. If I have to get well acquainted with other people's bodily fluids to live out this reality, then so be it.

I glance down at my assigned housekeeping list.

Five cabins down, seven to go.

Caribou Cabin is my favourite. It's one of the older cabins, lacking the high-end finishes that *Riverview* and *Otter* have, but there's something undeniably charming about it nonetheless. It's on the smaller side, with an open-plan kitchen and living area on the main floor, and a loft-style master bedroom upstairs. With the original cedar log siding, thick tartan bed linen, and an open fireplace and stone hearth, it's the epitome of cosy.

When I was a little girl, I always dreamed of living in a home just like this – one with sprawling wildflowers, and little mini me's running around in the front yard. The sweet smell of fresh bread in the oven, free-range eggs and a husband to love.

But I quickly learned that dreams and reality are often two distinctly different things.

And the older I get, the more I start to wonder if that sort of happiness was ever reserved for me. I'm more likely to end up back under the smog of the city in Rowenbridge, living on my own, having never known the love of a man at all.

I step out into the cool morning, puffing a stray hair away from my eyes, trying to pull myself up out of the doldrums. I lean over the log railing and look down on Braggan Valley.

The balcony wraps around the cabin in a horseshoe, with views across the lodge grounds and over the forest towards town.

It hasn't taken me long to get my lay of the land. The staff house and the main house are directly opposite each other, separated by a worn-out dirt road and a grassy yard. The lawn is decked out with picnic tables, a make-shift campfire, and a handful of faded red Adirondack chairs. Rugged mountains form the backdrop to the lodge and restaurant, with the runoff from the canyon waterfall filling the creek and flowing through the grounds towards the Braggan River. Sixteen newer cabins, including this one, hug the river on the opposite side of the main road.

There are certainly worse places you could find yourself for the summer.

I'd seen the pictures in the brochure, I'd scoured the internet and watched countless videos of influencers hiking out here, but nothing could have prepared me for how special this place would really feel.

I throw my gloves into my cleaning bucket, heading down the stairs and back out to the golf cart waiting for me at the front entrance. I sold my car back in the city, and apparently now my only options for transport are this somewhat unreliable buggy or sharing a truck with a man who despises me, for reasons I haven't quite worked out yet.

Speaking of which, I haven't seen Caden since he oh-so-graciously dropped my bags at my dorm and left me to fend for myself. Which suits me just fine, my back feels somewhat more relaxed knowing his eyes aren't boring into it, praying for my demise.

I'm finally done for the day, trundling across the gravel on my not-so-trusty steed, when I hear a familiar voice call out my name.

"Millie, darling!" Maura is dressed in floral pink overalls and rubber boots, pushed up on her tiptoes aiming a sprinkler at the baskets hanging over the reception entrance. "Come over here, will you?"

I hop down from the cart, heading in her direction to relieve her from the hose. I'm not much taller than her five foot, but the extra three or four inches I've got on her make me a little more qualified for this job.

"Beautiful day, isn't it?" I muse, successfully misting the flowers with water.

"It is just that." She smiles, raising her hand over her brow to shield the sun. "I know you're off this weekend, but I'm going to put your name down for a day hike up to Lake Ingrid. I hope you don't mind. I thought it'd be good for you to get to know the local area, try out some of the trails. You'll not believe the views up there."

"I don't mind at all... I need to get out there. I've been looking forward to busting out my new hiking boots since the day I arrived," I laugh.

I don't usually like being told what to do with my free time, but this just feels like she's looking out for me, like she really cares about me settling in and growing to love it here. There's something in the fibre of who she is that just feels like home.

"Excellent." Compost puffs out into the open air as she claps her hands together. "I'll add you to the list – you're going to have the most wonderful time."

She pierces a shovel into the ground, her voice breaking into a gentle lullaby as she returns her hands to the soil.

CHAPTER 11

Caden

"Camilla Adams?" I call the name for a second time, tapping my pen against the clipboard in front of me. No matter how many times we ask guests to arrive fifteen minutes before departure, there's always one who thinks the rules don't apply to them.

If it was up to me, I'd have left already. But Maura is always at my neck, telling me that good customer service requires a 'sprinkling of flexibility.'

Camilla Adams. I mull the name over in my head, realizing it sounds suspiciously close to Millie Adams. The same Millie Adams I have been successfully avoiding ever since I picked her up. I glance up at Maura, who's hanging towels over the reception porch to dry, adjusting each one as she goes. Her smug look is all the confirmation I need – my run of good luck is about to come to an end.

"I'm coming!" An out of breath screech rounds the corner of the lodge. "I'm h... I'm here." Millie bursts into the group, bending over at the waist, hands on her knees as she catches her breath.

I have no choice but to take her in.

She's dressed in the most obnoxious matching pink workout set. An inch of soft skin separating her sports bra from tight, high-waisted leggings. Her chestnut waves are wrangled into a loose braid, hanging over one shoulder.

I'm doing everything in my power not to imagine my fist wrapped around it.

I can almost guarantee the boots on her feet are brand new. They haven't seen a day's work in their life – not a single scuff.

She looks ridiculous, like my worst nightmare and best wet dream all rolled into one.

This is the last thing I need.

"Nobody told me I'd be transporting a flamingo out to the trail head," I snark. "Would've brought my *Exotic Birds* carrier if I'd known."

Continuing to play the dickhead seems like safer territory than letting the unchecked side of my brain take the lead.

"Funny." There's a deflated edge to her voice. She pulls a thick black sweater over her head, gesturing up and down her torso with her hands. "Better now?"

I nod, even though I'm not so sure.

There's something off about her this morning and I don't like it. I'm typically not in the business of caring about the woes of the staff, but for some reason worry eats at my gut as I notice the slight difference in her. We hardly got off on the best foot, but she had a little fight in her then and it seems to be missing now.

The minibus door slides open with a thunk as I signal for the guests to climb in and find a seat. I've been driving this hunk of shit around all week. The lingering smell of damp boots, coupled with the thick air from this early heatwave we've been having, means that I don't want to be stuck in here for a minute longer than necessary.

I'll be glad to get back to normal tomorrow morning. Back to my truck, back to Doug, and back to minding my own business. Fixing shit instead of carting people around like a chauffeur. Given that I'm under a family agreement, I don't have a signed contract or a formal job description. Maura just tells me what to do and I do it – that's how I make my money. That said, driving around all day in a four-wheeled Brussels sprout certainly isn't what I signed up for when I came back here.

I don't think the roads out here in Braggan Valley have seen a cop in years, but I take the drive slow anyway. It's too close to dawn for me to be careering around corners and chancing a run in with an animal. The elk herd have been grazing not far from here, and the bears haven't been shy about making themselves known so far this season either. We lose enough wildlife to careless drivers every summer. I'm not going to be the one to add to that list.

I've spent the best part of the last few weeks trying to avoid the girl at the back of the bus, but now my eyes are having to put in the work to stay away from her. She's distracting me without uttering a single word.

I allow myself a single glance in the rear-view mirror as we pull up on a turn. Her eyes are trained on the forest as we move through it. She's huddled up against the window, both hands tucked under her ear. A few stilted breaths are enough to tell me she's still wrapped up in whatever sadness she showed up with this morning. For some odd reason, I'm hell bent on changing that – even if it means sacrificing myself in the process.

I don't think it's possible for me to make her smile, but I'm certain I can fill her with rage, and that's got to be better than her looking like a sad Bambi.

I can't imagine Maura will be too thrilled to hear I'm on a personal mission to wind up her latest recruit, but I'll deal with the consequences later.

It wouldn't be the first time I've felt Maura's hand clip the back of my ear for my behaviour, and I'm sure it won't be the last.

The potholes in this parking lot are usually my ultimate bugbear, but today they'll be acting as accomplices in my master plan.

I decide on a crater deep enough to make the moon envious. Pulling a hard right on the steering wheel, the tires of the minibus drop into the hole with a *thunk* before I hit the gas.

I ignore the exclamations of the regular passengers, my attention trained on Millie as her head lolls from side to side, smacking against the window hard enough to pull her out of her trance.

If looks could kill, I'd be six foot under already.

I hadn't intended for her to hit her head quite *that* hard, but it seems I've succeeded in unlocking the rage I was hoping for.

"Sorry, hikers!" I puff out, putting my amateur acting skills to the test. "That pothole took me by surprise."

Millie's arms are folded tightly across her chest, her amber flecked eyes drilling into my skull, burning with a heat that feels something like hatred.

CHAPTER 12
Millie

What is *wrong* with this man?!

His face is painted with a smirk as we trundle through the parking lot, muddy water splashing up at the side of the minibus.

They say men fuck like they drive and, after that performance, I feel sorry for anyone who's had the displeasure of Caden between their thighs.

I'm torn between beating his perfectly round ass to a pulp or thanking him for the momentary release from my thoughts. There's a lump forming around my temple, and I can't be certain that I won't be going back to the lodge with a concussion, but at least the pain has pulled me out of my spiral for half a second.

I woke up on the wrong side of the bed this morning. Lately, there haven't been many mornings where I've woken on the right side. I should be used to it by now, the all too familiar tossing and turning, waking up drenched in sweat, having to convince myself it was all just a bad dream.

But it's never *just* a bad dream, it always continues to play out over and over as the day goes on, like a broken VHS stuck on repeat. The dreams start to blend into my waking moments until I can't escape my own memories. The maelstrom just keeps sucking me in until I'm drowning.

Today will be no different.

I'm seven years old. Not the kind of seven where you're obsessed with pink and write all of your secrets in a fluffy diary with a lock. But the kind where you've learned to listen to everything, to understand the meaning of every sound. The kind of seven where you know your mom's body has just been thrown against the wall.

I creep out onto the landing, careful not to step on the floorboards that creak, as if my presence would have any bearing on the rage flowing through him right now. One thick, veiny hand presses against Mom's chest, holding her against the door frame. The other claws at her hair, pulling her head back as he growls inaudible insults at her.

Her shirt is ripped open, exposing her chest. He pushes his body against her, pulling her into a demanding, smothering kiss. I haven't yet learned that not every kiss comes from a place of love. I'm still naive enough to think that this one means that her pain is over for now.

I'll soon come to understand that sometimes the stolen kiss is just the beginning.

I completely zoned out during Caden's introductory commentary, my mind stuck somewhere in the early 2000s. Taking deep breaths, I try to recenter myself, painting a borrowed smile on my face as I pull my backpack over my shoulder.

"... be safe and have fun. I'll be back here at 3 p.m." Caden nods as he winds up his instructions. I can only hope I haven't missed anything important.

I'm wildly unprepared for my first hike and my boots are already starting to gnaw at my heels.

I break into a slight jog to keep up with the other hikers as they split off into smaller groups, heading towards the trail head. Regardless of how unfit I am, there's not a chance I'm letting myself be left behind in bear country.

"Adams, wait up." Caden's grating voice pulls me back. "You're not going out there alone."

"I'll be just fine," I call out, refusing to turn around as I clamber through the first section of the trail, whacking branches and overgrowth out of my way. I'm already drawing longer breaths, praying my lungs make it through. "I have hiked before, you know."

It's not a lie exactly, just a significant twist of the truth.

"Looks like it." He chokes on a laugh as he catches up to me with ease. "Where's your bear spray? What's the plan if you fall over in those brand-new boots and twist your ankle?"

"I don't need your help."

"Don't get it twisted, Adams." He's already holding himself back to match my pace. "I'm not here to help you. I'm trying to protect my reputation. I always return my guests in one piece. Leaving you out here alone is like begging for a black mark on my clean record."

"Fine," I huff on an exhale. I don't want his company, but I don't fancy ending up in the inner bowels of a wild animal either. "I'll let you babysit me, if it makes you happy."

"You don't have a choice in the matter." He's six strides ahead of me, walking backwards with his arms folded across his broad chest as he nods for me to join him. "Come on, little Millie." He coaxes me with a baby voice. "I don't want to have to go back to the minibus for your stroller."

"You're an imbecile," I retort.

If humans came with block buttons, I'd be making use of the feature right about now.

The trail folds out in front of us, earthy switchbacks zigzagging up the mountain as the spring melt cuts through the ground in braided streams.

I've never seen anything so beautiful.

The fresh scent of pine rests in the air. I grapple to take it in, savoring the moment while catching my breath. I hadn't considered the impact the altitude would have on me, but I am struggling like never before.

The same can't be said for Caden, who looks like he is taking a leisurely stroll through the park. He stops every so often to wait for me, before taking off again whenever I'm within an inch of catching up to him.

For someone who protested so hard about sticking with

me throughout the hike, he's doing an awful job of being my guardian.

I can feel sweat pooling in every crease of my body. I didn't get the chance to check myself in the mirror before I left this morning, I was still in the process of dressing as I ran across the bridge towards the lodge. But I know I am looking a hell of a lot worse for wear just one hour into this hike, and I'll be looking downright hideous by the time we make it to the end of the trail.

I thought this was supposed to be fun.

I prepared this list before I came out here, things I wanted to do that I thought would make me feel like I'm really living. A bucket list of sorts. People come out here to hike, so I threw it on there. I was looking forward to the fresh air, crystal lakes, and the peace and quiet of nature. Yet, all I have right now is a blister forming on either ankle, a heart pounding out of my chest and soggy baby hairs spreading across my forehead.

There's no denying the beauty of this place, it's exactly how it looked online, if not better. But I'm starting to think that I'm maybe not cut out for this kind of thing.

There's something to be said for having grandma hobbies – reading, and knitting, and eating scones. None of those things have ever given me arrhythmia.

"What's taking so long, Adams?" Caden's muffled voice winds through the trees that separate us.

I stop, resting my hands on my hips, unable to walk and talk at the same time.

One gasp only goes so far.

"I'm not a daddy-long-legs like you, Caden! I wasn't gifted with the art of scaling mountains at birth."

"Did you just call me *Daddy*?" he splutters. "Damn, that's not how I saw this hike going."

"Uch." I make no attempt to conceal the disgust that's oozing out of me as I catch up with him. "In your dreams. How long until we reach the tea house?"

"Long." He's already strides ahead of me again, leaving me with nothing but a view of his backside in the distance.

I didn't know it was humanly possible for anyone to look good in zip-off pants. I was sure they were reserved exclusively for middle-aged men in hiking sandals and souvenir T-shirts. But it appears Caden has made some sort of deal with the outdoor–apparel-devil, because he looks like the furthest thing from a wholesome family-man right now.

CHAPTER 13
Caden

"Mmmmm," Millie moans, taking a bite out of the brownie slice she just spent twenty minutes waiting in line for. "This is *soooo* good."

"How much you pay for that?" I know for a fact Ingrid Teahouse uses the same supplier as we do, but somehow, they get away with slapping an exorbitant price tag on everything.

"Five dollars." Chocolate crumbs dust the creases around her mouth as she chews with her mouth full. "And it's the best five dollars I've ever spent."

Listening to this girl make noises like *that* over a square of overpriced chocolate might be the death of me.

I can't stand here for a minute longer.

"I'll be at the lake," I snort, leaving her to have her foodgasm in private.

Lake Ingrid is mesmerizing, the type of place that never gets old, no matter how many times you visit. I don't come up here often, but that's less to do with the beauty of the place, and more to do with my own baggage. I bend at the knees, dipping my hands into the glacial water, washing off the dust from the trail.

I pull my keys from my pocket, rubbing my thumb over the worn plastic of a souvenir keychain as I hold it out in front of me. The photograph has faded, but the mountains are just the same as they were all those years ago, you'd think nothing has changed.

But the people in the picture are gone now and that changed everything for me.

"What's that you've got there?" Millie's voice breaks through my thoughts as she pushes up on her tiptoes next to me.

"Just a picture of some old family friends," I shrug, shoving the keys back into the depths of my pocket. I don't know why I feel the need to lie, but sometimes it's easier than the truth. "Not that it's any of your business."

"Rude," she pouts, strutting away from me. "I'm just trying to be friendly."

"We're not friends," I remind her. "I wouldn't waste your breath trying to change that."

Slumping down on one of the rocks by the lake shore, she makes quick work of untying her boot laces – sinking her feet into the water, letting cool waves lap over her toes.

She's going to regret that when she has to wedge those swollen ankles back inside her boots.

The afternoon heat soaks into my skin, an apt reminder that the sun will be taking no prisoners for the hike back down. I slather sunscreen over my exposed arms, before dropping the bottle down at Millie's feet. I can guarantee she didn't think to bring anything useful with her in that backpack and returning her in one piece includes making sure she doesn't burn to a crisp.

I watch her apply the lotion, wondering where the fuck this girl learned to do life – she looks like an infant trying to feed itself spaghetti Bolognese.

Suddenly, having to babysit her seems like less of a joke.

She wipes her hands over her leggings, thick white smears still spread across her cheeks.

"Come here," I grunt.

"Why?" she replies, completely unaware that her face looks like it's been used for a very unfortunate form of target practice.

"You've got so much sunscreen left on your face that you look like a walking sperm bank," I answer. "So, unless you want to spend the rest of the afternoon looking like that, I'll need to help you rub it in."

She stomps in my direction, letting me know that babysitting duties are over, and we've progressed to the toddler phase.

I move my fingers across the bridge of her nose, taking in each of her freckles as I smooth the lotion into her skin. Her eyes catch mine, the light bringing out the caramel tones weaved through them.

My breath hitches.

I have no business being this close to her.

"Done." I toss the sunscreen bottle into my rucksack and sling it over my shoulder. "Let's get back on the trail."

I don't wait for her to follow.

"Wait!" She grabs my wrists, forcing me to turn around. "I'm not done here!"

"We've got to get going," I assert, pointing to my watch.

"The rest of the guests were already on their way down by the time we made it to the top. They'll be waiting for us til morning if we don't head back now – you're slow as death."

"The other guests can wait," she strops. "I hiked all the way up here. I'll be taking my time to enjoy it, and I need to get some pictures for my scrapbook. Start without me if you like, I'll come when I'm ready."

She walks off, swaying her hips with an abundance of sass that I'm quickly learning is her go-to.

"I'll wait." Not a chance am I leaving her alone to run into a bear, or worse, some creepy bastard on the trail. "But we don't have all day."

Pulling a tripod from her bag, she sets it up a few feet back from the shore, her tongue dipping out of the right side of her mouth as she concentrates on lining up her phone.

I keep a safe distance, propping myself up against a tree as she moves back and forth between poses. She looks every bit the tourist as she stands with her back to the camera, arms outstretched in the air, waiting for the self-timer to run its course.

She inspects the pictures each time, huffs of increasing intensity suggesting the results aren't quite what she was hoping for.

Pulling her phone from the stand, she spins in my direction, marching towards me with intention.

"I need your help." She holds out her phone, waiting for me to give her my palm. "I can't get the right angle."

"Last time I checked, photography wasn't included in the excursion." I've already gone above and beyond to make sure she doesn't die out here.

"I just need one good picture, Caden." She stands too

close for comfort, our height difference clearly apparent, as she looks up at me with doe eyes. "Please?"

"Fine." Anything to create some space between us.

Chestnut waves flow down her back as she releases her hair from its tie, her body a silhouette against the backdrop of craggy peaks and milky blues. I watch her through the screen, capturing each movement as the afternoon light seems to dance with her curves.

Fuck, she looks good.

I scroll through the pictures, lingering on the final shot – she's twisted to the side, head tilted back as she soaks up the warmth of the sun, breathing in the moment as if it's one worth remembering. It's ethereal. Everything about the landscape feels intentional – the wildflowers, rugged peaks, and icy waters. It all fits together perfectly, and Millie doesn't look out of place at all, like she was made to fit in with the mountains behind her.

She clears her throat, making me embarrassingly aware of her presence as she stands beside me.

"I made your butt look great in these, Adams." I avoid eye contact as I pass her phone to her, finally getting back onto the trail.

We trudge down the switch backs, over knotted tree roots, through patches of slushy mud and swarms of mosquitoes. Those blood-sucking dickheads are the bane of my existence every summer.

We've made it through most of the descent at a steady pace, but now that we're onto the final stretch, Millie is dragging her heels, stopping even more than she did on the way up.

I don't have time for this.

As peaceful as it is out here, there's a cold beer and a shaggy dog waiting for me at home, and Doug hates it when I'm late.

"Pick up the pace, Adams." I call out to her, waiting for her to catch up. "You know what humans and bears have in common? They both eat dinner at dusk."

The closer she gets, the more obvious her defeated glare becomes. A slight limp seems to pain her as she stumbles down the sloped path.

She's hurt.

My eyes trace down her legs – thighs, knees, calves, until I reach her ankles where a trail of blood runs along the neck of her left boot.

"You have got to be kidding me," I blurt. "Why didn't you tell me you were bleeding?"

Those stupid new boots.

"How do you expect me to tell you anything when you're always seven hundred miles ahead of me?!" she scolds. "I didn't pack my walkie-talkie."

She makes a fair point.

I sink down into a crouch by her ankle, inspecting the wound. Even if I was to clean this up and dress it right now, walking with a gouge this size would be impossible.

I push back to my feet, checking the distance remaining on my watch.

Less than a kilometer.

"I'll have to carry you."

Her eyes bulge out of her head.

"You will absolutely *not* be carrying me!" She pushes her hand against my chest, trying to move past me as her left leg pulls behind her. "I'm two hundred poun—"

I cut her off, bending down and sliding an arm behind her knees. "Ready?" I don't wait for her response as I throw her over my shoulder.

"Put me down!" She batters her fists against my lower back repeatedly, making this last stretch of the trail considerably harder than it needs to be. "I can walk."

"Stop struggling, Adams." I tighten my grip around her thighs. "You're injured. I'm not letting you go until I get you back to the van."

"That sounds like something a serial killer would say," she whines, kicking her legs, her butt jiggling against my cheek in a way that's entirely inconvenient.

"Serial killer or not," I say. "I'm still not putting you down."

"Ugh," she groans, her soft skin melting into me as she gives up the fight. "This is the worst."

The minute she stops fighting it, our bodies seem to fit together like they've known each other forever – much to my dismay.

CHAPTER 14
Millie

ELODIE

What do you MEAN he carried you down the mountain?

Over his SHOULDER?

I would simply pass away!!!!

I need all of the details.

Are you still alive????

MILLIE

Yes, alive.

Traumatized, but alive.

ELODIE

I can't believe his hands were near your butt!!!

You are BLESSED, Millie.

Do you know how many girls would sell
their soul to be thrown around by Caden
Thompson?!

MILLIE

Please don't.

I need to forget.

Pour me the stiffest drink you can find.

I can still feel the imprint of his hand on the back of my thigh. Every inch of my skin is tingling, my cheeks hot with shame. I have no idea how this man managed to carry me for a whole ten minutes, barely breaking a sweat, but I'm equally mortified and grateful that he did.

I pull my boots off, exposing the raw, bleeding flesh at my heels. I should've paid attention to all the articles I read about breaking in new hiking boots. I saw the warning signs, but I ignored them, like I do every time.

There are too many miles between me and a hot shower.

My skin is coated in a mixture of sweat, dusty earth and sunscreen. I'm exhausted and I need to wash everything off of me, including the way Caden's fingers felt digging into my skin.

I won't let my body remember how natural it felt to be near him.

I look everywhere but in his direction as we drive through the mountain bends. The journey seems to take twice as long as it did on the way here.

As we pull into the lodge parking lot, dusk is painting

the sky in swathes of lavender. It's a beautiful sunset – so beautiful that the rest of the hikers have pulled out their cameras to capture it, but I sure as hell won't be sticking around.

I've got to get myself far, far away from Caden and his ridiculously oversized hands.

I make no attempt at pleasantries as I leave, grabbing my belongings and scuttling over the creek towards the staff house in perfect agony.

I should've known better than to text Elodie about the debacle on Caden's shoulder.

All I want to do right now is lie down in silence and erase the last six hours. All she wants is to drag me through it all over again.

"So tell me." She gestures a hand towards me, pacing back and forth along the thin strip of carpet that separates our beds. "How did it *feel*? Were his hands rough and calloused? Did he make you feel safe? Are you falling truly, madly, deeply in love with the Beast?"

"He carried me over his shoulder like a bag of potatoes, El. There was nothing remotely endearing about it. I think you need to stop reading so much romance." I launch a copy of her latest cowboy smut fest in her direction to make my point.

"Respectfully, I won't be doing that," she replies, throwing herself down on the bed and flicking through the pages until she finds her bookmark. "I really wish you two would stop pretending to hate each other already. I want to fast forward to the part where you're fucking. Let me live vicariously through you, I want to hear all of the sordid details. You can't let all of this tension go to waste."

"Stop!" I blurt, my throat tightening as I pull my pillow down over my face. "I don't need to hear any more."

"Plus," she leans towards me, pulling at my pillow just enough to expose my ear, "I've heard he has a *massive* cock."

"Elodie!" I choke, rolling over to turn away from her.

Everything about that man pisses me off.

I don't care how big his dick is.

Or if the veins in his arms were handcrafted just to taunt me.

There will be no fucking.

Yet, even in my certainty, my mind can't help but wander to a place where his body is pressed up against mine. Our breathing entangled, shared hatred turning into something different entirely, crossing any lines that exist between us.

A single spark of untamed desire, igniting me in all of the ways it shouldn't.

CHAPTER 15

Millie

My body aches.

I shouldn't be *this* sore so many days after a hike. It feels like somebody has pulled out every muscle in my body, tied them up in knots, and then put them back in all the wrong places. To compliment my broken body, my ego is still in tatters after being carried down the mountain over Caden's shoulder.

My stomach cramps as I roll over, throwing my feet off the edge of the bed and begging for the energy to bring myself to standing.

Maura is headed into town for her weekly errands, and I'm unfortunately tagging along. I made arrangements to join her long before I realized how much agony I'd be in today, or how ridiculously early 7 a.m. would feel.

I could call off.

Maura wouldn't mind me rearranging my plans for another day where every step doesn't feel like certain death, but I promised Elodie I'd grab some of those apple turnovers she loves from Stella's. And who am I to come between a girl and her favourite pastry?

I throw on a pair of oversized grey sweatpants from the dirty laundry basket, inspecting them for any stains that might make it obvious that I'm wearing unwashed clothes. Satisfied there's no evidence, I finish the outfit off with my teddy-bear fleece and what is becoming my trademark half-assed bun.

Troll-under-the-bridge chic.

I make my way out of the staff house, tossing a water-proof anorak over my arm while wrestling my dusty pink rucksack onto my shoulders.

The cool morning is a tonic for my flushed cheeks. My eyes fall closed as I walk across the grassy yard towards the creek, letting alpine air fill my lungs.

With each passing day, I love it here a little bit more.

"You might want to watch where you're going." The husky voice comes from somewhere outside of me, breaking through my sweet reverie and reminding me that there are still *some* things I've not grown to love about this place. "It's my day off... don't want to have to save you from drowning."

I peel one eye open, assaulted by the man that comes into view.

Caden is jogging across the creek bridge, his T-shirt notably removed, tucked in at his waistband. A glistening sheen of sweat covers his torso. I follow its path over his pronounced muscles towards the deep *V* above his shorts. A lump forms in my throat as I take in the thick line of dark hair running down his lower abdomen, trailing off towards a place I have no business venturing.

"Eyes up, Adams," Caden goads, slowing his pace until

he's stationary in front of me, resting his hands on his hips. "City boys don't look like this?"

Damp hair falls across his forehead, framing his face as he catches his breath.

"Bore off," I balk, attempting to push past him towards the lodge. I don't plan on lingering here any longer when he's looking like *that*. "You'll trip over your ego if you're not careful."

I aim for a quick exit, but my butchered ankle drags behind me, voiding all attempts to disguise my suffering.

"Looks like you're struggling a bit on that ankle." Caden crosses his arms over his broad chest, watching me with amusement as I hobble away from him. "You just trying to get me to throw you over my shoulder again?"

"No," I mutter, returning a prompt middle finger in his direction as I work to leave his intolerable ass behind. "I'm *trying* to get away from you."

"Millie, love." Stella envelops me in a hug as I make my way into the bakery, the scent of cinnamon and vanilla rich in the air. "It's so nice to see you again, how are you getting on at the lodge?"

It's only my second time in the bakery, but Stella greets me like she's known me forever.

"Hi, Stella." I break the hug, feeling like it's already gone on too long. "I'm doing good, settling in now." I'm not sure how much truth there is to that. Things have certainly been getting better, but I'm a long way from *settled*. "I'm still learning everything, trying to turn my hand to a few of the jobs around the lodge. The weather has been gorgeous so far – you can't beat the sunrise from up there."

"Quite right." Stella nods. "I've lived here all my days, and I still pinch myself sometimes when I step out under those clouds. Anyway, what can I get for you this morning?"

I wince, noting the snaking line of customers in front of me. The younger staff member behind the counter laughs, shaking her head, as if Stella makes a habit of prioritizing locals over tourists.

"Just a couple of apple turnovers," I whisper, hoping not to draw attention to my unintentional queue jumping. "And a tray of cinnamon rolls."

"Right you are," she beams, making no attempt to quiet her own voice. "Coming right up."

A sea of wronged eyes bore into me as they catch on to the preferential treatment.

I mouth silent 'sorrys' as I bustle past them towards the cash register.

"There you are, honey." Stella hands me a brown paper bag across the counter. A quick count confirms that she's given me at least double the pastries I asked for. "How have the staff been?"

"They've all been great," I answer. "I'm fitting in really well." Another half-truth. Some of the staff have been lovely, but others are proving more *challenging*.

"I hear young Caden wasn't all too thrilled about your arrival," Stella adds, dropping change into my palm.

I raise my eyebrow.

She's not wrong. Caden wasn't shy about making his

feelings known when I arrived, but I didn't anticipate it becoming town gossip so quickly.

"Maura told me he asked her to send you home," she adds, as though reading the confusion on my face. "He was quite wound up apparently, blew up at her over dinner, barely touched his food."

Send me home.

"I... uh..." I try to swallow. "He wasn't the most welcoming, but I didn't know he felt so strongly about getting rid of me."

The revelation hurts me more than it should. I shouldn't care what he thinks, but as a founding member of the please-like-me-or-I'll-die committee, I do.

"Ohhh!" Stella throws a palm in front of her mouth, as though just realizing she might have put her foot in it. "Well, don't you worry about him, he'll come around eventually. That's just what Caden does, he puts on this tough, grumpy exterior, but he's soft deep down. A sweet boy once you get to know him." She throws her arm around my shoulder as she walks me back out of the bakery into the early morning. "You'll see."

I'm not so sure I will, he strikes me as many things but sweet isn't one of them.

Maura and I have entirely separate lists of errands, something I'm grateful for now that hot tears are brimming in the corners of my eyes. The last thing I need is for my new boss to watch me break down over the opinions of a man who hasn't even taken the time to get to know me.

I make my way down main street, going through the motions as I window shop and attempt to push down the emotions burbling inside of me. I drop a postcard for Mom

& Maddie at the post office, dip into the bookstore and candy shop, and then finally, step into the warm hug of The Coffee Pot.

I'm lost in my mind, replaying that first encounter with Caden, trying to work out the exact point where I went wrong. I barely register the cashier as she calls out to me, motioning for me to move forwards towards the service counter.

"You read?" she asks, nodding to the book in my hand as she folds a dusty red wave behind her ear. "We have a book club here every Thursday. You're more than welcome to come along, it's mostly romance books." There's a twang to her accent that I can't quite place.

"We really just drink wine and drool over smut," another girl chimes in, leaning over the cashier's shoulder before disappearing through a *staff only* door.

"Oh, no..." I shake my head, tucking the book further under my arm to conceal the exposed chest on the cover. "I just picked this up for my roommate. I think she's one cowboy romance away from going full yeehaw and running off to join the rodeo in search of a man."

"With that description, that's gotta be Elodie." She laughs, passing me my receipt and a stamped loyalty card. "I'm Brenna by the way, I'm guessing you must be Millie?"

"Uh, yeah," I reply, wondering how yet another person seems to know who I am before I've even had the chance to make my own first impression. "Yeah, that's me."

She hooks a thumb in the direction of the barista by the coffee machine. "Evan's brother Luke works out at the lodge in the kitchen."

I've met Luke briefly, tall, scrawny and quiet – one of the line cooks I'm sure.

"He did a pretty good job of describing you, babe," Evan adds, dusting chocolate over a love heart stencil before sliding my coffee across the counter.

"He did?" My eyebrows furrow together.

"Yeah," he nods, resting one dainty hand on his hip and the other over Brenna's shoulder. "I'd put money on him having a little bit of a crush, the way he was talking about the short brunette with the peachy ass," he shrugs, "and here you are."

"Huh," I laugh, shaking my head, "I highly doubt he has a crush, but I appreciate you hyping me up anyway. Lord knows I need all the good vibes I can get today."

"Well," he sighs, returning to the coffee machine and grabbing the next order from the printer. "Unfortunately, I'm here five days a week, so you know where to find me if you ever need an extra dose."

"Noted," I say, grabbing my coffee as I clock the long line of customers forming behind me. "Thanks for this—" I hold up the mug "—it was so nice to meet you both."

"Don't be a stranger, Millie," Brenna calls out, her smile soft as she adjusts her monitor to take the next coffee order.

Light rain starts to fall outside as I slump down into a padded armchair halfway between a wall of foggy windows and the open fire.

There's a lingering heaviness in me today that I can't seem to shift.

People all around me are making their own assumptions about me, good and bad, trying to place who I am, when I'm not even sure if I know that myself.

"Looks like there's a thunderstorm going on up there." Maura pulls out a chair across from me. "You need a listening ear?"

She places her tray on the table, passing me a slice of carrot cake and adjusting the knitted tea cosy on her pot.

I scramble for my wallet, pulling out some change and sliding it across the table towards her.

"For the cake, you didn't need to."

"Nonsense." She shoos my hand away, pouring herself a cup of breakfast tea, mixing in cream and sugar. "I'm glad we've got some time together this morning. How are things now that you're here?"

"Work is great," I say, trying not to let my mood over-shadow the gratitude I have for this job. "I've been getting used to the lodge side of things while it's been slower, and I think I'm an expert at cleaning the inside of a toilet bowl now."

She leans back in her chair, taking a sip, and holding me in place with a look. "I'm not asking about the work, Millie. I know you're doing a good job. I wouldn't have hired you if I had any qualms about that."

"Then, what are you asking?"

"I'm asking how you are... really." She loosens her cardigan at the shoulders, letting it fall back against her chair. "When we first spoke, you said you were looking for a change. It sounded like you needed an out, a chance to start over."

"Oh... yes." I sulk into myself a little. "I'm doing okay, but honestly, I thought this would be easier," I confess. "I thought getting some distance from where I grew up might help me, but in some ways everything seems harder. I'm pushing myself out of my comfort zone and my brain doesn't seem to like it."

I don't bother going into more detail – about the dreams, or the moments of panic, or how I'm finding myself triggered in ways I never have been before. If I'm too honest, I don't think I'd be able to hold back the tears for much longer – my sadness is a dam, just waiting for its release.

"These things take time." Her words are soft, bound by the sort of knowing that comes with age. "Be kind to yourself in the in-betweens, you don't have to have it all figured out."

"I know." I bite my lip, running a finger over the rim of my cup. "I just wish there was some sort of shortcut to the part where everything feels okay."

"I get it... I was like you once too, you know – starting over, not really knowing where my life was headed or how I was going to get there." She takes my hand across the table, rubbing her soft thumb over my knuckles. "It's okay to be scared, unsure, lost with it all. But you will find your way, darling. Maybe not right now but soon enough. Braggan Valley is a healer – this place has a way of giving people exactly what they need, when the time is right."

CHAPTER 16

Caden

I've got that old familiar weight on my chest this morning – the one that lets me know the day is going to hurt like fuck.

I'm feeling off, like I might boil over or break down in tears, and I can't afford to do either. I had to come out here to the river, to get away from the lodge for a bit and clear my head.

Grief fucking sucks.

You can prepare for the birthdays, the anniversaries, and the recurring memories that come with seeing the date they died on the calendar each year. But not so much the random Tuesdays, or days like today, where remembering comes out of nowhere, like a sucker punch to the gut. Reminding you that they're gone, and they're gone forever. The days where you wake up yearning for something you'll never have again.

I've been fishing all my life, but today I'm doing no better than the rookies I bring out here. I'm dressed the part in waders and rubber boots, up to my knees in the Braggan

River, but failing to catch a single thing, no matter how many times I cast out.

I think the trout can sense my mood, my negative energy moving through the water in ripples and pushing away whatever it comes in contact with. Nothing new there. That's what I do – keep the world out when things get dark, push everyone away so they don't have to deal with my bullshit.

You can't blame the fish for wanting no part in it.

Dad used to bring me out here whenever we visited from BC, bought me my first rod and showed me everything I'd need to know about this spot. This was our place. We'd come out here in the summers and catch up with Stella and Frank. It was a happy place then, but it doesn't feel like that now. If anything, it's rubbing salt into my wounds.

I miss him.

I miss them both.

I don't know whether to sit in sadness or anger or fall down on my knees and scream up at the sky, demanding the answers that I know I'll never be able to hold.

I've long forgotten their voices. I was so young when they died that I never had the chance to see it coming. It didn't cross my nine-year-old mind that there could be a world where they weren't part of it. I didn't have any time to prepare, to commit their voices to memory, to bottle up the moments we spent together so that I could go back to them when we didn't have any time left.

Instead, I was robbed. Robbed when they left and then robbed again every day since. Losing them little by little in the process of forgetting, until I'm not really sure if I'm remembering them right at all, or just clinging to the hope that I do.

I rub my thumb over the keyring in my pocket, one tiny reminder of the 'us' we were, before we lost it all.

You'd think this would all get better with time, that by thirty-three I'd have learned how to move through this feeling. But I'm still here struggling, letting the loss eat away at me until there's nothing left.

A tug at my line pulls me out of my thoughts and back to the river. I draw back on my rod slightly, slowly reeling in against the tension, but it breaks all too soon, and the first fish of the day swims off, taking any hopes of a successful catch with it.

"Fuck this shit." I make my way out of the reeds towards the bank, throwing my rod onto the grassy mound in frustration. I should know better than to throw my toys around like a toddler, but I can't help feeling like the world is conspiring against me today, kicking me when I'm already so far down.

Doug lifts his head. He's been sleeping in the bed of the truck, wrapped in blankets while I've tried to shake off this mood. On days like this, he keeps me going. I don't know what I'd do without this scruffy mutt depending on me for his every whim, dragging me out of bed even when I don't want to see the light of day.

He bounds down towards me, using the tailgate as a launch pad, and lands in an awkward lump by my side. I give his greying jowls a scratch and slump down next to him, letting my head rest in the dewy grass as my tired eyes fall shut.

I want to forget everything, to clear my mind until it's

completely blank, so I can get back to the lodge and help Maura with the set up for the day. It's one of the biggest weekends of the year. We've got wood to chop, deliveries to pack away, furniture to move. She needs me, and she definitely won't benefit from me sulking in the corner, wishing things had turned out different.

Doug repositions himself over my chest, his full weight pressing down into me, as though he can sense the anxiety mounting within me as I run through a mental inventory of all of the things I need to do when I get back to the lodge.

"I wish you were here, Dad," I call the words out loud, thankful there's nobody around to see how mad I've become. "I wish I could talk to you, that you could tell me what to do."

"I'm always here with you, son."

I jerk, certain I'm losing my mind, but careful not to open my eyes for fear of losing his voice, or the image of him that's slowly being etched in my mind.

"Dad?" The words are mine.

He's standing in the river, knee deep, just as I was, summoning me to come join him under the warmth of the sun. I don't move from my spot by the water's edge, but a younger version of me runs across my mind, bounding into his arms, creating a splash as he goes.

I watch the two of them, trying to slow down the seconds as the boy wriggles free of his father's arms and dunks his tiny hands into the cool water.

"These waters—" Dad points to the shallow ripples, a mirror image of the two of us reflected, both adult men now "—hold more than just fish. They heal too. You did the right thing coming out here, trying to clear your head, to straighten

it all out. There's no better place to find the answers you're looking for. Life hasn't treated you kindly, Caden, but despite everything, you've turned out to be a good man. The kind your mom and I would always have hoped for, son."

"It doesn't feel that way," I reply, honesty feels like the easiest thing in the world now that he's here with me. "It feels like I'm failing every day, like I'm less of a man with all of these feelings getting in the way, keeping me from the things I should be doing."

"Oh, Caden." I wish I could bottle his voice. "A good man is someone that the ones you love can depend on, a man who sticks to his word – that's you. I've never seen you let anyone down. Not Maura, not Josie, not Doug, not even those god-awful city slickers." He laughs at that, his face fading now, waning with each word spoken. "You're not failing just because you're hurting, Caden. I see you being so incredibly strong. It's okay to break down, to cry, to yearn. That doesn't make you any less of a man. The ones who love you don't need you to be perfect, they just need you to be you, to show up, to stay. Promise me that you'll keep choosing to stay, son."

I reach out to him, trying to hold him, to give him my promise, if only to keep him here with me a little longer.

But he's gone.

And when I open my eyes, I realize he was never really there in the first place – just my mind playing tricks on me, reminding me how much I've lost.

CHAPTER 17

Millie

Maura has the entire staff packed like sardines in tight rows in front of the restaurant entrance. She's clinging to her clipboard, using her pencil as a pointer as she walks back and forth across the gravel – a self-appointed drill sergeant. There's a tense energy around the lodge, like we're all on high alert, scared to put a foot out of line.

Maura is one of the sweetest souls I've ever met, but there's an air about her today that makes me feel like getting on her bad side would hurt like hell. I'm begging the ground to swallow me up every time her eyes move in my direction.

Unfortunately, there's no escaping my fate.

It's the weekend of the Barnhoff wedding, and with over 150 day guests and about as many moving pieces throughout the proceedings, the entire Braggan Valley Lodge team has been pulled in to help in some way.

Even Bill, who's usually out playing golf and flaunting his semi-retirement, has been saddled with the arduous task of steaming the tablecloths. And then steaming them a second time once Maura scolds him for the several missed creases in the fabric.

I'm listening intently, waiting for my call.

Parker should take a leaf out of my book. Despite working at the lodge for five summers, he somehow doesn't seem to have the sense to adapt his behaviour to complement Maura's current warpath.

"Parker!" Maura's voice booms across the gravel parking lot. "If you're so interested in horseplay, maybe you should take your resume to the Holden Stables and get out of my kitchen."

Chef Raphael scoffs. "*Her* kitchen?" He's clearly offended that Maura has laid claim to the four walls that he dedicates his entire life to.

"Technically, it is her kitchen," Parker shrugs. "She owns the place, you're just the chef."

"*Just* the chef!?" Raphael seethes, spinning on his heel.

"I'm kidding... I'm kidding." Parker dives behind Luke to shield himself, both hands raised in the air in surrender. "You're the best there is, Chef."

Maura continues with her delegation, separating the team off into groups of three or four, assigning tasks with little to no explanation.

"Nina and Millie," Maura calls out. "You'll be on the food & liquor deliveries. Liquor will be here in ten minutes, followed by Carter Food Services within the hour. Once that's done, you can help Beth and Ivar polish cutlery."

She might as well be talking in gibberish, because not one word of that made sense to me.

I was hoping I might be paired with someone who knows what they're doing, but one look at Nina confirms she is just as clueless as I am. She just arrived at the lodge a few days ago, this being her first job straight out of high school.

Great.

"Caden!" I bristle as Maura calls out his name, summoning him from his truck. "Get over here! You can help the girls with the heavy pallets."

No. Fucking. Way.

I don't want to laugh a gift horse in the mouth, but I'd rather do this alone than have Caden assigned to help. I'm not at all ready to be in close proximity with him after hearing what he really thinks of me.

"Surely not!?" It sounds like the feeling is mutual. "Don't you need me out here chopping logs? The cabins are full all weekend and they'll no doubt want to use the main pit by the creek, too."

"Yes." She chews on the end of her pen, contemplating his offered escape plan. "You're right, I do need you to stock the log shed."

At that, he relaxes, realizing he's off the hook.

"After you take care of the food delivery that is," Maura adds, the touch of a smirk dragging at her upper lip as she walks away.

"But..." His shoulders tighten again as he attempts to carry on with his protest, but Maura is long gone, already assigning housekeeping duties to Elodie and the twins.

Caden sighs, pulling his cap down further over his eyes and leaning back against his truck in defeat.

"*Idiot,*" I mumble under my breath, not knowing why I'm calling him one, but feeling good about it nonetheless.

"You'll need to pull out all of the baking supplies and make sure the newest ones go to the back." Parker has thrown on his whites, losing his clown attitude and actually becoming useful as he explains rotating inventory to Nina. "First in, first out."

Seems like sound logic.

I head to the wine cellar, ready to tackle the liquor delivery with his instructions. I pull out the older wines, filling the shelves with the new ones and meticulously straightening each bottle with the label facing forward. There's something satisfying about getting them all lined up perfectly.

I'm taking my time, taking full advantage of the distance this task is putting between me and Caden. I can breathe a little easier when his irritating presence isn't taking up so much of my personal space.

"Adams, need your help."

I *always* speak too soon.

"Have you ever thought about using your manners?" I ask, a much harsher bite to my voice than I was expecting.

He's holding the door open expectantly, as if he thought he could summon me, and I'd just hop right up at his beck and call.

"Oh, I'm sorry, let me try that again." He huffs out a laugh, as though he thinks my request for basic human decency is over the top. "Your royal highness, would you please be so kind as to accompany me to the walk-in for our assigned duties?"

I look to the empty boxes to my left, hoping they've somehow refilled themselves with additional bottles of beer so I can refuse his request.

No such luck.

"Let's go, Princess." He taps his foot eagerly on the tile flooring. "We don't have all day."

I shoot him a look that I hope feels like molten lava, as I reluctantly get to my feet and barge past him in the direction of a thick white door held open with a milk crate.

"Why is it so cold in here?" I ask.

"It's a fridge, Adams." His brow furrows as he follows me inside. "You do know what a fridge is, right?"

This is the largest fridge I've ever seen. What sort of fridge has a hallway and six-foot shelves?

"Of course I know what a fridge is... I just didn't know *this* was one. It's bigger than the rooms in the staff house."

"Right." He shakes his head in disbelief, wasting no time getting back to ordering me around. "Here's how this part works, I call out the item and quantity, you check it off the list. Got it?"

He hands me a clipboard, ripping open the first of several cardboard boxes stacked outside the ridiculously-large-fridge.

"Why can't Nina do this?" I grumble.

"Are you injured?"

"No."

"Have a sick note?"

"No." *Sick of your shit, maybe.* I roll my eyes, battling to keep my innermost thoughts to myself.

"Then you're perfectly fit for the job." He picks up an open palette, sliding it onto the produce shelf next to me. "Beef Tomatoes, 5 kilos."

I groan, searching through the spreadsheet in front of me, hoping to find the tomatoes before giving Caden the satisfaction of pointing them out.

Bingo.

I nod as I check them off the list.

"Heavy Whipping Cream, 2 crates."

Another nod.

"Portobello mushrooms, 2 kilos."

This time I forgo the nod, hoping he'll take the movement of my pen as confirmation that I've checked them off.

"Mushrooms, 2 kilos," he repeats, waiting for my response as he pushes the crate into its spot on the shelf.

"Are you expecting me to provide confirmation each time?" I'd probably consider reining in my sass a little if I wasn't still so mad at him for trying to sway Maura's opinion of me.

He turns towards me, resting his hands on his hips.

"I don't know what's wrong with you today, but whatever it is, you might want to think about dropping this attitude real quick." His nostrils flare as he stares me down. "Sure Maura's being a pain in the ass, but this is a big weekend for the lodge. The Barnhoff wedding is huge – their reviews could make or break us, we rely on shit like this to get us through the slower months in winter. If you're not going to be helpful, then you might as well go home."

"Pffft... go home." A bitter laugh tumbles out of me. "That's fitting."

96

"What is your problem?" he grunts, taking a step closer to me.

"My problem, put plainly—" I cross my arms over my chest, refusing to be intimidated by his broad frame towering over mine "—is you."

"*Me*?" He laughs, returning to the stack of boxes. "Go on then, do tell." He pulls the clipboard out from underneath my arm, holding it out in front of me. "And check off the chicken breasts while you're at it."

I severely dislike this man right now.

"I bumped into Stella in town last week, she told me about some of the not so nice things you've had to say about me. I'm clearly not your favourite person, but did you really have to try to get me sent home? Before I'd even had the chance to start? That seems like a low blow, even for you."

"Ha! Stella is two things: the best baker on planet earth, and the biggest gossip in Braggan Valley. I'd take anything she says with a pinch of salt." He leans over me, pointing out a checkbox on my list. "Chilli Jam, 2 counts."

"There's no smoke without fire though, is there? Why would she make this up?" I drag an aggressive line across the paper. "You know, I didn't take you for a coward. But if you're going to talk shit about me, the least you could do is quit lying and say it to my face."

His eyes darken, a black storm swirling in their ocean blue as his jaw flexes. Leaning over me, he plants a hand on either side of me, gripping the top shelf.

I try to take a step backwards, but I've nowhere to go.

"Listen, Millie." His breaths are ragged. "You can say what you want about me – that I'm a dickhead, or ill-mannered, or straight up rude. Those things might all be true, but don't call me a liar. That's not who I am. If you want me to be honest, then I'll be honest. Just don't blame me if you don't like it."

He pushes off from the shelf, taking a few steps away from me, removing his cap and running a hand through his mussed hair.

His dark heat lingers around me, pinning me in place against the cool metal shelving.

"When you arrived, I did want you gone. I was at my wits' end with Maura meddling in my love life, trying to set me up at every turn. Then you showed up with your tiny little waist, that fat ass, and those fucking freckles, looking every bit my type." He pauses, bursting open another cardboard box before spitting out the rest of his words. "I thought it was all part of Maura's elaborate scheme to get me hitched, and I made no secret of telling her I wanted you out."

I don't know how to make sense of what he is saying.

Stella wasn't lying, but she didn't give me the full story either.

"I'll admit I got the wrong end of the stick, and Maura handed my ass to me for it."

"And what about now? Do you still want me gone?" I don't know why I ask, and as soon as he replies I wish I didn't.

"What's it to me, Millie?" He throws the last of the supplies on the shelf, signing his name across the delivery invoice before heading for the exit. "I couldn't care less whether you stay or go."

CHAPTER 18

Caden

I couldn't care less whether you stay or go.

I replay the words over in my head, wishing I could take them back. Not just because saying them out loud makes me sound like a complete asshole, but because they're also starting to feel like the furthest thing from the truth.

She infuriates me.

And yet, I can't seem to get enough.

She's everywhere I look, doing dumb fucking shit.

This morning, I looked out of the kitchen window to see her immersed in sunrise yoga by the creek with Elodie. It might've been the perfect advert for the stretch on her yoga pants had her downward dog not looked so much like a constipated chihuahua trying to squeeze out a shit.

If she's not falling over something, waltzing around with her eyes closed or finding the most inane way to complete a task, then she's putting herself at risk by wearing those stupid over ear headphones everywhere she goes. It's like she forgets that we live in a National Park with wild animals that would happily eat her for breakfast.

She's clumsy, and uncoordinated, and careless.

But aside from all of that, I can't help but notice that she's kind too. I've caught her in her sweeter moments – laughing with Maura, or taking the time to chat with the quieter new hires while they're still settling in. Throwing the same ball for Doug over and over again.

There's a softness to her that I wasn't prepared for.

Then in the moments where she thinks nobody is watching, she takes enough deep breaths for me to know that what I've seen so far is just what's on the surface. There's a side of her that she doesn't show to the world freely.

And that's the side that draws me in the most.

CHAPTER 19
Millie

"If Ella Barnhoff gets cold feet, then I'm next in line for that groom." Elodie refuses to sit down, captivated by the nuptials unfolding in front of us. "The groomsmen are so dreamy, too. Do you think any of them are single?"

She holds up her phone, zooming in on the five men lined up by the altar.

"I don't see any rings," she squeals, filling in my silence with her excitement.

I sigh, pulling grass from the dirt beside me as I try to distract myself from paying any attention to this circus dressed up as a celebration of love. It's been the talk of the town for weeks, locals have coined it *The Barnhoff Wedding*, erasing the groom's last name as if he's not even a part of it at all. Everything has been about Ella and her semi-famous golf pro father. I hate to think how much it has all cost, but I'm sure it's barely made a dent in Everett Barnhoff's bank account.

Across the creek, mismatched wooden chairs are

adorned in lavish organza bows, arranged in long rows, separated by a gravel aisle scattered with soft pink rose petals. Guests are filtering in, slowly taking their seats as the groom nervously bobs from one foot to the other under a 10-foot floral archway.

Chatter filters across the grounds as the clop of hooves melt into the melody of a harp. The guests rise from their seats as an ornate cart pulls up by the aisle entrance. Mr Barnhoff steps out of the cabin, extending a proud hand to his daughter who seems to be lost under a marshmallow of tulle and satin. A sheer, lace-trimmed veil is draped over her face as thick blonde curls roll over her shoulders towards the small of her back.

I can't deny that she looks beautiful. Ridiculous, but beautiful.

Elodie pants, holding back her squeals as she climbs on top of the picnic table to get a better view. "Mills, get up here! I can see the whole thing. Ella looks stunning, and Barnhoff is giving DILF."

A chorus of oohs and aahs continue from the guests as the bride moves down the aisle towards the man waiting for her.

I clock the groom, his eyes filling with tears as he takes in his bride and offers Everett a strong handshake. He crumbles when Ella stands in front of him, letting the crowd see his vulnerability in the face of the woman he loves.

Cameras flash as videographers run the perimeter, trying to get the perfect shot. There's an entire row of seats dedicated to the press.

I wonder at the authenticity of it all.

All of these people here, the money spent, the time planning for this show. All with the best intentions and hopes for the future. Nobody goes into a marriage thinking they are going to get divorced, it's a promise to forever... but that's rarely how it ends.

"I've never seen somebody look so miserable at a wedding," Elodie prods, interrupting the runaway train of thoughts. She jumps down from the bench, flopping down on the ground beside me.

"Technically, we're not at the wedding," I point out. "I never did receive my wax stamped invitation in the post."

"Special guests," Elodie shrugs, throwing an arm around my shoulder and pulling me into a hug. "I don't know how you can't just love seeing two people in love."

I snort a laugh, but don't offer any words in return.

"I've still got some time," she continues, counting out the months between now and October on her fingers. "I'll make a hopeless romantic of you yet."

"Good luck with that," I reply.

"Come on," she drags out the words, pushing against my arm playfully. "You seriously don't want to fall in love someday?"

"I'd kill to believe in that kind of love," I confess with an honesty even I wasn't expecting. "I've just never seen it work out that way."

Elodie straightens a dark tartan sash across my chest, pulling it taught and fastening the edges with a thistle brooch. The

Barnhoff's have insisted on honouring the groom's Scottish heritage, throwing an excessive amount of tartan at almost every corner of the venue.

I look myself up and down in the mirror, taking in the person staring back at me. I look different somehow. There's a golden tint to my cheeks, the result of hours spent outside over the past few weeks. It's proof that I'm changing a little each day that I'm here, even if some days I feel like I'm right back in the starting blocks.

"Let's go, Mills." Elodie claps her hands gesturing towards the door. "You can get back to being a die-hard over-thinker after dinner service."

I roll my eyes, following her out through the staff house towards the kitchen door of the restaurant.

It's my first shift in the restaurant, a true baptism of fire, working the most high stakes dinner service of the season. I'm trying to fake it til I make it, but I'm certain I look as shit scared as I feel.

The restaurant manager, Bella, is speaking in a hushed tone as Chef Raphael throws his hands around, making no attempt to silence his disgruntled thoughts.

"You know this happen too much, Isabella." He slams a fist on the steel counter. "I spend all day on lamb. Now over-cooked, taste like mutton. Fast food, not fine dine."

Bella grabs his wrists, pulling him closer to her as she stabs a finger into his chest. I don't catch her words, but I can't imagine they are any less pointed than his.

"You tell Barnhoff be quiet, no more speech." Chef Raphael pulls a knife from the magnet on the wall, chopping fresh cilantro with speed and precision as he lays down his demands. "Tell him, or I leave, and wedding eats slop."

Bella sighs, throwing a middle finger in Chef Raph's direction before returning to the dining room with a plastered-on smile.

We're paired off based on two factors: people who have served before, and people like me, who wouldn't know what foie gras was if it hit them in the face.

I've somehow drawn the shortest straw in the batch and wound up stuck with Brett Stevens.

I haven't spent much time with him outside of the occasional run in at the staff house kitchen, but I've heard enough about him from the other girls to know this pairing is unfortunate.

He snorts, looking me up and down, as I fumble with my apron ties at my waist. He has some nerve looking at me like I'm the worst thing to happen to his day, when he walks around in public with a haircut that looks like someone has dumped a bowl of instant noodles on his head.

Holding out a large brown tray across his arms, he nods towards the pass where Parker is ladling up piping hot bowls of soup.

"Grab the bowls, put them on the tray," he snarls. "And don't bother spilling any."

I follow his instructions, kicking myself for not biting back at his demands.

As we make our way into the dining room, I rack my brain trying to remember which shoulder I should pass the bowls over.

Left or right? Left or right?

I opt for the right, and continue moving round the circular table, trying to dodge flailing, half-drunken arms as I go.

"Left," Brett scorns. "Service is always from the left."

He continues muttering insults under his breath, leaving me feeling suitably chastised by the time I make it to the final couple on the table. I grab the last two bowls, placing the first in front of a woman with greying red waves, before turning my attention to the man next to her.

My body tenses, the air sucked straight out of my lungs as my eyes land on the likeness of a man I've spent the best part of my adult life trying to forget.

My father.

Heat sears through my skin as shock renders me paralyzed, my fingers molded to the ceramic of the bowl. I take in his rusted brown beard and thick head of chestnut hair. Soup runs down the inner sleeve of my white button down, scalding my arms as it follows its rushed path. My hands shake but my feet are planted where they are.

I notice the differences, he's taller and stockier, with a distinct Scottish accent. My father was short, born and bred in Rowenbridge with the classic Saskatchewan twang. Those things should make it make sense for me, but my brain can't help but notice the similarities. The way his nose crooks just so, and his eyes hold that distinctive blue-grey that I could never forget. Panic wraps around my brain like poison ivy, squeezing the air out of my lungs until I'm gasping for it.

The dining room moves around me in indistinct smears, a kaleidoscope of imposing, blurry images.

Five things you can see, Millie. Tell me five things you can see.

I try to focus on something, anything else. But I'm seeing double as the man rises to hover over me, the second version of him looking even more like my father.

His brow furrows with gentle concern.

"Are you alright there, lass?" He extends a hand towards my elbow. I flinch at the contact. Pulling back, I drop the empty bowl onto Brett's tray and stumble towards the kitchen.

"Can't breathe." I gasp. "Air... I need air."

I burst through the swing door, picking up speed as I try to recenter my dizzied vision, my sight set on the back exit.

"Whoa, lady!" Parker shouts, as he feels the full force of my weight against his shoulder as I barge past. "You ever heard of the no running in the kitchen rule?"

"Clearly not!" Chef Raphael shouts. "You stay out of my kitchen, dumb girl!"

I burst out into the early evening, hoping the cool rain will soothe the searing pain clawing at my heart.

Instead, I run straight into the barricade of a rock-hard chest and the very last person I want to see.

CHAPTER 20

Caden

I've been meaning to fix this light outside the kitchen door for months. It's not safe for the cooks to be out here in the dark when we're surrounded by wild animals.

It's one of five jobs on my list to make the kitchen area safe, let alone up to operating standards.

That's the thing about summer at the lodge, there are never enough hours in the day to get shit done. The jobs just keep stacking up on top of each other, and I'm the only one pulling a finger out of their ass to complete them.

I'm just about to get stuck in when I hear Chef Raph's distinct roar bellowing from the kitchen.

Stay out of my kitchen, dumb girl.

That's not happening.

I drop my toolkit & storm towards the entrance.

He thinks he can get away with throwing his weight around, knowing nobody likes to stand up to him, but I will. He can't be treating the staff like shit, regardless of the type of kitchens he was trained in. This is Braggan Valley, and that's not how we do things here.

I'm just about at the threshold when the door swings open, followed by a short figure bouldering into me.

She looks up for a second, catching her breath as tears brim in her rich amber eyes.

Millie.

She pushes off my chest, stumbling and making it a few paces before she bends over and retches up over a pile of logs.

The same logs I just chopped this afternoon, but I'll have to worry about that later.

"What's going on?!" I demand.

She doesn't reply, instead steadying herself before taking off in the direction of the canyon trail. It's no kind of night to be out on the trails with the storm forecast.

I'll need to go after her, but first I'm dealing with the overgrown wankstain we call Chef.

I yank open the kitchen door, coming face to face with Parker, the colour bleached from his cheeks.

"What the fuck happened there?"

"I don't know, man." Parker holds his hands up. "She just came running through from the dining room like she'd seen a ghost."

I feel my jaw tighten as my eyes fall on Chef Raphael. It doesn't sound like the tears were his fault, but he's overdue for some home truths anyway.

"Raph!" I point. He meets my stare. "Learn to watch your mouth or you'll find yourself out on your ass. You're not above anyone here. Next time you think about raising your voice, remember who signs your paycheck. Maura won't stand for this shit, and I won't hesitate to throw you under the bus if you *ever* speak to Millie like that again."

I don't give him any time to retort, slamming the door shut behind me. It's not lost on me how hypocritical I sound after the way I spoke to Millie yesterday.

I grab Doug's leash from the passenger seat of the truck as I whistle for him. He comes on demand, hurdling across the creek to meet me just before the trail head.

The rain is coming down hard, slashing at my cheeks as I take long strides along the trail, following the tiny footsteps Millie has left behind.

My boots squelch as the storm picks up, leaving behind a stream of mucky slush where the worn path used to be. The wind is thick, stealing my breath as I try to push against it.

When I finally find Millie, she's sitting dangerously close to the edge at the canyon overlook. The loaded waterfall is gushing through the rock in deafening bursts.

"Millie! Get back here! You shouldn't be over there," I roar, climbing over tree roots to get closer to her. "It's not safe."

"Leave me alone, Caden," she gasps, her voiced drowned out by the rushing water. "I want to be alone."

"Like hell am I leaving you alone out here." The frenzied sky lashes down on us, Doug lets out small whimpers as rain soaks into his thick coat. "Get your ass back over this railing."

She glares up at me, mascara streaked down her freckled cheeks. Her white button down is completely soaked through, brown waves weighed down against the cotton.

I wrap Doug's leash around a tree, freeing both my hands to help her back over the railing. "Please, Millie." I'm not too proud to beg right now. The canyon is dangerous, and I'm not going to stand around letting her become another statistic. "You need to come back where it's safe."

She teeters slightly as she clambers to her feet. My heart leaps out of my throat as I lunge forward, tugging her into my hold and dragging her back over the railing.

I expect her to pull away, but she clings to me, her hands digging into my back, lungs begging for air between painful sobs. My arms hang in midair for a second, useless while I decide what to do with them.

Fuck it.

I wrap them tightly around her waist, letting her sink into the warmth of my flannel beneath my jacket.

"What happened, Millie?" The question comes out as a whisper.

"I... I just saw that man... and I froze." She draws in a breath. "I thought I could do this... but I don't know that I can... it never goes away, it's everywhere I am. It's everything I am."

She's not making any sense.

If someone hurt her, it'll be the last thing they do.

"What man? Who did this, Adams?"

She shakes her head. "It's not... it's nobody here... it wasn't his fault." The words make their way out between disjointed cries. "It's nothing."

"It's not nothing, Millie. *Nothing* doesn't hurt like this. Whatever it is, I need you to tell me." I rub a thumb across her shoulder, pulling her closer to shield her from the storm. "Let me help you."

Something between anger and misplaced possession claws at my lungs.

I never want to see this girl cry again.

She straightens, pushing away from me and letting my arms fall back to my side. I feel an instant loss, a void without her cradled beneath them.

"I'm fine," she affirms, rubbing her eyes with her wet sleeves. "I'll be fine."

She looks anything but fine, but I won't labour the point while we're out here. "Let's get you back down the trail," I say with as much composure as I can muster. "You need a hot bath and some fresh clothes."

She looks at me with confusion. "There's not a bath in the staff house."

"No... there isn't," I confirm.

Doug raises an eyebrow at me as I untie his leash from the tree.

CADEN

Where do you keep those bath things?

Bath grenades???

Make the water fizz and are a pain in the ass to clean up?

I'm hoping Maura has her phone on hand. If not, I'll happily march into that wedding covered in mud to get my answer.

. . .

AUNT MAURA

One: You're supposed to be working right now.

Two: If you've finally brought a girl back to the main house, I can't wait to meet her.

CADEN

It's not like that.

Also, not helpful.

Answer please.

AUNT MAURA

Oh Caden... you HAVE brought a girl home.

How splendid.

CADEN

...

AUNT MAURA

The bath BOMBS are in the glass jar in the vanity in the back bedroom.

Remember to use a condom. Safety first, ejaculation second.

Jesus Christ.
    She couldn't be further off base.

I've never crossed that line with any of the staff, and breaking that tradition with Millie is the last thing on my mind.

Especially not tonight.

All I care about right now is finding a way to erase this sadness from her completely.

CHAPTER 21
Millie

Can somebody please tell me why I'm in Caden Thompson's bedroom?

The scent of sandalwood & leather fills the air. It's masculine and woodsy – an exact match for how Caden smelt when he held my head against his chest earlier, letting me sob into his flannel. It's a scent that's becoming familiar, starting to feel like a piece of Braggan Valley – a worrying reminder that I've spent far too much time around him for my own good, mostly under less than favourable circumstances.

Doug pads around me, looking for the most comfortable spot to slump down on. I don't know how old he is, but his movements are coated in a stiffness that acts as a reminder that his life will be painfully shorter than ours. He clambers across my knees, letting his weight sink into my stomach as he pushes me back against a mountain of pillows.

I have no business kicking back in Caden's bed like this, pressed into the sheets he sleeps in every night.

"Get off me, you big slob." I wrestle with Doug, trying to push him off, but his stubborn body doesn't move an inch.

Caden reappears, holding a pile of fresh plush towels. His eyes fill with a heated glare, raking over me, as he takes in my position on the bed. A cloak of something akin to anger falls over him as his jaw rocks back and forth beneath his stubble.

"Sorry," I blurt, holding my hands up as Doug finally shifts to let me move. "I didn't plan on making myself so at home, but this dog of yours had different plans."

"Bath's ready," he grunts, pulling some clothes from his drawers before passing them to me. "Towels and fresh clothes for when you're done."

"I can't go back over to the staff house in your—"

"—yeah, I know. I'm not into how it looks either, believe me. But it's that or heading back in your towel which is even worse."

I'm mortified as I weigh up the options.

"Bathroom's on the left." Caden gestures to the open door, a light flickering glow emits from the room. "Front door will lock behind you when you leave."

"Right," I answer, realizing I'm being dismissed.

"Right," he repeats, nodding once before closing the door in my face.

That'll be that, then.

The bath is filled to the brim, bubbles resting on the surface in soapy clouds. After weeks of tolerating the narrow shower stalls and temperamental water pressure back at the staff house, I'm drawn in by the thought of this sweet heaven.

I flick off the main light, leaving the candles set up on the corners of the tub to coat the room in subtle warmth. Easing myself into the warm water, the bubbles soothe my weather-beaten skin. I tilt my head back, letting my hair spread beneath the water, my tired eyes closing as I sink a little deeper.

A silent tear runs down my cheek as I feel the weight of the past few hours press down on my chest.

I wish I could've left all of this behind in Rowenbridge, instead it's followed me here and, on nights like these, it feels worse than it ever has before.

God, I need my mom.

I don't know how long I've been lying here, running my fingers through the sudsy water, letting thought after thought weave through my mind, but I should probably get out soon before I overstay my welcome.

A gentle wrap of knuckles moves across the bathroom door.

"Hey, Millie." Caden's voice is dry as he clears his throat.

"Mhmm?" I push up on my elbows, bubbles rolling off my skin.

There's a pause, the space between us heavy with tension while I wait for him to respond.

"I'm... I'm sorry about yesterday." The wall divides us, but I picture him right outside, leaning back against the door frame as he talks. "I don't like how I spoke to you, and I didn't mean what I said. It wasn't right. I let a rough day get the better of me and I shouldn't have. If you were to ask me again today if you should stay or go, I'd answer differently. I'd tell you the truth." He pauses, drawing in a breath. "I'd tell you that I think you should stay."

Heavy footsteps recede, getting quieter and quieter until the creak of his bedroom door confirms that he's left me here alone with his words.

I think you should stay.

The water drains from the bath, leaving behind an oily pink residue that I can't seem to get rid of no matter how hard I scrub. I hold up the clothes Caden looked out for me, comparing the drawstring waistband of a pair of grey sweatpants against my hips.

If I can get these over my thighs, it'll be a miracle.

I pull the faded concert T-shirt over my head, squinting my puffy eyes in the mirror to make out the artist's name under an illustrated white horse. *STAPLETON.*

My wet hair falls out of my scrunchie in chaotic waves as I wipe at my red cheeks, removing the troughs of mascara running down them. It's a good thing Caden didn't stick around for formal goodbyes. I look awful, and for some reason, I find myself caring for what he thinks about that.

I look down at my soggy trainers, recoiling at the thought of having to squelch over to the staff house in them. I opt for bare feet instead, the better of two less than favourable options.

Tiptoeing my way through the hallway of the main house, I make every effort to be as quiet as possible, squinting through the peephole to ensure nobody is around before I make my dash across the lawn.

The coast seems to be clear.

I release the front doorknob with a gentle click and make my first efforts towards a step when a quiet voice pulls me out of my skin.

"Sleep well, Millie."

I leap backwards against the door, closing it with a slam, sending shudders through the foundations.

So much for a quiet escape.

Maura stands in the soft light of the main house kitchen, steeping a tea bag in the mug in her hand.

"Oh...uh..." I'm flustered. I can't find the right words as I hold my damp clothes against myself, trying to shield Caden's clothes from view. "It's not... This isn't what it looks like."

She smirks, shaking her head as she takes a sip of her tea.

"Really, it's not." I feel instant guilt, like I've been caught out doing something I shouldn't be.

"I heard you had a rough start tonight." There's a warmth in her voice. "It seems like Caden was just trying to help you out. He sent me a flustered text about looking for *bath grenades.*"

"Well... yes, actually," I laugh with a shrug. "He offered me a hot bath after the storm, and I couldn't say no to that. I just don't want you to see me sneaking out in Caden's clothes and get the wrong idea."

"Don't worry, love. That's not what I thought. Caden's not like that, he's never brought a girl back here." She takes a half step in my direction. "I've always thought he was saving that for someone special."

A swarm of butterflies passes through my gut at that admission. He's never brought a girl here, and he offered to

119

run me a bath like it was nothing at all. I don't like the way my body reacts to those facts, at all.

"It's nice to know that he does still have a soft side after all," Maura quips on a yawn. "I best get to bed – early start again tomorrow. You let me know if you need anything, Millie. Be kind to yourself."

She rubs my shoulder and pulls the front door open, letting me step out into the cool evening.

I stand there for a while, gazing up at the clear night sky, asking it for answers.

CHAPTER 22
Caden

Dawn moves across the sky as I step out onto the front porch, almost falling my full length over a loosely tied plastic bag at my feet. I tear it open to find the clothes I lent Millie last week, laundered and neatly folded with a note on top.

Thank you. That bath did the trick. M x

I throw the bag to the side, kicking off my morning routine with a porch coffee as the birds wake up. I don't know how I'm ever supposed to look at those sweatpants again, knowing they've been wrapped around Millie's perfect ass.

I've not seen her since that night, and there's a part of me that's begging for that to change.

A big part.

They say the first sign of addiction is denial, and I've spent the best part of the last week trying to convince myself that I'm not into Millie. But truthfully, she's quickly taking over my thoughts. Morning, noon, and night. Ever since I walked in on her lying back on my bed, looking all flustered, tangled up in my bedsheets.

I need my fix.

Need my eyes on her.

And whenever my dick brain steps aside for half a second, I'm caught up in the more serious stuff – worrying about whatever the hell happened to her in the dining room, and what I can do to fix it. Seeing her with that pain behind her eyes nearly brought me to my knees.

This is fucked. I don't do *this* – the wanting, and waiting, and wondering.

I've had my fair share of women, between situationships back in BC or the more recent one-night stands in Aspen Ridge, but I've never caught myself catching feelings. I've never been interested in attachments or commitment, so I just don't go there. The friends with benefits lifestyle has always suited me just fine, even more so when we bypass the being friends part and just take what we need.

But that's not what this is. I'm fawning over this girl like I care, like there's something at stake.

I barely know her, yet I find myself wanting to, in every way.

There's no denying the reality of this.

I'm addicted.

And I want her.

But I'm not sure I'm not what she needs right now.

I'd rather be at the river. I need the space and time to clear my head. I had every intention of packing up and heading out fishing for the day, but Maura intercepted me just as I was getting the truck ready. She has a bad habit of presenting me with to-do lists the length of my forearm whenever I have better plans. I'm not even halfway through today's selection of tasks and the afternoon is already slipping away.

Blistering heat sears my skin as I throw my axe down for a third blow on the same chunk of wood. I've lost my knack today, missed the spot more times than I can count.

You'd think this unseasonably hot June weather would put guests off lighting fires, yet I can't seem to keep up with the restocks of the log shed. Sweat clings to my white T-shirt, leaving me looking like a perfect contender for the wet tee night at The Ridge.

I pile fresh logs into the back of the golf buggy, ready to cart them round to the cabins at Maura's request. My hands are full when Doug startles, bounding up from his spot in the shade and darting past me in the direction of the creek.

Fuck.

I've been lax with keeping him on his leash out here, he's so old now that I've started doubting his ability to chase after anything, but I might be about to eat my words.

I plant my axe in the chopping block, grabbing the leash off the barrow's handle, ready to break into a sprint after him.

My heart beats in an uneven rhythm as I scan my eyes over the open yard until they finally land on him.

And *her*.

Not a wild animal then, but that's done nothing to ease my heart rate.

Doug spins excitedly in circles, jumping up at Millie's knees and lapping up all of the attention as she bends at the hips to give him gentle scratches and belly rubs. She's unintentionally giving me a view that I have done nothing to deserve.

Fuck, she looks good.

Dark high-waisted shorts float around her hips, cinched at her waist where they meet the ruched material of a wraparound bathing suit. Her wet hair is secured in a loose bun, with tousled waves falling in bangs on either side of her face.

It looks like she's had the afternoon by the river that I was hoping for.

I turn back towards the wood pile, biting down on my knuckle as I try to think of anything that might help clean my mind out right now.

"Caden!" I'd recognize Elodie's signature Newfoundland intonation anywhere. My mind was so focused on Millie that I hadn't even noticed she was there.

She's all long limbs and wild blonde curls, her arms wrapped around Parker's shoulders as he carries her across the lawn on his back.

Poor guy.

He's been firmly placed in the friendzone for 3 years, taking the small wins where he can and never once overstepping, just waiting for her to promote him.

It's honourable really.

"Oh, hey Elodie." I let Doug's leash hang in front of me, hoping it provides some sort of distraction from the evidence of my attraction to Millie, which seems to be retreating at an unbearably slow pace. "Parker." I nod.

I've got no interest in looking at another guy when my dick is still half hard.

Elodie hops down from her trusty steed, patting his back before steadying herself against him as she slips her feet back into her Birkenstocks.

"Parker here tells me you were Millie's knight in shining armour on Friday."

I can't tell if she's presenting it as a question or a statement, and I really don't want to talk about Millie right now.

I just did what any good person would have done.

I shake my head and pull the axe from the block, hoping she'll catch the hint that I have shit to do.

"Right, Parker?" She nudges him but doesn't allow him the time to answer. "Apparently, you stopped her from falling to her death off the canyon edge during the storm and valiantly carried her back to safety."

"I just said you went after her." Parker shrugs. "Elodie took that and ran with it, you know how she gets. Sorry, bud."

"You read way too much romance," I mutter, lining up a fresh log ready to split.

"Hmmph." Elodie folds her arms in a huff. "Millie said that too. I'm sick of all of the romance slander. Those books are sent from th—"

Elodie's rant continues in the background, but I lose

track of the words as my eyes snag on Millie walking towards us with Doug hot on her heels.

Seems I'm not the only one with a little soft spot.

I feel my Adam's apple bob in my throat, the afternoon heat suddenly suffocating me as I try to maintain my composure and appear unbothered by her presence.

"Hi," I blurt, pushing both hands into the pockets of my work pants and rocking back and forth on my heels.

"Hi," Millie responds in kind, holding my eye contact for no more than half a second before directing her attention towards a patch of seemingly interesting grass by her foot.

I can't think of the right words to say.

I can't even think of the wrong ones, something I'm usually incredibly good at.

"Jesus," Parker attempts a whisper, leaning into Elodie, "it's so much worse than I thought, that man is so far gone."

I shoot him a glare.

He needs a reminder that people in glass houses really shouldn't throw stones. I'll happily give it to him at some point, but right now I just need space to breathe.

"I better get back to work." I pat the side of the golf cart, prompting Doug to clamber up into the front seat and signaling the end of this painful encounter.

"Laters, loser." Elodie blows me a kiss, falling into a light skip as she heads back in the direction of the staff house. Parker scurries behind with her backpack slung over his shoulder.

I shake my head as they leave.

"Bye, Caden," Millie smiles softly, "see you around."

I watch her leave, my eyes follow her as she makes her

way across the grassy yard, the gentle sway of her hips keeping me transfixed.

See you around.

That rubs me the wrong way. I crank the golf cart ignition and trundle over the dirt road towards the cabins on a slow rumble.

I have no interest in just seeing Millie around, I need more of her than the occasional stolen glance or passing hello.

I want all of her, the versions of her that nobody else gets to see. But I can't expect her to give me those parts of herself, when I have nothing to give in return. I'm not made for forevers, I've never been the sticking around kind of guy. I'm the one who packs up and leaves before he's left. No matter how much I want her, that's who I am deep down. And I'm not interested in hurting Millie with a goodbye.

I don't know why I'm even walking down this path in my mind.

I've always mocked Parker for the whole friends-without-any-of-the-benefits thing, thinking he drew the short straw, but maybe he's onto something. Maybe it's the easiest way to hold on to a little bit of what you crave in a person without making promises you can't keep.

Maybe that's what I need with Millie.

Maybe that's what *she* needs right now.

A friend.

I could spend more time with her, get to hear her infectious laugh every day, watch the way her button nose scrunches up when she's thinking too hard, and show her all the best spots around the valley.

We don't have to make a mess with our feelings. I just need to be around her.

Friends.

How hard can it be?

"Doug." I rouse him from his sleep as we pull up on the verge by the first cabin, ready to decant fresh firewood onto the porch. "I'm going to need your help with this one."

CHAPTER 23

Millie

The front door slams.

Today was my birthday, and I'm certain he forgot. I'm almost glad. Big occasions seem to bring out the worst in him. I'd rather go without a cake and gifts than risk him blowing up.

Mom took me out for a cinnamon bun during my lunch break, she does what she can to make us feel special, but she knows as well as I do that it's safer to act like these days don't exist. Like most of my birthdays, my twelfth has come & gone just like any other day.

His footsteps are irregular as he makes his way up the stairs. He's stopping every so often, the banister creaking as it takes his drunken weight. Slurred words grow louder as he moves closer. I pinch my eyes shut, hoping that he'll bypass my door and go straight to bed. Or better still, that he'll pass out where he is without getting the chance to hurt any of us.

The turning of a doorknob and light spreading across the floor lets me know that I haven't escaped his hell tonight.

His stench fills the room; the clinical smell of the hospital, mixed with stale beer and cigarettes. The juxtaposition of his two lives. I keep my eyes shut, body angled away from him and pressed into the mattress, hands gripping the duvet cover. I know what is coming. The sound of his zipper comes first, followed by a damp warmth spreading through my bed linen and coating my skin.

"Elena," he calls into darkness, "your daughter's pissed the bed again." His voice is coated in a smirk as he staggers back out into the hallway, leaving me sodden and shivering in the mess he's left behind.

The lounge has plenty of chairs, but I always find myself in this one, rocking back and forth. It's a little worse for wear, with its stitched-up arms and sagging upholstery, but there's something soothing about it.

Whenever I wake in the small hours, I come out here and sit by this window, talking to the stars as if it's just us. I get lost in the night sky, trying to forget the nightmares and memories that have crept up on me in sleep.

I've taken to reading Elodie's romance books to pass the time, making sure I return them before she wakes up. I can't give her the satisfaction of knowing that I've fallen in love with the characters between these pages. At times, I find myself craving that kind of love, the words reigniting a spark of hope in me that a love like that might exist. But I know these stories are just fictional. I'm not naive enough to believe that my life might pan out like that one day.

All of my romantic relationships to date, if you can even call them that, have hurt me more than they've healed me. They've been heated, and toxic, and messy. The same story on repeat, over and over again. It's like my brain is hard-wired to search for the familiar chaos that it's always known. And all I ever knew growing up was a man who didn't mind hurting me – who chose to, no matter how many times I begged him to stop.

Some nights I can't help wondering how different my life might have been had my father been a better man. He was my first heartbreak. I've spent so many years searching for the love he didn't give me in other people, throwing myself into loving the wrong kinds of men, hoping that my love would one day be enough for them to treat me right.

So no matter how much these love stories tempt me, I won't do that to myself again.

I won't beg another man to love me.

The early morning silence is broken by the creak of the front door. The staff house makes no secret of being from the middle ages, its bones groaning with each push or pull.

I clear my throat, rising to my feet. "Umm, hello?"

Caden's broad frame moves through the dim light of the kitchen. We haven't spoken properly since I left his bedroom last week.

"Jesus *fucking* Christ!" He leaps back against the row of fridges, panting with his hand splayed against his chest.

"I don't know why you're scared." The words form around my held back laughter. "You're the one breaking and entering *my* house."

He clocks his fit watch. "It's four a.m. I was hardly expecting anyone to be kicking around here."

"Why are *you* kicking around here?"

"Need some breakfast." He pulls open Parker's food locker, grabbing a loaf of bread and inspecting it like he's expecting to find something living there. "Don't mind me."

"You can't just waltz in here and steal someone's food in the middle of the night."

"You're right, I shouldn't. But I'm starving and the last piece of bread to exist at the main house looks like it's growing a beard." He mashes a banana into the bread and stuffs it into his mouth in one bite, his eyes locked on mine in challenge.

There's an ease between us that I wasn't expecting. I thought we'd have to walk around on eggshells for a little longer, feeling awkward around the edges.

"You shouldn't speak with your mouth full, it's not very becoming."

"You can try and teach me manners all you want, Adams," he scoffs another bite, "but at thirty-three, I think I'm a lost cause."

He hops down from the bar stool, dusting his hands off on his sweater and scraping the rest of the crumbs onto the floor with one swipe.

Men.

"You know there are no maids around here." I pull the spot sweep from the wall, nodding to the mess he's just made as I forcefully clasp his fingers around the broom.

"Shame," he shrugs. "I'd quite like to see you in one of those silly little frilly dresses."

My cheeks flush as I make a quick return to my spot in

the lounge, diving back into the pages of my book as if it's the most riveting thing I've ever read. My eyes trail over the same sentence, not taking in a single word. I'm going to need to put some serious distance between myself and Caden if this is how he's going to act, I don't trust myself to be anywhere near him with the sort of images his words have just put in my mind.

I'd quite like to see you in one of those silly little frilly dresses.

Caden falls into the chair across from me, dragging his palm across his beard as he settles. He leans forward, elbows digging into his spread knees as he stares right at me with his signature ocean blues. Apparently, nobody taught this man manners *or* how to read the room.

I pull at my pyjama top, fanning the material against my chest.

I need air.

"Why are you up so early, my little maid?" He bites down on his lip to hold back his laughter, his eyebrow raised as if he's testing my response.

Jesus.

"Couldn't sleep." The less words, the better at this point.

I concentrate on my breathing, working out each exhale in a steady, even flow. Returning my eyes to the page, I focus intently on conjuring an image of Cowboy Jack and forgetting about the distraction of a man sitting across from me.

He places his boot in the stirrup, swinging a thick thigh over Brandy's back and adjusting himself in his Wranglers as he gets situated. Long, blonde hair falls around his shoulders as he brings his Stetson down on his head. He extends a hand towards me, pulling me up until I'm seated in front of him, his arm secured around my waist, my butt taut against his thick, hard...

I snap the book shut, realizing a second too late that my mind wasn't painting a picture of Cowboy Jack and his flowing blonde locks at all. Instead, I'd planted myself between the thighs of a whole different man all together.

My body heats with shame.

There's nothing outside the window to look at, but I keep my gaze focussed on the tiny glimmers of light that come and go as the leaves dance with the wind and the moon.

"I'm heading out on the water this morning. Want to catch the sunrise over Lake Braid, only reason to be awake at this ungodly hour."

"Okay."

Don't invite conversation. Keep yourself to yourself, he will leave eventually.

"There's enough room for the two of us in the canoe. You fancy it?"

No.

I shouldn't spend any more time with Caden than absolutely necessary.

But it *would* give me the chance to score canoeing off my summer bucket list.

"I'll bring Doug?" he adds, as if he knows that'll sweeten the deal for me.

And it does – the soft spot I have for that shaggy old dog and his slobbery hugs is growing at an alarming rate.

CHAPTER 24

Caden

"You're going to need a toque." Millie has come down from the staff dorms in an entirely inappropriate outfit for heading out on the lake at this time in the morning. I assess her choice of clothing: a flimsy, cropped T-shirt with mid-length sleeves and paper-thin active leggings. Not a jacket or sweater in sight. Does this girl know we are in the mountains? "And double up the rest of the layers while you're at it."

"It's June!" she protests.

"And it's also 4 a.m.," I retort. "Go get dressed in something that doesn't scream 'I want to freeze to death today' or we're not going anywhere."

"I forgot you were my father, Caden. Silly me..."

I bite back the joke on the tip of my tongue as she saunters back towards the stairwell indignantly. I already took it too far earlier with the maid comments.

Friends don't flirt.

That being said, I did take great pleasure in seeing the

instant crimson flush to her cheeks paired with the momentary flash of fire in her eyes.

Millie returns a moment later, padded out so thoroughly that I swear she's only done it to mock my request for additional layers. She's gathered her unruly waves into two thick braids and tucked them under a cream woollen hat with faux fur bobbles on either side. A matching knee-length puffer jacket and sheepskin mittens completes the look. It's not any more practical than the first, but at least she'll be warm for the drive.

I make a mental note to grab an extra flannel and windbreaker from the main house before we head out – there's not a chance a life jacket is fitting over that puffer.

"Better?"

"You look like you've taken inspiration from the teddy bear factory, but yes," I answer, cranking the door open and gesturing for her to go first. "Let's go, Adams."

I help Millie up into the passenger side of the truck with a boost, careful to keep my hands squarely on her waist, not an inch above or below.

Doug quickly follows, clambering up into the footwell and resting his shaggy head on her lap before she even has the chance to sit back or fasten her seatbelt.

Millie seems to slot so easily into every area of my life. In the short time she's been here, it's already hard to imagine this place without her.

I knew name-dropping Doug would seal the deal on convincing her to spend some time with me. As soon as I mentioned his name, she matched his puppy dog eyes and quickly agreed to let me take her out on the water.

The sky is still pitched black, save for the milky glow

from the moon barely dusting the tips of the mountains in light.

I had no intention of boosting out here to catch the first glimmers of pink this morning, but there's something pretty special about seeing the sun bring the Braid range to life for the first time. And I want to be there to catch the look on Millie's face.

I find myself wanting to catch all of Millie's happiest moments.

A blend of soft breaths and sleepy grunts makes its way over to me from the right-hand side of the truck. I sneak a glance to find Doug cocooned in Millie's lap, his snout cozying in at the nape of her neck. She's resting her head on his, her mouth slightly open.

It's a good thing I know this road like the back of my hand and don't need help navigating. She's out cold, but I'm grateful for the company, regardless.

I drop my speed a little, careful on the bends to make sure I don't wake her.

Whenever I come out here, I'm flooded with the bitter-sweet memories of our final summers together as a family before the crash. We used to come out here every thanksgiving, just before they were due to close off the road to vehicles for the winter. Mom would pack up an array of pastries from Stella's, and she'd always make sure to get extra cinnamon buns to stop us fighting over them. Josie had a penchant for wanting whatever I wanted at that age, and I hadn't yet grown to understand just how much I'd do anything for my little sister. So we'd always have at least six cinnamon buns between us. We'd sit out on the boat wrapped in thick blankets with flasks of hot chocolate, and sticky smiles and all of the love in the world, not knowing how soon we'd have to learn to live without it.

No matter how old I get, or how much time spans from the last goodbye, drives like these pull me right back into missing them so much I can't breathe.

I roll down my window, letting in the chill of the morning.

Millie shifts to the side of me. I can't imagine it's comfortable trying to catch up on lost sleep in that gigantic jacket, never mind with a seventy-pound lump of fur adding to the warmth. I gently let a little air in her window, hoping the cool will help her too.

This road is about as well-maintained as the old shed out the back of the main house. It's no wonder thousands of tourists find their cars in the ditches out here every summer. I keep my eyes focused on the road in front of me. It winds tighter as we get closer to the lake parking lot, gradually switching from patchwork potholes and asphalt, to pure gravel.

Millie shifts again, but this time it's more of a jerk, and it's followed by another in the other direction. Her face is tight as she flicks her head from left to right as though she's trying to shake something off.

I slow to a crawl, concern for Millie instantly erasing my own sadness.

"Stop. Please! Just stop!" Millie cries out, thick tears rolling down her cheeks from tightly closed lids.

"Hey... Adams." I shake her with my free arm, trying to rouse her from her nightmare. I know too well how painful those can be, and I can't bear to see her fighting this one right now. "Wake up... hey... wake up."

"Dad, please!" She's gasping for air as she writhes in her chair. "It wasn't her fault! Stop hurting her... please!"

I slam on the breaks, veering to the side of the road, just shy of the ditch. Doug startles, moving off her lap.

I'm rounding the truck and yanking her door open before I even know what my plan is. Spinning her knees, I pull her towards me.

She wakes with a gasp, her eyes glassy and disoriented, not fully taking me in.

Doug whines from the foot well, hating seeing her like this just as much as I am.

"Millie, you're safe." I pull her into my chest, not knowing if it's the right thing to do, but needing to comfort her however I can. "It's okay, it was just a nightmare. You're safe, I promise."

Her arms are dead weights by my side. I step back, bringing my palms up to her cheeks. She's somewhere else entirely, still trapped between this moment and whatever hell she was remembering.

"Millie, look at me."

Her eyes meet mine. She swallows as she pulls at the jacket wrapped around her body, struggling for air. I pull at the zipper in one swift movement, freeing her arms and throwing the piece-of-shit puffer into the back of the truck. Her shirt is soaked through.

"I'm... I'm sorry," she stutters. "It happens sometimes... the dreams. I'm sorry, Caden. I didn't mean to fall asleep, I'm so sorry."

She's barely back to reality and her first thought is to apologize. I don't like that she thinks she has to go there.

"Drink." I pass her the chilled water bottle I packed

earlier, waiting for her to take a gulp before I respond. "Don't bother saying sorry to me for something that you can't control, Millie. You hear me? You never have to be sorry. Sometimes the dark shit just finds us when we're sleeping, but it's not something you have to apologize for, it's not your fault."

"I just—" she wipes at her cheek, as fresh tears replace the old ones, "—I thought I was over this. I'm so fucked up. I'm sorry, you shouldn't have to deal with this."

"Look at me." I tuck her bangs behind her ears, resting a finger underneath her chin. She looks terrified, lost, broken. I'd do anything to take away her pain right now. "It's not your fault. You're not fucked up. And even if you were, you think that'd phase me? We're friends now – you think I'm the type of guy who only sticks around when things are going good?"

I drape a blanket over her shoulders, pulling it tight around her, hoping it'll bring some warmth back to her.

"You'll always be safe to be yourself with me, Millie. Even when shit gets rough... *Especially* when things get rough. You don't ever have to be sorry."

CHAPTER 25
Millie

I fasten the final button on the flannel Caden pulled from his backpack and turn back towards the truck, stumbling through leaves and broken branches as I go.

I couldn't convince myself to get changed out in the open, which seems ridiculous, given that I've shown Caden some of the most vulnerable, naked parts of myself over the past few weeks. I highly doubt seeing me standing in my underwear, with all of my flaws on show, could be any worse for him than seeing the crazy, bawling, stuttering moments of panic he's had to endure recently. I had him pinned as a grumpy, antisocial moron, with the emotional intelligence of rock, but he's been the one person who keeps showing up. Giving me exactly what I need, at exactly the right time, without a second thought.

His kindness has come so effortlessly.

The original picture I built up of him in my head is slowly crumbling at the edges.

He's turned the tailgate into a make-shift breakfast bar,

flipped down and laid out with mismatched mugs filled with frothy hot chocolate, a handful of granola bars, slices of cooked ham and a Tupperware filled with hazelnut spread.

Interesting.

"I just grabbed what we had," Caden explains, letting embarrassment coat his features. "I wasn't expecting guests, otherwise I'd have swung past Stella's yesterday."

"Not at all," I reply, grateful for the snack now that my belly is rumbling. "I actually happen to be partial to spreading chocolate on my ham. It's my favourite way to start the morning."

He scoffs at my sarcasm.

The early morning sky has gradually been descending through the colour chart, changing from obsidian to navy on the drive here, and now sitting somewhere closer to indigo.

"You'll probably want to ditch the shoes," Caden states, dropping a pair of ridiculously large flip-flops at my feet.

I slip off my sheepskin lined boots, hopping around on one foot as I remove my socks and stuff them inside. Caden catches the corner of my eye, shaking his head as he unties the canoe from the truck bed.

I look ridiculous – like a much shorter, much curvier version of Caden. I don't fill out his clothes quite right. The same flannel shirt that perfectly holds his frame falls just above my knees and barely buttons over my chest. Yet, some part of me secretly likes being wrapped in these clothes that belong to him, even with the obvious sizing issue.

I take tiny steps towards the water's edge, my toes clinging to the silicone base of the flip-flops, hoping to keep them on my feet.

"What size are these? And did they once in fact belong to a behemoth?" I ask.

"They're a thirteen." Caden laughs. "I don't know if I'd call myself a behemoth, but I'll leave you to be the judge of my size."

"Excuse me?" I splutter.

"I said I'm a size thirteen," he smirks, knowing exactly what he's just said and where it sent my thoughts. "My feet, Adams. We're talking about feet."

"Right." I nod, begging my mind to think of Caden's feet and *nothing* else.

I thought I'd seen Doug in his cutest form, but that was before I'd seen him in a life jacket. He looks adorable right now, snuggled up in the middle of the canoe, completely at ease. It's hard to believe that this hasn't always been his life. Elodie told me that Caden found him one day abandoned on the side of the highway, he brought him back to Braggan Valley with no idea if he'd make it, given how down and emaciated he was. Life hadn't treated him kindly, but Caden showed up and chose to stay.

"Here!" Caden calls. I duck out of the way of a low flying object, realizing all too late that it's my own life jacket. He tuts, brushing past me to pick the jacket up off the ground and dust it off.

"I can swim, you know. I don't need this." I gesture to the garish orange flotation device.

"In that water?" He raises a brow as he pulls the jacket over my head. "No chance. You'll go into shock before you even have half a chance to call for help. I'm not taking that risk. No PFD, no canoe. Got it?"

"Uch, fine," I relent, throwing the lifejacket on and

fumbling with the straps and zippers, trying to work out how to fasten myself in. You'd think they'd consider making safety gear like this easier to use if we're expected to wear it.

"Let me help you," Caden offers.

"I'm fine," I blurt, my little-miss-independent act rearing its head again. "I've got this."

He doesn't argue, leaning back against the tree in front of me, his arms folded over his chest as he watches me struggle.

This went a lot better in my head.

I've got myself tied up in knots, clips in all the wrong places, and I can't seem to reach around the back far enough to untwist the waist strap.

I feel like I'm suffocating – wrapped up in string like a pork roast at the grocery store.

"Still doing fine, Adams?" His trademark smirk spreads across his face.

"A little less than fine," I confess, throwing my arms down by my side in frustration. "Can I reconsider your offer?"

He makes his way back over to me, loosening all of my handy work and pulling the jacket off my shoulders, rotating it 180 degrees before feeding it back over my arms.

I had it on upside down. *Great.*

He's standing all too close as he pulls the zipper up over my chest. Taking his time with each clip, he secures me in the vest like I'm precious cargo.

"As you can see," he gestures to the canoe, where Doug has already fallen back into slumber, "I don't get into the habit of taking the things I care about out on the water without making sure they're safe first."

He pulls the final strap taut around my waist with one hand, my body stumbling toward him as he runs his fingers over each fastening, ensuring they're in place.

"Perfect," he affirms, his eyes holding mine for just a second before he makes his way towards the canoe. "Let's go."

I follow after him silently, my chest momentarily robbed of air.

The morning is silent as we push off from the rocky shoreline, save for the soft ripples of our paddles moving through the turquoise water.

When I say *we*, I really mean Caden.

He's fully in control of this voyage. I've barely let my paddle touch the surface.

I'm captivated by the way the jagged peaks cast shadows over the lake, splitting it into two entirely different shades of blue. Behind the mountains, the sun is slowly lighting up the sky, wispy clouds melting into the morning in swathes of pink and orange.

There's something almost ethereal about being out here on the lake with nobody else around. Just two humans and a dog, sharing this corner of the earth with nature as dawn welcomes another day. My worries are a little further away, it's like they can't quite reach me out here. The gentle sway of the morning waves mixed with Doug's rhythmic exhales is the perfect soundtrack, there's no need to fill awkward silences or scramble to find things to talk about.

We get to just *be*.

Caden offered to take me home this morning, said he'd turn the truck around right there and then, drop me back at the lodge if that's what I needed. But I didn't want to go

145

home, and he didn't press the issue, just hopped back in the driver's seat and carried on towards the parking lot.

I'm grateful for that. It's not often people trust you to know your mind, and let you have your way when you're in the midst of your own chaos.

We fell into ordinary conversation about ordinary things. He told me about his sister, Josie, and her 'punk-ass man-child' of a boyfriend, his old life firefighting back in BC, and that one year Doug dragged the Turkey off the table when Maura wasn't looking and ruined Christmas dinner. His stories turned the tears brimming in my eyes into ones filled with laughter.

"It's beautiful, huh?" Caden's velveteen voice breaks through my thoughts.

"So beautiful," I muse. "The clouds look like cotton candy. Like a painting... but it's real, it's right there."

"Mhmm," he hums. "I don't know that a painting could ever fully do it justice."

He's right.

This is the sort of place that needs to be felt.

"Thanks for bringing me out here." I sigh softly. "You don't know how much I've been needing something like this."

He's silent for a beat, letting my words rest between us.

"You wanna talk about it?" He drags his paddles through the water, pushing us a little further into the lake. "Either to me, or to the water? I always find that this place brings a little healing."

I run my fingers through the opaque ripples, wondering if there is some magic to all of this.

Maybe it's because we're out here in this safe haven,

away from reality, or because he's been so selflessly kind recently, but I feel like opening up to Caden. Even though I hardly know him, it feels like trusting him would be the easiest thing in the world.

I want to give him my truth, I want to let him in. I just don't know where to begin. I've carried this around for so long that I don't even know where the hurt starts and I end. It's all so intertwined within me, buried and blended into the essence of who I am, that some days I feel like I can't separate myself from those dark moments. All I've ever known is what I've been through, and its endless aftermath.

"My dad was kind of fucked up." A tiny laugh bursts out of me. It's the understatement of the decade. It's like I'm programmed to make light of everything that happened, using humour as the chaser for a reality that's too hard to swallow. "He's been dead seven years, and I still can't seem to move on. I'm still so stuck."

"He was fucked up? In what way?"

"He was a doctor, well-respected in the community, forever doing the right thing for the world to see. You'd think we had the perfect life, but behind closed doors, it was completely different. We lived in a broken home, but the kind where the cracks are on the inside – ones you'd only notice if you were really paying attention."

I pause, waiting for him to fill the silence, to end the conversation, or sugar coat it with a positive anecdote. But he doesn't.

"Mom tried to leave so many times, but men like that know what they're doing – they chip away at every part of you until you can't trust your own thoughts. They make you think you'll be nothing without them. I think she was scared that leaving him would be worse for us."

It's not until I wipe my cheek that I realize I'm crying.

"Nobody noticed, or if they did, they turned a blind eye. The older I get, the more I think it's the latter. We had the bruises, the excuses that didn't make sense. My grades slipped, Maddie was constantly acting out – but still, nobody asked. For years we stayed and hurt at the hands of my father, until the day he died. That should've been our chance to move on, to start afresh free from the hell of him. But even now, I can't seem to move on – my mind keeps pulling me back into that old life, asking me to remember."

"Millie, I'm so sorry." Caden's voice is tight. "Is that why you moved out here to Braggan Valley? To get away from it all?"

"Mhmm." I nod. "I came out here thinking a new place might give me a fresh start, that I'd have a chance to move on from these stupid dreams, and the flashbacks, and all of this unshakeable sadness within me." I feel my throat tighten around the words. "I wrote this silly list of things I wanted to do when I got here – thinking I'd be able to throw myself into life in the mountains without carrying the weight of this around with me. I just wanted to hike, swim in lakes, and ride horseback with the wind in my hair. I wanted to feel free... I thought I *would* feel free. But instead, I'm scared to allow myself to feel the sun on my face for fear that the darkness is just waiting on the sidelines to come and take it away."

I suck in a breath, feeling shame roll over me. All Caden wanted this morning was to come out here and enjoy a peaceful sunrise with Doug, instead he's had to listen to me offloading all of my trauma like a bloody dump truck.

"I think you're brave."

"What?" I'd call myself many things. Naive? Maybe. Hopeless? *Definitely*. But never brave.

"I think you're brave," he repeats. "You've clearly been through a lot, and I don't even know the half of it. I'm just hearing what you tell me, and I'm sure you're holding back on the worst of it. Yet, you still chose to come out here. You still chose to believe there was some good in the world, and that you were going to try and find it for yourself. Don't you think that's brave?"

"God, what sort of drugs are in this water?" I joke, in a fruitless attempt to diffuse all of the pent-up emotion within me. "You've seen me break down far too many times already this summer."

"You don't have to hide yourself from me, Millie." Caden's voice is strained. "I care about you – every part of you. And I don't want you to hide from me."

He cares about me?

Those words feel like a comfort I haven't done enough to deserve.

"I just wish he'd chosen to be a better man, you know." I move my paddle through the water, giving my hands something to do as raw emotion coats my words. "There were tiny moments where I thought there was still some good in him. I'd cling to those moments so tightly – the odd warm embrace, chinks of pride when I did something right, a night of drinking that didn't end in violence. But those moments were always short lived. He'd return to the reality of who he was soon enough, and I'd be robbed again of the father I deserved. That's the part I find hardest to let go of. I think there's still a little girl inside of me who holds so tightly to the could-have-beens."

Caden doesn't speak, as though he knows there's more I need to say.

"They say time heals all wounds, but I'm not sure it's healing mine at all. If anything, I'm getting worse." I pick at the ragged skin around my thumb. "I'm still so *angry*. I'm angry for that little girl and the childhood she didn't get, and I'm angry that after everything he's done, he's still hurting me now. I'm angry that all I know of love is heartbreak, and that I learned it from the man who was supposed to love me the most. I'm just so angry."

I let the tears fall, and as they do, I realize it's not anger I'm feeling at all. It's raw, unrelenting agony. Devastating loss burning through the foundations of my heart, tearing all of those moments away from me. It's all of the things I wanted disintegrating, falling around me and leaving me behind in the ash, because they were never mine to hold.

That kind of love was never meant for me.

CHAPTER 26
Caden

My heart feels like it's trapped inside a vice. We're still about twenty minutes out from the lake shore, but all I want to do is wrap my arms around Millie and let her crumble inside them.

I ache to take away even the tiniest fraction of the hurt she's holding on to.

We're not so different, me and her.

Sure, her tits are way better than mine and only one of us knows how to change a light bulb, but at the core we're more alike than I realized. Just two adults trying to get over the things that happened to us when we were kids, hoping there's something better waiting for us at the end of it all. I know too well how it feels to have your childhood stolen from you, and I hate that she knows that feeling too.

"I get it, you know." I'm nervous as I say the words.

I don't tend to open up about this stuff. Took me years to see a therapist, and even then, my first few months of sessions were a train wreck.

But I'll do anything if it helps Millie feel less alone.

She turns over her left shoulder to look at me, the canoe rocking slightly as she does. I'm going to need her to turn back around, it'll be easier to have this conversation without seeing the look of sympathy on her face.

"Millie!" I grunt. "Don't go rocking this thing – Doug will kill me if we get him wet, and I forgot my water wings."

At that, she lets out a cross between a laugh and a snort, facing forward again and letting her paddle rest across her knees.

"My parents are dead."

Her laughter cuts, replaced by a gasp that sounds like she's just taken an arrow to the lung.

In hindsight, I could have started this conversation off a little better, but I've never been able to master socially acceptable grief or talking about this stuff without making it awkward.

"Oh, Caden, I'm so sorry. I didn't mean to bring th—"

"No, listen," I interrupt. "I'm not telling you this for pity, or to make it about me. I got plenty of that growing up and I don't need any more of it. I'm telling you this because I know where you're at. When I say you don't need to apologize to me for breaking down or telling the truth, I want you to know that I mean it."

She nods, and I can tell she's biting back on the words she wants to say. She's the kind of girl who wants to heal the world around her because she knows how it feels to be broken.

"What happened?" she asks.

"Car crash." I feel my throat tighten as I swallow. "I was nine, Josie was three. It was a freak accident, something to do with the brakes on my parents' SUV. They ran straight into the path of a trucker on the highway. Nobody was at fault, and it wouldn't have mattered anyway, they were all gone before the emergency services had even arrived on the scene."

Doug pads towards me, resting his head on my feet and laying a weighted paw on my calf.

"Happened on Christmas Eve, nonetheless. Wasn't very festive of them."

"Caden..." Millie's tone is scalding, but I can tell she's holding back the very same laugh that I've come to crave.

"Sorry." I laugh. "Coping mechanism."

"At least the trauma makes us funny, right?"

"Right," I agree, even though I know I haven't been funny for a long time. I haven't been much of anything until recently.

"I'm sorry you had to go through that so young, Caden. I can't even imagine what that must have felt like."

"It's been years since then, but I still remember that night like it was yesterday. I have dreams too, flashbacks – like yours. Wake up drenched in sweat, and then I'm glad it was all a dream, until I remember that it wasn't."

I wasn't there. I didn't see what happened, but my mind does a good job of filling in the blanks. I've pictured my mom's face watching the truck career towards them. And I've wondered at the final thoughts going through my dad's head as he yanked on the steering wheel hopelessly, knowing he could do nothing to save the woman he loved.

"There's some nights where I'm standing right there at the side of the road, watching them burn in the car and there's nothing I can do about it. I want to run, but my feet won't move. I try to call out to them, but there's no sound. I'm just stuck in that spot, watching them go – like a useless prick."

I don't mention that in those moments, I sometimes find myself wishing that I *had* been there that night, that I'd died right there with them in that car. At least then I wouldn't have had to go through this life without them.

"It took me years of therapy – and countless therapists – to start believing that maybe time is a healer. The pain never gets any smaller, but you do learn to live around it. These things happened to us when we were kids. That shit is part of who we are... we don't get to forget the way it changed us, but we do get to decide how we live from here on in."

I'd started to forget that until she showed up. But somewhere between the freckles on her nose and the sass on her lips, I've found something to live for again.

"I guess you're right," she sighs.

"I'm always right, Adams."

"You're always up your own ass," she counters.

"I think you might be obsessed with my ass."

She throws her fist up in the air, middle finger raised in my direction, but doesn't refute my claim. I don't blame her – it is a fine ass, after all.

There's a newfound ease between us as we flit between deep conversations and the familiar territory of taking the piss out of each other. Even in the silences there's an unspoken promise that we don't have to be anything other than ourselves.

"You wanna know something?" I ask.

"Sure do."

"Everyone thinks I rescued Doug, but that's only half

the story." I smile down at him, choosing to ignore the fact that he's slobbering all over my pants. "He rescued me too. Kept me going on the days when my mind was dark and getting out of bed felt like the hardest thing in the world. He gave me something to live for, and he's been filling my life with those tiny somethings ever since."

"Tiny somethings, huh." Millie contemplates the words. "I like that."

"Tiny somethings." I nod. "You've just got to find yours, Millie."

CHAPTER 27
Millie

"Why won't this piece of crap do what I tell it to do?!"

I slam my hands down on the keyboard, hoping my aggression might force the hotelier reservation system to work with me instead of against me.

I don't feel like admitting to user error this morning.

You'd think after working under Ackermann in the office at the factory for so many years, I'd have managed to figure out this whole technology thing, but it's still not my strong suit.

Elodie chortles from behind the merchandise clothing stand, where she's been folding and refolding the same *Braggan Valley Lodge* sweater for at least thirty minutes.

"Need some help, technophobe?" She laughs.

"No," I reply, the stubborn edge to my voice lasting only as long as it takes me to realize I do, in fact, need her brains for this. "Actually, yes... I'm trying to upgrade the Eden family to Pinemartin Lodge so that I can place this new booking for twelve in the riverside cabins. Every time I drag

the booking over to its new spot, I get this error message—"
I turn the monitor towards her, "—and it moves back to
where it was before."

She doesn't even look at the screen as she gives her
response. "Click on the little house next to the Eden's lodge
booking. If you unassign them from their current cabin, that
should work."

It does.

"Thanks," I tut, burying my head back in my to-do list
for the morning. With July fast approaching and the influx
of bookings for Canada Day next weekend, tourist season is
officially upon us. We're already booked out on weekends
until September, and the weekday slots aren't too far
behind.

I've been picking up extra shifts with Elodie, trying to
learn the ropes at reception so that I can level up from toilet
bowls and laundry hampers to spreadsheets and error
messages.

"So, Millie, what did you get up to yesterday morning? I
had to eat breakfast alone. You were gone for *hours*." Elodie
drags out the last word as she leans over the reception
counter, stealing a grape from my snack box and dropping it
into her mouth with a pop.

"Canoeing," I answer bluntly, hoping that will placate
her, but I know full well that Elodie is never placated with
minimal information.

She needs the full lore.

"*Canoeing*?" she questions. "Since when are you into
canoeing? And with who?"

"Caden." I try to give a nonchalant shrug, but it comes
off more like an anxious twitch. "I couldn't sleep, and I ran

into him in the staff kitchen. He said he was heading out to the lake with Doug, and asked if I wanted to join him."

Amusement etches her features. "I knew it!" She beams. "I knew from that first hike that Maura sent you out on that this was going to be a thing!"

"Settle down, El. It's not a *thing* – Caden and me... we're just friends." The words don't feel right as I say them. After yesterday, what we have feels deeper than a friendship, but I won't kid myself that we're anything more. "Now if you don't mind, I've got work to do."

"Sure, sure," she laughs, moving on to re-stacking the pile of illustrated children's books she already organized this morning. I wish I had her natural ability to avoid labour so effectively.

I fix my mind back on the paperwork in front of me, punching numbers into the calculator as I try to work out the direct booking discount for the week. I gawk at the prices. Even with ten percent shaved off, I'd never be able to afford a night in one of the cabins. Apparently, you *can* put a price on those views, and it's well beyond my pay grade.

Elodie clears her throat, tapping her pen on the reception desk. I'm too focused on updating the online prices, checking my work twice for mistakes, to turn my attention towards her.

"Eh hem." She clears her throat again, this time with three deliberate thumps on the counter.

I lift my head in annoyance, sucking in a breath as two piercing blue eyes collide with mine, knocking the wind out of me.

Caden leans back against the double door entrance to the reception area, one foot crossed over the other, thick arms folded across his broad chest. He's been working on the renovations to the main hotel rooms today, they're finally being refinished to make additional space for the influx of guest bookings this year.

I let my eyes trail over him, taking in the skintight charcoal shirt under his flannel and the way his work pants hug his thighs. I can't say I wasn't hoping for him to find a reason to come past reception, not just because everything from his tousled hair to his tattered work boots makes him every bit my type, but because the more time I spend with him, the more I crave his presence.

In a turn of events that I never could have predicted, I've come to the realization that I like being around him.

"Oh, Caden... hiiiii." Elodie bounds over to him, leaning against his shoulder. "We were just talking about you. Millie was telling me all about your little date out at Lake Braid."

"It wasn't a date," he bites back with so much assertion that it stings a little. "We're friends."

"Jeez, no need to bite my head off." Elodie laughs. "It just sounded so romantic, forgive me for getting my wires crossed."

"Stop meddling, El." Caden shakes his head as he moves past her towards the front desk. "Morning, Adams."

"Morning," I murmur, clicking through old reservations on the screen, trying to distract myself from the man holding his weight against the counter in front of me. "Do you need something?" Another pretend click. "I'm kinda busy."

"I need the list."

"What list?"

"Your bucket list."

"Why do *you* need *my* bucket list?" I whisper, hoping

159

that Elodie has made her way into some far corner of the office, and can't hear any of this.

Elodie hearing that Caden has any interest in my wants for the summer would only feed into her delusions.

"Because I've been up all night thinking about you, Millie. About the things you said about wanting to feel free." He runs a palm over his beard, as if he's thinking carefully about his next words. "I can't take away the past, or the shitty things that have happened to you. But I can help you with the parts that come next. This place is special to me, Millie, I want it to feel that way for you too. I don't want you to leave here without the moments you came for."

"You don't have to help me, Caden."

"I know I don't have to. I *want* to. And I'm gonna need that list."

I've been so caught up in Caden's words that I didn't notice Elodie slipping in next to him.

"He needs the list, Millie," she states, backing him up like his right-hand man.

A defeated sigh leaves me as I lean down, pulling my journal from my tote and flicking through the dog-eared pages until I find the list in question. Ripping the paper from its binding, I drop it onto the counter, hanging my head into my hands as they begin to read through the entries.

"This is mildly embarrassing," I groan.

I know for certain there's a couple on there that I would have rather kept to myself, but I'm eternally grateful that I had some sense and decided against scribbling 'have my first orgasm' down as number thirteen. The thought of Caden reading those words sends chills down my spine, and not the kind I was hoping for.

Millie's Summer Bucket List
1) Go hiking
2) Learn to Bake
3) Horseback Riding
4) Wild Swim in a lake
5) Go on a date
6) Learn to Drive Stick Shift
7) See the Northern Lights
8) Lose 30 lbs
9) Go Canoeing
10) Spot a bear
11) Backcountry camp
12) Get into reading

"This is a good start." Elodie nods, unfolding her glasses from her pocket and sliding them over her nose. "I think we can do better, though. There's plenty you've missed here if you want to have the best summer of your life."

Caden runs his finger over the words as though he's back in high school, studying for his year-end assignments.

This is ridiculous.

"Pass me a pen," Elodie says, holding her palm out towards me. "I'm scoring hiking off the list – you already achieved that back in May when Caden had to carry you down the last stretch at Lake Ingrid over his shoulder, remember?"

"Thanks for reminding me." I roll my eyes, sinking back into the office chair and wishing I'd never agreed to hand over this list. "It's funny… somehow, the most embarrassing moment of my existence had slipped my mind until you mentioned it."

Elodie slaps Caden on the shoulder, pointing to the second entry on the list. "It's Millie's birthday next week, that's the perfect opportunity to tick off number two."

He nods, his brows furrowed in concentration as he makes a note in the margin.

"Horseback riding!" Elodie practically squeals. "You bet your bottom dollar I'm coming with you on that one, I need to meet my summer quota of hot cowboy sightings."

"You know it's just the Holden's working the stables, right?" Caden says. "Hardly the world's finest cowboy stock."

"You've gotta be kidding me." Her face pales and then quickly refills with a deep shade of crimson. "Those men have full permission to do unspeakable things to me. Johnny, Reid, Wyatt, Lawson, Beck – the lot, all objectively fuck-able. And the *cousin*s, what were their names again?"

"Colton & Tanner Briggs." Caden seems entirely uninterested in the fantasy unfolding in Elodie's mind. "Tough luck, though, Colton's out on the circuit and Tanner's in Texas. Rarely back in this neck of the woods."

"Five out of seven isn't bad."

Five out of seven. I hope that doesn't mean what I think it means.

Caden stiffens as his eyes travel down the page, an anguished look that I can't quite place moving across his face beneath his ball cap.

"Ohhhhh." Elodie laughs. "Go on a date – I like it. I

162

heard Brett Stevens has the hots for you. Maybe he'll be the lucky guy?"

I screw my nose up as bile swirls in my gut at the thought.

Brett is the most intolerable human I've encountered in the whole time I've been here. I'd much sooner commit to a life with one hundred cats and a battery powered rabbit than go on a single date with that boy.

"Over my dead body." Caden works his jaw back and forth as he spits out the words. "Millie's not going on a date with Brett Stevens. End of story." He gestures towards the list. "Continue."

Elodie fails to hide her smirk as she continues reading through the list. "Number seven: see the Northern Lights. You'll have to stick around till fall then, they're brightest up here in September."

I don't want to think about leaving yet; it feels like my time here is just beginning and moving way too fast all at once.

"Pen," Caden grunts, waiting for Elodie to drop it into his palm, before dragging a thick line through the eighth entry. "Don't even think about it." His eyes hold me in place as he says the words. "You wanna learn to run, or climb, or swim faster, sure. But you're not gonna play some weird numbers game with the scales as if they define you. Not happening. You're just fine the way you are."

Elodie gives me a knowing look, the kind that a man wouldn't pick up on if his life depended on it, but I know exactly what it means. She pulls a pamphlet from the visitor information rack, fanning it across her face dramatically just out of Caden's line of sight.

"Number thirteen." She narrows her eyes into slits as she tries to read the words. "Do something that scares you."

Confusion pulls my attention towards the final entry. I drag the paper back across the counter towards me.

"I didn't write that," I say, it comes out more like a question.

"No, I did," Caden interrupts, taking the list from me and folding it into a square before shoving it down in his flannel pocket. "You'll thank me for it. Now if you'll excuse me, I've got shit to do."

He leaves, taking the scent of cedar and sweet tobacco with him, leaving dusty footprints on the carpet and a tightness in my chest as he goes.

CHAPTER 28

Millie

I'm woken by the distant ringing of a cell phone, lodged somewhere down the side of my bed or tangled up in my bed sheets. As soon as I grab it, the call rings out.

Ugh.

I slump back down onto the bed, pulling a pillow over my head to block out the early morning sunlight beaming through the window. The ringing starts again, I squint with one eye at the name moving across the screen.

Maddie.

Panic instantly floods my gut as I push myself up to a seated position and slide my finger across the screen to answer.

"What's wrong? Maddie... Is everything okay?"

"Good morning to you too, sis." Sarcasm is thick in her voice. "I was just calling to wish you a happy birthday. Mom's here too."

She pans the camera over to Mom, who takes her hands off the steering wheel to give me a double wave.

"Happy birthday, darling!" She's wearing business casual office attire. After I moved to Braggan Valley, she started working for the City of Rowenbridge, processing applications for a host of local support programs.

It seems to be doing her good.

I take in both of their faces, letting momentary relief flood me as I realize they're both okay. Nothing bad has happened, everyone is safe. I wonder how long it'll take me to see an incoming phone call and not immediately think the worst.

The relief is short lived as it dawns on me that they've both just wished me a happy birthday, which means today is going to be the kind of day I want to be over before it's even started.

"Try to have a good day, darling." Mom is leaning towards the camera as she pulls up on a red light. "I know you hate birthdays, but we love you, Mills. Today and every day!"

"Thanks, Mom." I try on a smile, but it looks as fake as it feels. "My birthday wish is for you to stop driving like you have nine lives, please keep your eyes on the road."

"Oh, she's crazy, sis! Nearly ran down an old granny at the Broadville intersection on the weekend." Maddie regales the tale as if it's hilarious, not borderline alarming. "Side note: can you try and convince her to let me stay off school since it's your birthday?"

"No, Maddie." You've got to respect a girl for trying, but she's far too smart to be skipping class and letting her grades fall the way mine did. "You can't take the day off just because your sister who lives in the next province over is turning twenty-eight. It's not even a big birthday. Nice try, though."

I really do hate birthdays. I can't remember a single one that hasn't left me feeling like there's a dead weight pressing down on my chest. It's one of those days where you're supposed to be happy on the outside, regardless of whatever is going on inside your head. I learned pretty early on that having to wear that mask around was exhausting, and I'm yet to grow out of feeling mounting dread every year when my birthday rolls around.

My skin is sticky, a result of the intolerable summer heat we've been getting, and not helped by the queasy feeling in my gut about whatever Elodie has planned for this morning. She crept out of the dorm well before her usual alarm, and that girl usually sleeps like a log.

It doesn't take a brain surgeon to work out that she's up to something.

I can't bear the thought of putting on clothes before showering the night sweats off my body, but my grumbling stomach is begging me to head to the kitchen for a slice of toast to start the morning. I slip my legs into a pair of cotton pyjama shorts, and swap my drool covered nightshirt out for the first clean vest top I can find. The less fabric clinging to my skin right now, the better.

Pushing all of my weight into the door, I eventually manage to hit the right angle and burst through into the staff kitchen. Caden really needs to take a look at those hinges before someone gets injured.

I rub my hand over my shoulder, inspecting the area and expecting an instant bruise to form.

"Millie!" Elodie's voice is eager as she bounds across the distance between us, enveloping me in a suffocating hug before I even have the opportunity to grab a slice of bread and throw it in the toaster. "Happy freaking birthday!"

She lets me go, only to drag me further into the kitchen, pulling out a bar stool for me as I take in the decorations strewn across the island – there's glitter, and giant balloons, Polaroids with some of our first pictures together, and a hot pink gift box tied with layers of organza ribbon.

She slides a plate in my direction, loaded with fresh hash browns and an interestingly coloured sauce drizzled over eggs and bacon. Suddenly, I don't know how I ever thought I'd be satisfied with a measly slice of toast.

My belly rumbles in anticipation.

"The girl is nuts," Chef Raphael blurts from the sink, pointing towards Elodie as she scuttles towards the bathrooms. "She tells me cook you Eggs Benedict on croissant, but make hollandaise pink. PINK!" He scrubs furiously at the spatula in his hand, as though the request has caused him severe emotional distress.

"Thanks for breakfast," I laugh, hoping my manners will keep me far away from the bad books Elodie is currently residing in. I have no interest in being on the wrong side of him twice in my life.

A rough hand slides across the small of my back as a hot, familiar presence moves behind me. I immediately curse myself for not opting for more coverage as my nipples pebble beneath the thin, white fabric.

"Happy Birthday, Adams," Caden's voice whispers against my ear. "I hope it doesn't suck."

I fold my arms across my chest, trying to conceal the way Caden's body pressing up against mine just made me feel. He's gone before I have the chance to get used to it, dropping down on the stool next to me and digging into his own breakfast.

I look around the room, taking everything in. I can't believe how much thought and effort Elodie has put into making this morning special. It's the kind of birthday Mom would've wanted to give me all of those years ago when she was just doing her best to get by.

"This is too much," I choke out, tears threatening to fall before I can get any more words out. "I don't... I didn't do anything to deserve this."

"That's just the way Elodie is," Parker replies as he arranges banana slices on top of his pancakes in a lopsided smiley face. "She doesn't hold back. If she loves you, she's going to love you hard. Don't doubt for a second that you deserve that kind of friendship, Millie, you mean the world to her."

I gulp, shaking my head and pushing off from my spot, ready to bolt. My mind starts to whir – goading me to remember that nothing can be this good without something much worse coming right after.

"Hey." Caden grabs my hand under the counter, rubbing his thumb over my knuckles. "You're okay." He doesn't move from his stool, digging into his breakfast with his opposite hand, calming me without making a scene or drawing attention to us.

I focus on his calloused skin moving in deliberate, gentle strokes over mine – perfectly in time with the voice in my head as I count backwards from ten, deep centering breaths bringing me back to the present.

"I'm okay," I whisper, easing myself back down onto my stool, clasping Caden's hand in mine between my knees as though it's my lifeline.

I'm ridiculously full.

You can say what you like about Chef Raph, but he's a damn good cook and I couldn't have stopped myself from finishing that plate even if I wanted to.

"Millie, I can't wait anymore." Elodie is so full of energy this morning that she's almost vibrating. "Please open your gift." She shoves the box in my direction, grabbing my plate and glass as she goes, making room for me to unbox whatever is inside.

I release the organza bow, taking off the lid to reveal another layer of shredded tissue paper. Inside is a smaller box, and inside that is a vintage-style Polaroid camera encased in dusty pink leather, a hand-made beaded bracelet with my initials between two hearts, several rolls of mountain-themed craft tape and a stack of mismatched paper off-cuts tied with an elastic band.

"For your scrapbook." Elodie's words are hurried, a nervousness scattered within them. "Do you like it? It's okay if you don't... I can take it back, it's all thrifted, it's no big deal."

"El," I interrupt her dizzy rambling, but I'm still at a loss for what to say. "I... this... I love it. It's perfect."

This time it's my turn to suffocate her in a hug.

I squeeze her tight, realizing how lucky I am to have found a friend like her – someone who knows me so completely, who seems to get the inner workings of my soul, and doesn't ask me to be anything more than I am.

"My turn." Caden clears his throat, passing me a small rectangular box, coated in velvet from the pocket of his jeans.

"You got me a gift?" I ask, confused.

"Mhmm." He shakes it off like it's the most normal thing, but I've never had a man buy me a gift before, especially not for my birthday. This is the furthest thing from normal for me. "Nothing fancy; don't get your knickers in a twist."

I take the box from him, popping the lid open.

A thin silver chain lies on a bed of pillowy silk, with a dainty butterfly pendant attached, light bouncing off an opaque stone at the centre of its wings.

A small hand-written note is affixed to the roof of the box, I pluck it out, bringing the message closer so I can read the tiny lettering.

The butterfly;
Fragile, but courageous.
Happy Birthday, Adams.
From Caden

My airways tighten as I try to swallow.

It's beautiful.

And *thoughtful*.

It's like he's taken the conversations we had out on the canoe and molded them into something tangible, something

I could keep. A reminder that even when shit gets rough, I'll always find a way to keep going.

"Thank you," I whisper the words, my eyes transfixed on the intricate details of the necklace. "I... uh—"

The words are like cotton wool on my tongue, I can't get them out. I don't quite know how to articulate the way this has made me feel.

Seen. Understood. Known.

"Let me help you," Caden gestures towards the box, "if you like it, that is? Otherwise, I'll take it back to the Dollar Store." His smooth laugh bursts through any tension between us.

"I hope you're not trashing Dollar Village," I chide, dropping the chain into his waiting hand. "That store is my lifeline."

"That's worrying." He quirks an eyebrow in my direction. "You might want to reevaluate your life if that's the case."

"Hey!" I huff, folding my arms across my chest. "It's my birthday! Save your insults for another day."

"As you wish." He plants his hands on my shoulders, spinning my body away from him. "I'll start a list to keep track of the good ones."

His calloused fingers glide over my skin as he pulls my hair to one side, his movements both commanding and gentle. The necklace falls against my chest, careful hands fastening the closure at my nape.

He lingers for a second, his breath filling the sliver of space between our bodies.

I run my fingers over the butterfly pendant, feeling its ridges between my thumb and forefinger as I burn.

I burn for Caden Thompson.

And I don't know what to do about it.

"Better get dressed, Birthday Girl. We're headed out straight after this." Caden's voice is cool as he steps away, reminding me that he doesn't burn for me in return.

"Headed where?" I ask, keeping my gaze down, embarrassed by the realization that I might have just *felt something* for the man I once swore I hated.

"Stella's," he mumbles, tearing another bite out of his bacon roll. "Oh, and Adams..."

"Yeah?"

He leans in closer to me, leaving just an inch between us as his hot words spill out.

"I like this top—" he pulls at the material covering my chest, "—but unless your intention is to distract me from our baking lesson, you might want to consider something a little less... transparent."

CHAPTER 29

Millie

The sweet smell of apple and cinnamon hits me as soon as we pull up in the parking lot outside Stella's. The bakery has a different look to it this morning, the usual backlit cake displays are nowhere to be seen in the shopfront. Instead, lace curtains are drawn across the windows and a handmade cardboard sign is affixed to the front door. I squint to read the message.

Closed until noon - Private Baking Lesson - come back soon! Stella.

As if Stella has closed the entire bakery just for this.

I push open the door, glass beads jingling as I go.

"Millie!" Stella places down the tray of breakfast rolls in her hands and bustles around the front counter towards me. "Happy Birthday, sweetheart." She pulls me into a warm hug, leaving me coated in flour and doughy handprints.

I'm starting to regret my choice of double layers of black for clothing, but there was no way I was leaving my dorm room in anything close to white after Caden's earlier comments. I made sure to find my thickest vest top and follow it up with a long-sleeved cardigan, buttoned right up to the neck.

"Thanks, Stella." I try to dust off what I can from my midriff, but I seem to make more of a mess of myself in the process. "You really didn't have to do all this," I note, gesturing to the closed curtains.

"It's nothing," she replies, shooing away my comment with her hands. "Teaching you to bake is my pleasure. Plus, I get to spend some time with my bonus nephew. It's not often that happens these days."

Caden bends, leaning into a hug. "Thanks, Aunt Stell," he gives her a squeeze, "but don't be acting like I don't come around here to see you. You know I'm at that door every time there's a new pie to try."

Stella tuts, rolling her eyes as she signals for us to follow her into the back of the bakery. I hadn't really given much thought to what it'd look like back here, too preoccupied with the sugar laden treats out front, but I'm taken aback by how big this space is. Two large industrial steel counters line the back wall, with another forming an island in the middle of the room. Pantry shelves are stacked high with baking sheets and plastic containers, and there seems to be at least two of each appliance – stoves, walk-in fridges, stand mixers. I can't believe all of this is kept by one woman in her sixties and a few high school part-timers.

Stella squeezes in between Caden and I, throwing down a recipe book on the counter with a thunk, a plume of icing sugar swirling in the air.

"Now." She licks her index finger as she flicks open the first page. "I've already made you some pastries and a peach crumble to take back to the lodge later, so it's up to you what you'd like to bake this morning. Have a flick through and decide on a recipe."

This recipe book is a tome – it seems to originally have been some sort of Filofax, but is now twice the size, with newspaper clippings, photographs, and recipe cards stapled inside. Some of the entries are handwritten, and look to be older than Stella herself, while the more recent ones are printed on fresh white paper. I thumb through the recipes, lingering on each page for a second as I drool a little at all of the options. It's impossible to decide, there's cakes and cookies, pies and pastries, and I want all of them.

"Take your time, Adams." Caden sighs, leaning over the counter, anxiously tapping his thumb against the steel.

"Patience is a virtue," I remind him.

"Well, consider me short on virtues, then. I just want to get to the tasting part."

I pull out a recipe card for a two-tier lemon sponge, separated by a layer of tangy curd and covered in sweet butter icing. Nothing goes harder than a lemon dessert, and the recipe is significantly shorter than some of the others in the book, which seems like a smart choice given my inexperience.

"I'll be baking my own recipe," Caden states.

"You can bake?" I ask, embarrassed that this man can bake, and I've never so much as cracked an egg into a mixing bowl.

"I can do lots of things, Adams," he boasts, selecting an array of utensils from a drawer beneath the island.

I busy myself, grabbing the ingredients we need to get started from the pantry, while Stella sets up a baking station on the opposite side of the island. It's a simple list, but I still find myself lost between the shelves trying to source everything we need. *Sugar, butter, flour, eggs...* It's no secret that my wide hips don't need any of these things, but birthdays were made for cake.

I watch intently as Stella talks me through each stage, showing me the techniques and then giving me the chance to try it out myself – measuring, mixing, whisking. Her hands move with ease through the steps. I try to follow, but my wrists are too rigid, my measures too clumsy.

By the time the cake pans are in the oven, I'm exhausted.

I slump down in the wooden chair by the back window and rest my forehead on my fingers.

"Baking is no joke, huh?" Stella pulls up a chair next to me.

I lift my head, dragging my forearm across my brow to wipe away the residual sweat from my whisking. Caden is still clattering around in the thick of it, pans and bowls and baking paper strewn over the counter. I'm not sure how much of the flour made it into his batter, but there's at least half a bag on the floor.

"I love to see Caden like this," Stella muses.

"Hmm?"

"He seems to be coming back to himself." She pours hot tea into a mug, sliding it across the table towards me. "For a while, I thought we had lost him again."

"Lost him? What do you mean?" I ask.

"He's been through a lot, that boy. He grew up here after his parents passed, and we all got to recognize when he was withdrawing into himself. I started seeing that again this year, he stopped doing the things he loved. No ice fishing, no trips back to BC, less of the back country stuff. None of us wanted to see him back in that dark place. But he seems to be living again, there's a spark back in him that's been missing for a while."

I read between the words, hearing everything she doesn't say.

I watch him as he clangs around the kitchen, haphazardly piling up dishes in the deep sink, belting out some country song or another. I've not known him for long, but even in this short time he does seem different from the first day I met him, like he's rolled his shoulders back and let himself breathe in life a little.

"I brought these with me this morning." Stella places a shoe box filled with old photographs on the table between us. "I thought you might like to see some older pictures from the Valley – it's changed a lot in recent years."

"I'd love that."

Time seems to fall away as we sift through the pictures, it's like a walk down memory lane. The mountains in the background look the same, but the town itself has changed so much.

"Here's the day we opened the bakery." Stella's hair is darker, a coiffed bob resting on her shoulders as she snips a ribbon in front of the store.

"Oh, and here's the day Frank asked me to be his wife." She passes the photograph to me with careful hands. "It was simple as it could be – no fanfare back then, no elaborate declarations for the masses. We were just two people agreeing to keep falling in love, over and over again."

I run my thumb across the weathered photograph, the two of them sat on a park bench with ice creams in hand.

Stella beaming at the camera, Frank's head tilted down, his eyes locked on her.

"How did you know?" I don't know where the question comes from. "That you loved Frank, I mean?"

"Oh, well..." she laughs, "I didn't know. Not for some time. Frank played the long game, asked me to court him more times than I can remember. I always said no, had my sights on some cowboy over in Aspen Ridge who I hardly remember now. I thought he was the man I'd marry."

"And then?"

"And then it crept up on me... loving Frank. We didn't have that love at first sight sort of beginning. We were childhood friends, and that was all I wanted from him. Until I realized that nobody cared for me the way Frank did. I thought love was supposed to be explosive, filled with lust and wanting, arguing and breakups – that's what I'd seen in my kid years. But what we had was soft, what we had felt so natural that I didn't recognize it for what it was. It was love, and when I finally realized that, I knew I couldn't give my heart to anyone else. So I gave it to Frank."

I swirl a teaspoon around in my tea, scared to speak for fear of letting out the raw emotion sitting in my throat.

"There are all kinds of love in this world, Millie. When you find it, your heart will know, but it might take a while for your head to catch up." Stella pats my back as she pushes up from the table, hobbling towards the oven on seized hips to silence the shrill beeping.

I continue looking through the photographs, pausing on a more recent photo, printed in colour and stamped with a date in the late nineties. I recognize it. It matches the photo from Caden's key chain, the one he was looking at when we hiked to Lake Ingrid.

There's a woman on the left, roaring red curls falling over her shoulders as she points towards the camera, trying to redirect the attention of the toddler secured to her chest, granola bar in hand, eyes fixed on her mother.

On their right is a man who looks to be in his late thirties, tall and built, his strong features a perfect match for the adult son he never got to meet. His head is thrown back in laughter, hands on his hips as he lets the little boy in front of them take center stage.

Caden.

He's dressed in knee-length shorts, with stripy socks that rise to mid-calf and chunky white trainers covered in a thick layer of dirt. A gummy smile stretches across his face from ear to ear. His legs are spread wide, arms outstretched, fingers forming peace signs in the open air. He looks like the happiest kid in the world.

A kid who had no idea just how much he was set to lose.

My heart aches for every version of that little boy, the one who didn't know what was coming, and the man in front of me now, who's had to live through every moment since.

CHAPTER 30
Caden

I've been busy distracting myself, cleaning every bowl within an inch of its life, going over them twice for good measure. I can't let my mind go where it wants to go, which is right to the thought of Millie in that vest this morning. I'm finishing up with a final wipe of my section of the counter space, when I feel Millie's arms snake around my waist from behind.

Fuck, no.

This is bad.

This is really, really bad.

Blood rushes to my cock as my mind starts its inventory of all the other ways I'd like to have her wrapped around me, not one of them appropriate or polite. I thought my libido was starting to die down now that I'm moving towards my mid-thirties, but with Millie around I feel like I'm fresh out of grade 12. I'm suddenly incredibly grateful for Stella's insistence that I wear this goofy apron; the extra coverage is saving my ass right now.

"Is everything okay back there?" I ask, knowing that the longer I can smell Millie's sweet, fruity scent pressed up against me, the harder it's going to be for me to convince my cock to step down.

"Thanks for this, Caden... for bringing me here on my birthday, organizing all of this." She pushes off from me, walking backwards towards her baking station. "This means a lot to me."

You mean a lot to me.

More than I'd ever bargained for.

"It's cool. It was really just part of my selfish plan to try more of the recipes from this bible."

I hold up the recipe book in one hand.

Stella raises a brow. "You've tried everything in that book, Caden. I think I baked it back to front when you were going through your first growth spurt in high school."

"Sometimes I can't help myself." I shrug. "When I want something, I can't stay away. I've got to keep coming back for more."

Millie pulls her apron back over her head, tightening the strings around her waist. Her silhouette is perfect, even under all of the layers she's wearing right now. I can't help wondering how it would feel to hold her. *Properly.* I want to know how every inch of her body would feel under my hands, I want to run my fingers along each line, every curve and fold. I want to watch her let go beneath me.

And I want her to want that too.

I was already doing a terrible job of staying on the right side of our friendship, but seeing her this morning in that shirt, feeling the exposed skin on the small of her back and the way she heated at my touch, pushed me over the edge.

I'm done being friends.

She was made for me, and it's about time I do something about it.

I've been checking on my muffins every five minutes, hoping by some generous twist of fate they've finally started to rise. I went for double chocolate muffins, with a vanilla cheesecake filling, hoping that I'd be able to combine two of Millie's favourite things into one cupcake case. I had visions of her being wowed by my baking skills, biting into one of them and doing that cute little moan that sends me into orbit each time, but instead I've got flat muffins and zero chance of impressing her.

Stella's also bound to hit me around the back of the head with a baking tray when she sees the disaster I'm about to pull from the oven. She spent two whole years of her life babysitting me after school, teaching me everything there is to know about baking, and this is how I turned out.

I scan back over the recipe, trying to work out at which point I went wrong; which of the steps I missed, or ingredients I completely forgot to include. I want to blame the oven, or the utensils, or the type of flour, but there's no doubt this is all my own fault considering how distracted I've been.

Stella is working with Millie across the counter, showing her how to use the stand mixer to beat together sugar, butter, milk, and lemon flavouring to get the perfect buttercream topping. That funny feeling is back in my gut, the one that feels somewhere between hunger and fear. Watching Millie fit in so well with everyone around here, seeing how loved she is, throws me off my axis a little. It's like she was meant for Braggan Valley, like a missing puzzle piece that was just slotted in. This place had no idea she was what we were missing, but if you took her away now, we'd all feel the void.

"How is it?" Stella asks, kneading a ball of dough to the left of Millie.

Millie drags a finger through the buttercream, sucking it into her mouth with a pop.

"Sooooo good, oh my god!" She turns to face me, holding out the bowl. "You want a taste, Caden?"

Yes, I do.

I make my way around the counter, taking a deep breath in through my nose as I get closer to Millie. I place the bowl down on the counter, taking her hand in mine and dragging her index finger back through the frosting. I meet her eyes as I bring her finger to my mouth, rolling my tongue over the icing and sucking as I savor the tangy lemon taste.

"Delicious."

I don't drop eye contact as I let her hand go, her round cheeks flare red under my gaze as she bites down on the inner corner of her lip. I don't know what's gotten into me, but I do know that I never want to stop tasting Millie Adams.

The back door barely takes my weight as I push out onto the patio, hoping for a cool breeze but it's equally stifling out here. There's no escaping what she does to me. I want her, and not just her body, I want every part of her. No matter what she gives me, I find myself wanting more of it. I'm in too deep for a girl I've barely touched, but I can't help feeling like she's it.

I know that I don't want a world where Millie isn't part of it.

And it terrifies me.

I pull my keys from my back pocket, rubbing my thumb

across the faded picture in the cracked key chain frame. It feels stupid, speaking to a set of keys, but it's all I've got.

"I don't know what the fuck to do, Dad." I blow out a breath. "I don't know if I'm ready for this. Don't know if I can handle it."

I know he can't really answer, but I look up to the clouds anyway, watching them move across the baby blue morning and hoping he can at least hear me up there.

"I like her, I really do."

If there's a chance that I've found something like what my parents had, then I shouldn't hesitate. I should grab it with both hands, but there's still a part of me that's holding back, scared to fall for Millie only to have her ripped away.

"I haven't done this before." I run my hand across my jaw, my beard grazing the skin. "I could fuck it all up, lose our friendship."

I pace back and forth across the gravel, kicking stones as I try to make sense of the chaos unfolding in my head.

I feel torn between the safe choice, and the one that feels right, the one that I seem to be more drawn to each day.

"Maybe I just need sex. It has been a while."

Pulling my phone out, I scroll through my contacts. There's plenty of girls I could call, I could show up in Aspen Ridge and be at a hotel ten minutes later, my face between the legs of someone I barely know.

But that's not what I want anymore.

My cock goes limp at the sight of any name that's not Millie's.

I don't want something temporary, or shallow, or transactional. Not when I know how it feels to be around her.

Everything else pales in comparison.

Fuck.

"What if I'm falling in love with Millie?"

I hear the slam of a dustbin lid behind me and a clatter of metal by the door.

Turning back towards the bakery, I find Stella crouched by the cardboard skip, hiding from me as she pretends to break down boxes for recycling.

Eavesdropping like it's her god-damn job.

"How much did you hear?" I probe, pulling her up to stand beside me.

"I don't know what you're talking about." She pouts, but her eyes are gleaming and it's a sure-fire sign that she heard everything.

"Say nothing," I warn, pointing a finger in her direction and shaking my head as I make my way back inside.

"This is exciting." She smirks, abandoning the box she was flattening and following behind me. "My lips are sealed."

About as sealed as a busted biscuit tin, I'm sure.

Millie has finished frosting the top layer of her sponge and is now delicately placing candied lemon slices between the piped swirls of buttercream. She's concentrating so hard that her nose is scrunched up, and she's sticking her tongue out of the right side of her mouth.

I glance through the oven window, accepting defeat as I realize all I'm left with is flat, burnt muffins. Dropping the baking tray onto the island, I throw the oven gloves over my shoulder, crossing my arms over my chest.

It's a disaster.

Millie lifts her head, clearly concerned by the smell of

186

burnt chocolate. Her eyes clock the crusty, congealed lumps of flour and cream cheese lining the muffin cases.

"Uh, Caden..." she skirts around the words, "they look, uh, lovely. Albeit a bit burnt and an interesting shape, but lovely."

"Caden!" Stella's voice is shrill as she stabs a fork into one of the muffins, holding it up in front of my nose, forcing me to examine my failure. "What sort of crime against baking have you committed here? Have you no respect for this kitchen?!"

At that, Millie loses her composure, falling into wheezy laughter. She dips to the ground, crouching and holding her belly as she tries to contain the screeches bursting out of her chest.

"Caden, they're so ugly." She falls back against the dairy fridge, pawing at her eyes as tears roll down her cheeks. "They look like little lumps of horse shit."

Her cackling gets more and more frantic each time she looks back at the abomination I've left on the counter.

But I'm not even mad.

I'd fuck this up again if I got the chance, just for this moment.

Hell, I'd set myself on fire time and time again if it meant being able to promise Millie laughter like this on her birthday for the rest of forever.

CHAPTER 31
Millie

"El, I'm dying out here."

We haven't had a single day under thirty since the start of July. I wasn't made for this sort of weather. I was made for tartan scarves, pumpkin spiced lattes and watching raindrops race down the side of bus windows. And as much as I don't want to wish time away, I'm truly ready for this month to be over.

"How much longer?" I grumble, feeling my thighs rub together at the hem of my shorts and hoping we're within a few steps of the spot Elodie has mapped out for us.

"Millie, you're being dramatic. We can still see the parking lot, and you're not the one carrying an inflatable paddle board on your back."

She makes a fair point, but I'm not sure she's ever had to walk like a duck for days because of raw skin between her legs.

I should not have worn these shorts.

A short trudge brings us to a quiet spot on the far side of

the lake. I drop my backpack, falling into a heap on the grass as I try to regain the oxygen I lost on the walk over here. Elodie wastes no time unzipping her paddle board and working the foot pump until it looks a little less like a deflated balloon. I don't know where she finds her energy, but I wish she'd share some of it right about now.

Parker rolls out a picnic blanket, dropping heavy objects on each corner to keep it in place. I size up the distance between my current spot and the icy cold beverages inside the cooler on the far side of the blanket. Crawling, I make my way over and pull out a can of pop, cracking it open with a hiss.

"Nothing could ever cure me quite as fast as one of these." I hold up the can towards Parker before taking several long glugs and relishing the feeling of quenched thirst.

"I think you're addicted to that stuff," he points out, though I have no interest in taking in his criticisms right now.

Dipping my toes into the cool waters, I let the waves lap at my ankles as I take in the mountain views. There's barely a cloud in the sky, it's a picture-perfect day.

By the time Elodie has finished blowing up the paddle board, Parker is already halfway across the lake on a blow-up doughnut ring, a beer in his left hand, and a portable speaker in the other. He's got the right idea – the inflatable rings, I can understand. I'm not so sure about the idea of having to stand up and work your core muscles on this paddle board.

I throw one leg over the front of the board, situating myself cross-legged as Elodie assumes her position behind me on her knees. I'd agreed to come out here this afternoon on the condition that I'd play no part in steering this thing,

Elodie would have to do the paddling, and I'd just get to soak up the rays up front. I let my hand rest in the water, creating a gentle ripple as we push off from the lake shore.

"You've been spending a lot of time with Caden recently." I don't miss the slight inflection in Elodie's tone, she's looking for gossip, but she's not going to get any from me.

"Yup."

"What's going on there?"

" Nothing."

"You guys fucking?" she probes.

"No?!"

"You don't sound too sure about that one, Mills."

"I've told you before, we're just friends. He's just helping me with my bucket list. That's all."

"Yeah." She scoffs. "I once asked Caden to help me carry my groceries from the bus stop to the staff house and he looked at me like I'd just pissed in his cereal. I don't think he's doing this because he wants to be your friend."

"He said so himself. You *heard* him – we're just friends."

"Have you ever stopped to consider that what he's saying out loud and what he's thinking inside might be two entirely different things? God, you're hard work sometimes, Mills."

I'm starting to think that Elodie brought me out here just to trap me on this floating device and quiz me on things that I don't have the answers to. I don't *know* if Caden is saying one thing and meaning another. I don't *know* if his flirting is dead end or if he's hoping for something more. I don't do this sort of thing, and I don't know how I'm supposed to know.

Relief flows over me as we float back in the direction of the shore. I throw my feet into the water with a splash, escaping Elodie and her incessant line of questioning as I wade through the lake weed.

She's relentless.

I smooth another layer of sunscreen over my face. I've been applying double layers daily in the hope that it might help reduce the invasive crop of freckles taking up residence on my cheeks. With all the time I've been spending outside, I seem to wake up with even more intricate patterns between the tiny dots, and I don't like it. Mom's been telling me they're a sign of beauty all my life, but I'm still no closer to believing it.

Parker clicks at a gas lighter, setting up his portable BBQ and throwing down burgers on the lattice grill. There's only three of us here, but he seems to have packed enough meat and cheese to feed a coach full of hungry kids after a field trip.

"Are you judging my cooler supplies over there?" He pushes his sunglasses down his nose and squints his eyes at me.

"What? No!"

"You know you're a terrible liar, right?" He laughs. "If you're not saying what you're thinking, then it's almost definitely written all over your face."

"That's not true!"

"Believe me, you're an open book, Miss Adams." He flips a burger, the scent of charred beef wafting in the air. "Just count yourself lucky that Caden's never learned to read."

"Yeeeeeehoooooo!"

I watch from the top of the grassy mound overlooking the lake as Elodie and Parker take turns throwing themselves from a rope swing into the water below. Elodie wraps her legs around either side of the tire, hands clinging to the rope as Parker pulls her back and releases her over the lake. There's a splash followed by screeches of laughter.

It's not a steep drop, no more than 10 feet, but it's enough to put me off going anywhere near the edge.

Parker takes a run and jump, pushing his feet into the inner ring of the tire as he ploughs through the air and shows off with a back flip as he lets go.

I've never met two people so childlike, so filled with ease in every moment of their lives. I'm caught off guard by the envy that starts to bubble within me. It's like I'm watching from the corner of the room, unable to access what they have. I'm always too scared, always holding myself back. I don't know what it feels like to throw caution to the wind and just go for something.

"Millie! You've got to try this!" Elodie treads water as she shouts up to me.

I let her invitation hang there and pull my glasses down over my eyes. I want to be able to do it, but I'm stuck. I've just watched them both do it, I know it's not that far down, but I can't convince myself to take a single step closer to the edge, let alone on the swing.

Plus, I'm not so sure that the branch is fit to hold any more than 200 pounds, and I'm not eager to test it.

Elodie climbs up the side of the hill, digging her nails into the muddy bank for support. Her natural curls are falling out of her hair tie on either side of her face. I lie back against the warm grass, throwing a hand over my eyes to shield myself from the sun and to avoid her pleading.

"Camilla Adams." She stands over me, one foot on either side of my hips, dripping water over my midriff. "I command you to get that perfectly round ass of yours in the water, immediately."

"I'm not going in, I'm scared of heights." I push up on my elbows. "And if you could stop dripping on me like a wet dog, that would be greatly appreciated."

"It's all in your head." She steps away from me, taking a run towards the swing. "Look, watch!"

I hear the splash as she hits the water, but I've already fallen back against the ground. I've come so far this summer, but there are still so many moments where anxiety takes the wheel. I *know* healing isn't linear, but I can't help beating myself up when I feel the fear taking control again, standing in the way of the things I want to do and the type of person I want to be.

"Number thirteen." I sit bolt upright, turning at the sound of Caden's voice. "Do something that scares you."

He smirks as he slowly walks towards me, pulling off his T-shirt, leaving him in nothing more than swim shorts and a pair of slides.

"What are you doing here?"

"Got off work early. And just as well I did, looks like *someone* is being stubborn." He holds out his hand to me expectantly, pulling me up to my feet as I grab it. "Get up here, we're crossing this shit off the list."

I take in his broad chest, the thick muscles of his thighs, the ribbed waistband of his shorts that would be so easy to slide a hand under. Heat rushes to my core as he drags me in closer to him.

"Let's go."

"I can't... I can't do it." I shake my head, glancing back over at the swing.

"You can do it, Millie." He brings his lips to the shell of my ear. "I know you can."

"But the swing—" I inspect the branch above, "—what if it breaks?"

"Fuck the swing." He takes my hand in his. "We'll jump together. Do you trust me?"

"I... I don't know." I look back over the lake, my heart thumping beneath my rib cage, Caden's hand gripping mine against his chest. "I don't think I can do it."

"I've got you, Millie, you can do this." He leaves the slightest kiss on my brow, so gentle that I'd have missed it if I wasn't paying close enough attention. "On the count of three?"

Against my better judgement, I let Caden guide me closer to the edge. My shaky legs barely hold my weight as the voices in my brain implore me to stop, to turn around, and run.

"Ready?"

"No." I squeeze my eyes shut, taking tiny nauseous steps towards the drop. "This is a terrible idea."

"One... two... three." Caden pulls me with him, and

when I open my eyes, we're falling, the mountains blurring in my periphery as we sink into the water below.

I throw my head back with a gasp as we surface.

I did it.

"That's my girl." Caden pulls me in against his protective body, spinning me around in the water, as though we're caught up in a dance that's just for us. "You did it... And I'm so fucking proud of you."

CHAPTER 32
Millie

"What the fuck is this shit, Elena?!"

"I'm so sorry." Mom scurries around the table to take his plate from him. "I can make you something else."

"You think I work all day to come home to a dinner that's burnt to shit?" He snatches the plate from her, throwing it across the room with a smash.

Maddie's lip quivers and I grab her hand under the table, hoping she'll be able to hold back her tears for long enough not to provoke him.

"Useless! You're fucking useless!" He swipes a hand across the table, sending condiments and a glass vase flying off the edge. The flowers he bought as an apology yesterday fall in a watery clump on the floor. "Can't cook, can't keep this place clean. Can't keep me happy when I come home to fuck what's mine."

Mom gives me a pleading look across the room. I bundle up Maddie against my hip, creeping backwards as I leave the room and take her to bed, hoping to shield her from the worst of this fight, but knowing she'll hear it all.

I hold her against me, letting her use my shirt to mop up her silent tears.

"You're good for nothing, Elena." There's another clatter, followed by the shattering of glass and a pained cry that I can tell mom tried to hold back. "And those fucking kids, they ruined us. Ruined you as my wife, ruined the life we had together."

"Richard, please. Don't bring the girls into this. It's not their fault. This is all my fault."

I bite my lip, trying to stay strong for Maddie. I don't want her to see how much his words are hurting me too.

"I'm going out." The front door clicks open. "And that pussy better be ready for me when I come back."

Momentary silence follows the slam of the door, before Mom gasps for air and folds into gut wrenching sobs.

"It's okay, Madds. It's gonna be okay." I kiss her forehead, tucking her in under the comforter and placing her teddy bear under her chin. "Wait here, I'll be back in just a minute."

Mom sweeps at the broken glass as her body shakes. I take in the open space, the smashed television on the floor, the contents of the dinner pot all over the kitchen tiles, cracks snaking through each of the family pictures on the wall.

It'll all be back to normal tomorrow.

He'll replace the TV, take down the frames, buy some gifts and make his empty promises. He'll convince us that it's all in our head, that it was never that bad – and he'll do it so well that we'll start to believe him.

And then we will repeat the cycle all over, and over, and over again.

"I'm so sorry, Millie." Mom falls into my chest, wrapping her arms tightly around my waist. "I promise we're going to leave, we're going to get out of here. We just need some more cash, then we will leave."

I run my hand over her forehead, feeling blood seeping into my nail beds as I try to hold together the woman I didn't break.

CHAPTER 33

Caden

MILLIE

You up?

CADEN

Tell me this isn't a booty call, Adams?

MILLIE

No.

You wish.

CADEN

If you're not after my fine ass, then what can I do for you?

MILLIE

I had a bad dream and I can't sleep. I feel like a loser, but can you come over?

Shit.

I throw my beer down on the bedside table and search the floor blindly for anything I can find to throw on. These flannel lounge pants and an old T-shirt will have to do.

I dart through the dark hallway and out into the evening, forcing my toes into Bill's Crocs as I go. I shouldn't be out this late without a torch and bear spray, but I don't have time to fuck around.

I've got to get to Millie.

I punch in the code for the staff house.

"Incorrect code," the irritating AI voice spits back at me. "Enter the correct code and then press pound."

"I'm *trying*, you dumb fuck." This house hasn't been renovated in decades, I don't know why Maura decided we needed to install some robot in place of a classic lock and key situation.

If we really needed to incorporate fancy tech around here, I could think of a hundred other problems to solve first – like chopping wood so I don't have to.

I can't seem to get my fingers to work fast enough, the code errors out twice more before the lock finally clicks.

I pull the door open, almost taking it off its hinges as a shudder reverberates through the first floor of the building.

"Millie!" I call into the darkness. I'm usually more respectful late at night, but I don't give a fuck how much noise I'm making right now, I just want to make sure she's okay. "Millie!"

"Shhhh!" The aggressive whisper comes from the dim light of the kitchen. Millie steps into the hallway, marching towards me to scold me. "You can't come in here shouting like that at this time, you'll wake the others."

"Don't care." I step closer to her, tilting her head up towards me. Her eyes are red and bloodshot. "You've been crying."

"No shit, Sherlock." She laughs, patting at her cheeks. "I'm fine. I just don't want to be alone right now."

I follow her into the lounge, slumping down on the couch next to her.

"You don't look fine, Millie." I pull her body in next to mine, hoping she'll find some comfort in it. There's no resistance as she falls into me. "You don't have to wear a mask around me, you know?"

"I know." She shifts, letting her head rest against my shoulder. "It was just a dream, but sometimes they feel so real, you know? It felt like I was right back there."

I rub her arm, knowing that words won't take away any of the things she's going through.

"I think it's the therapy." She lets out a huff, running her thumb over a loose thread on her shirt. "I've done a couple more sessions, and it's bringing a lot to the surface."

"How's it been?" I ask, giving her the chance to talk if she wants to, but hoping she doesn't think I'm prying into this personal corner of her life.

"Weird!" Millie laughs. "She keeps asking me where I feel things in my body, but I don't even know what that means. I'm all thoughts and words, but 'sitting in my body' feels foreign to me. Plus, there's so many awkward silences where she expects me to say something – so I'll just blurt out the first thing that comes to my mind, or whatever I think she wants to hear."

"I get that – therapy fucking sucks, until you start to realize it's working." I cycled through therapists and strategies for months before I saw any sort of change in me, let alone a breakthrough. "I once told a therapist to take her Filofax and shove it up her ass."

"You didn't." Millie's jaw drops, her tone scalding.

"I did, I'm not proud of it now, but I was just a kid. Maura had to beg her to take me back. In the end, she ended up being one of the best therapists I ever had, but it took me a while to open up. You'll get there, Mills."

I'm proud of her for even trying. I know firsthand how easy it would be to walk away, to leave all the broken pieces on the floor for somebody else to clean up.

Choosing to heal so your hurt doesn't hurt others takes guts.

"I think I'm just so used to putting on the brave face for the outside world, that it's hard to take that off for this random person sitting across from me with her stupid notepad and pen, scribbling away like her life depends on it."

"It's the worst," I agree. I'm sure there've been some interesting things penned about me on notepads during my time.

"I know it's good for me." She sighs. "I know in the long run it'll help. But it's hard. And I hate that it's bringing even more of these memories up for me, making me think about everything and how it's changed me."

"I know, baby, I know."

She jerks back, pushing her palm into my thigh as she glares at me. "Did you just call me *baby*?"

I *did* just call her baby. What the fuck is wrong with me? *Get it together, Caden.*

"Uhh, yeah..." I scrape a hand through my messy hair. "I

don't know where that came from. Don't overthink it, was just a slip of the tongue."

"You know I'm already overthinking it." Her eyes trail down my body. "Um... what the fuck are you wearing?"

I look down, finally taking in the shirt I picked up off the floor. It's part of the pyjama set Maura bought me two Christmases ago, a cotton T-shirt made up entirely of pictures of Doug, organized in a collage with his name in bold neon lettering across the top.

"I'm not sure I have an explanation for this one." I shrug. "A certain damsel in distress needed me, I didn't exactly have time to sift through the wardrobe for my best button down."

"Thanks for coming, Caden." She smiles softly, but I can still see remnants of her sadness in her eyes. "Even if it looks like you picked your outfit out of a dumpster... it means a lot."

"I'm always here, Millie."

I'd drop everything to be the thing that she needs, to make sure she never feels alone.

She needs a shoulder to cry on? I'll be it.

If she calls, I'll come.

I'm starting to realize there isn't a single thing I wouldn't do for her.

"The stars are so bright tonight." She stands up, making her way over to the window. "Stargazing feels a little bit like therapy too. Looking up at them all, scattered across the darkness. You realize you're just an insignificant speck on a floating rock, somewhere in the vastness of the universe. It makes all of the problems in the world feel a little smaller for a while."

I join her, bringing my body firm against her back as she looks out at the night sky. It's clear, but there's still a fair amount of light pollution from the lodges. We'd get a better view from the overlook.

If she wants to spend the evening watching the stars, then I'm gonna make sure we do it properly.

"Let's go, Adams." I bend at the knees, scooping her up and throwing her over my shoulder like that first time on our hike out at Lake Ingrid. Except this time she's in frilly satin shorts and my willpower is working overtime to keep my hands where they should be.

"What are you doing?!" she demands.

"I know a better place," I point out. "Just trust me."

"Are you kidnapping me?"

"If that's what you're into," I laugh, pulling open the staff house door and stepping out into the cool breeze of the evening.

I drop the tailgate and help Millie climb up into the truck bed. She wastes no time wrapping herself up and falling into the mountain of pillows and comforters I threw in here as we swung past the main house. We're parked up on an old logging road, about ten minutes east of the lodge. It's always been my spot to come when something is weighing heavy on my heart, it only seemed right to bring Millie out here after the rough night's sleep she's had. The views of the town from here are incredible, but lying back and staring up at the stars beats that by a long shot.

Millie points her index finger up towards the sky, tracing a dot-to-dot line from one star to the next.

"Orion's belt. I studied the stars in fourth grade for a science project. I've been obsessed with the sky ever since." She yawns. "I love seeing the way it changes. The clouds, the sunsets, the way the moon impacts everything. I can't believe we get to experience it all for free."

"It's pretty special," I agree.

"When I was a kid, I used to look out the window late at night and whisper secrets to the moon. It felt like my diary, somewhere I could put all of my big thoughts and feelings, without the fear of someone finding them." She sighs at the memory. "Sometimes, I still find myself doing it now, it's a silly little habit that's hard to break."

"It's not silly if it helps," I say. "I love learning all of these little things about you."

"You do?" She turns to face me, propping herself up on her elbows.

"Yeah, I do." I keep my eyes trained on the sky. I don't mention that I feel like I'm saving all of these moments up, obsessing over them like a little boy with a toy train collection, taking care of each one like it's the most precious thing she'll ever give me.

Always wanting more.

I take her hand in mine, facing her palm up as I draw tiny shapes across her skin. Her deep breaths turn into sleepy sighs, more drawn out with each breath as she falls into a light sleep.

She turns on to her side, shuffling closer towards me.

I keep drawing those tiny hearts over the line across the centre of her palm, letting them turn into letters and then into words, spelling out the truth that I can't find the guts to say out loud.

CHAPTER 34

Millie

"Yeeeehaw!" Elodie is galloping around the gravel parking lot out front, dressed in bell bottom jeans, a floaty white blouse, and a pair of cowboy boots that look like they've only just made it out of the box.

"You ever been on a horse?" Caden asks, packing up a cooler into the back of the truck.

"No, but first time for everything, right?"

"I don't know that you need all this get-up for a one-hour trail ride up to Lake Braid," Parker laughs.

"Oh, hush. This outfit deserves to see more of the world than just the confines of the rodeo grounds once a year."

"That's true, you do look kinda hot in those jeans," he adds.

"Parker!" Elodie slaps his shoulder, pushing him away. "Keep those thoughts to yourself, buddy."

I wince.

You've got to respect Parker's relentless attempts to crawl

out of the friend zone, no matter how many times Elodie kicks him back in.

"Let's go." Caden taps the hood of the truck impatiently before opening the passenger door and extending his arm towards me to help me up.

We wind through the alpine, gaining elevation as we make our way out to the trailhead at Lake Braid. Caden has pulled some serious strings to get us booked on to a private trail ride at Holden Stables, the same stables that have been sold out since the start of the summer season.

The scent of hay and manure hits me as soon as I hop down from the truck and make my way over to the corral. There's ten horses fenced off, all different colours and sizes. I've never seen a horse up close. I had no idea just how huge they could be. Each of them has a brand on their hind quarter, the initials M.R.R standing out against their coats. I move slowly around the wooden fencing, taking in each one and trying to give off cool, calm, and collected energy. I read last night that horses are extremely perceptive, they'll be able to tell if you're nervous and that might throw them off.

Or worse, they might throw *me* off.

I feel my anxiety ease a little as I stop in front of a mare with unique markings across her flank, splattered patches of rusty orange and cream. I push up against the fence post, getting close enough to scratch her long nose as she nuzzles against my hand. Her nostrils flare as she nods her head up and down, her tongue flicking out across my cheek.

Euch, gross.

"Looks like this is your girl." I turn my head to glance over my shoulder, coming face-to-face with a real-life version of one of the cowboys from Elodie's smutty novels. He's decked out in leather chaps stretched over tight denim wranglers, a thin plaid shirt buttoned up to the collar, and a belt buckle that threatens to blind me if the sun hits it just right.

Holy shit.

"Yeah, uh... it... licked my face," I stutter. "The horse did."

"Yeah... Pepper has a bad habit of marking her territory with a French kiss every now and then." He laughs. "I'm Wyatt, by the way. I run the summer trail ride program out here for the ranch."

I look down at his extended hand. His short blonde waves and chiseled jawline may have turned me to stone.

"And you are?"

"Right." I nod, letting my hand fall into his. "Millie. Millie Adams."

"Nice to meet you, Millie Adams." His handshake is firm, which is more than can be said for mine as I fawn in front of him.

I feel a warm, commanding presence behind me, the comforting scent of sandalwood and leather confirming it's Caden. He runs his rough fingers down my spine, resting his palm on the back of my hip.

"I've got this one, Holden." He takes the riding helmet from his hands, turning me round to face him. He's mere inches from me, the heat of his body melting into mine.

If I didn't know any better, I'd think he was trying to mark his territory too.

Wyatt raises his hands in surrender, jogging backwards towards Elodie and Parker with a smirk across his face.

Caden runs a finger under my chin, checking the room between my jaw and the helmet strap as he secures it in place.

"You didn't have to dismiss Wyatt like that." I huff. "I wanted to ask him some questions about this horse."

"Pepper?" he asks. "There's nothing that I can't tell you about that girl. I worked a few summers out at Moon River Ranch, was there the year she had her first foal."

"*You* were a cowboy?"

"Ranch hand," he grunts. "Shoveled shit and fixed fence posts all summer."

"Interesting... Did you also have a pair of those leather chaps?"

"Might've done."

"Hot." I fake rolling my eyes back in my head. "Wear those next time."

I turn back towards the corral, hoping he doesn't catch the flush rising in my cheeks.

I feel his weight against my back, pushing me up against the fence post. His hand wraps around my braid and with a little tug, he pulls my head back to look up at him.

"Are you flirting with me, Adams?"

"Me? Flirting with you?" I push my hips back, arching my back and resting my ass against his zipper. I don't know what's gotten into me, but I think I'm done waiting on Caden making the first move. "I would *never*."

"*Fuck*." He slides his hand under my top, dragging his pinky across the top of my leggings. This is new territory, but I'm not mad about it. "Carry on like that and you're going to be the death of me."

"That's what I was hoping for." I slide out from underneath him, walking away and relishing the feeling of his eyes boring into my back.

I'm pretty sure that man is going to need a minute to recover.

CHAPTER 35
Caden

"Cade," the call comes from across the corral, "this big guy's for you."

The horse looks like it's been on double feeds for the past year. I hadn't planned on galloping off through the alpine, but I have my doubts that I'm even going to make it up the first incline on this one.

"Where'd you find this lump of lard, Holden?"

"Ain't nothing wrong with Fergus. I had to find a weight match for all that ass you're packing." His hand comes down hard on the back of my thigh.

"Did you just spank me?"

"I did." He laughs. "And I'd do it again, baby."

Jesus.

I check the tack before throwing myself up onto Fergus. I wouldn't put it past Wyatt to try to make a fool of me out here. We used to spend hours thinking up pranks to make the days go faster back on the ranch. It's good to see him again, even if he's already ribbing me like he used to.

It feels good to be back in the saddle, too. I've missed it. I've missed lots of things.

That's what happens when you find yourself stuck in the phase of surviving instead of truly living. You don't realize you're being swallowed into the darkness until you're right there, with no desire to get out. It's not until you start feeling the light seeping in again that you realize how buried you were.

Millie's last to get on her horse. She's pacing back and forth by Pepper's side, wringing her hands together and biting the corner of her lip. She looks like she's ready to bolt as Wyatt pulls the mounting block up on Pepper's right hand side.

"Hey, Adams," I wait for her to look up at me before continuing, "you've got this, there's nothing you can't do."

She nods, but it doesn't look like I've done much to help drown out her fears.

"So, we're going to take it nice and easy—" Wyatt begins demonstrating how to get in the saddle, "—left hand on the horn, left foot in the stirrup and then a big swing right on over. Easy as."

"Easy as," she repeats, still glued to the spot.

"I'll be right here to help you up." I watch Wyatt as he stands far too close to Millie. He places a hand on her waist as she positions herself against Pepper's flank. "Okay, on the count of three, big swing and pull yourself up and over."

He slides his hand down her thigh, resting it just below the crease of her ass.

Not on my fucking watch.

"Holden, keep your goddamn hands to yourself!" I snarl, jet black jealousy searing through me.

He laughs, counting down, "Three, two, one..." Millie swings her leg over, darting her eyes from Wyatt to me and back again. "This your girl, Cade?"

How do I answer that? How do I tell him that yes, she's mine, but she doesn't know it yet? That if he touches her like that again, he's going to regret it? Hell, I'm fighting to stay on this horse right now instead of going over there and chopping his hands clean off.

"Not for you," I clip. "Just keep your hands where I can see them."

"Roger that." He chuckles, walking closer to me so he's just out of earshot of the rest of the group. "You ever considered growing some balls and asking her out?"

"Get fucked, Holden."

I squeeze my heels against Fergus, hoping he'll take the hint to pick up the pace to catch up with the rest of the group. Instead, he keeps his head low, grazing on weeds that'll probably send him to an early grave.

"Heads up, Fergus." I pull the reins up, trying to steer him back onto the trail. "Did Wyatt put you up to this?"

He grunts, shifting half an inch forward.

I can barely make out the other horses further along the trail, but my eyes make no mistake when they hone in on the full hips moving up and down rhythmically on the back of Pepper.

I need to be close to her.

And I need Wyatt Holden to be so much further away.

"Come on, fat boy," I dig my heel in a little harder at Fergus's flank, "even Doug is a better wing man than you, and he fucking sucks."

Fergus lifts his head, grunting twice before taking off at a gallop with an earth shattering whiny. I fumble for the reins, instead having to hold on to his mane as he careers through the trail.

I'll be surprised if I make it through the day with both eyes still in their sockets at this rate.

"Hey boy." I finally clasp the reins in my hand, pulling at the bit assertively. He slows a fraction, letting me catch my breath. "You ever heard of a gentle trot?'

The trail opens up as we hit the meadow, wildflowers scatter through the long grass in a tapestry of lilac, pink and yellow. The group have stalled ahead at a small turquoise lake, long noses dipped in the water trying to cool off from the afternoon heat.

Millie is resting her body across Pepper's neck, hands weaving the strawberry blonde mane into several individual braids.

Not bad for a girl who was five seconds out from a panic attack thirty minutes ago.

I can't help but admire the way she's thrown herself into so many things recently, regardless of how shit scared she's been.

Fergus has returned to a slow crawl, his hooves moving through molasses as I try to catch up, not helped by the slight incline of this final stretch.

"You need me to give you some riding lessons, Thompson? What the hell was that?"

I flick my arm across my face to bat away a fly, wishing I could do the same to Wyatt.

"You've given me a defective horse."

"A defective horse... you know how ridiculous that makes you sound, right?" Wyatt smirks, scratching at Fergus's neck as he shoves a carrot between his gnarly teeth.

"I don't know what else to call this thing." I jump down, leaving Wyatt to look after his beloved beast while I join Parker and Elodie at the water's edge.

The afternoon sun is catching the subtle flecks of gold in Millie's chestnut waves as she holds out her phone, trying to take a selfie with Pepper.

"How's the ride?" I ask, my annoyance with Fergus melting away with each step I take towards her.

"Going better than yours," she chuckles, sitting up and repositioning herself in the saddle. "Let me show you."

Pepper is graciously obedient as Millie pulls up her reins and guides her through the wildflowers in careful circles. Her face is tight with concentration, teeth digging into the right corner of her lip. I try to keep my eyes focused on Pepper's hooves, but they keep being drawn back to the saddle and the way Millie's core grinds against it as she moves.

"I'm a natural, right?" she asks, pride spread across her sun-kissed cheeks.

"You're a natural, alright," I confirm, fighting for my life, and suddenly grateful that I only ever invest in high quality denim.

CHAPTER 36

Caden

We're going to have to hire a contractor if we've got any hope of getting these rooms online before the end of the month. I've barely got any work done in weeks. The main lodge renovations should have been finished now, but I can't focus on a single task for more than five minutes.

Every minute of my day is filled with thoughts of her, all of the things I want to do to her, and everything I want to give her.

I'm ready to give her all of the things I've never even considered giving to someone else.

I wipe at the sweat beading at my forehead, throwing another plank of wood into the scrap pile. I think Maura might use the off cuts of wood to make a crucifix for me if she ever finds out how much money I've wasted this month. I've had to cut boards for the same section of paneling at least three times already.

I'm distracted.

Letting the tape measure recoil, I accept that I'm not

going to get any further along with this project today. With the temperature sitting over thirty, and Millie taking up every corner of my thoughts, I'm as much use here as a chocolate teapot.

I prop open the back door with my toolbox, stepping out into the afternoon to cool off – disappointed to find there's not even so much as a slight breeze, just blistering sun. I wasn't built for this. I've always preferred the frost of winter and days like today back up my testimony that summer sucks.

I swat a mosquito on my arm, watching my own blood seep out of its tiny body.

Little fuckwit.

Pouring a trickle of water from my bottle over my forehead, I lean back against the siding of the lodge and close my eyes. I'd take this moment to pray for summer to be over sooner, if it didn't mean that I'd be willing Millie's departure closer.

I can't hold that thought in my head for any length of time. Having her here only to lose her again feels like a punishment I'm not quite sure I deserve.

My skin prickles as I catch the sound of soft, feminine mutterings getting louder as they move closer. I can already picture Millie lost in her own world, headphones over her ears, paying zero attention to her surroundings.

She rounds the corner, jumping back with a fright as she almost comes into contact with my shoulder.

"Holy shit!" she exclaims, dropping the basket of laundry that was resting on her hip at my feet. "You're not supposed to be there."

"Oh really, where *am* I supposed to be?"

"Well actually—" she nods in the direction of my unfinished work, "—inside that lodge until the renovations are done. Maura's a few days out from disemboweling you for your tardiness."

"Pfff, don't I know it." I take another swig of water, trying to stave off the headache that's forming between my brow.

"This heat is unbearable." Millie lets her weight fall onto one hip as she tosses her hair up into a lopsided bun.

"It is." Stifling now that she's close enough to touch and I can't do anything about it. I'm in the right mind to grab her and push her up against this wall, taking her lips in mine like I've been craving for far too long.

"What are you thinking? Your face just did that weird thing."

"What thing?"

"The thing where your jaw goes tight and you look like you've seen red."

Shit.

"I'm just too hot." It's not a lie, just a slight omission of the truth. "I'm going for a dip at the lake when I'm done to cool off. Come if you want."

Come if you want.

Like that has ever convinced anyone to go anywhere. I need to cut my bullshit and tell Millie how I feel. The summer is too short for me to keep stumbling around my words like a coward.

"If you want to see me in my swimsuit again, you could just say that, Caden," she laughs.

She has no idea how much I want that.

"Don't get ahead of yourself, Adams." She wouldn't be

getting ahead of herself at all. If anyone is, it's me. I'm starting to see a future with her that she never promised to give me.

"I'll be done at four," she says, hip checking me as she moves past me towards the laundry room. "Meet you at the truck."

I've reversed the truck up towards the shore at a secluded spot on the side of the lake. It's a little detour off the main road, an old hiking trail that's rarely used anymore. I come up here often enough in the summer that the branches have stopped growing across the tracks I've driven into the dirt.

It's the perfect spot for some privacy away from the tourists and prying eyes.

I pull a length of rope from the truck bed and loop it around the tow hitch, getting it set up for Doug. He's splashing around in the water, the waves bringing out his inner puppy as he paddles after the sticks Millie tosses and drops them at her feet. It doesn't take long for him to tire, flopping down in the shallows when he's had enough, his tongue lolling out of the side of his mouth.

I can't stand to see him ageing. I know it's just the way things go, but I'll be fucked when the day comes that I have to live without him.

I roll a blanket out in the shade of the truck, pouring fresh water into his dog bowl before whistling for him to come back to me. He moves slowly, shaking the damp out of his coat before he slumps down, looking about as grumpy as you can expect a long-haired dog to look in this heat. I tried to leave him at home, but he was having none of it. He likes to be wherever I am.

Knotting the rope around his collar, I leave him enough length to roam around the clearing without venturing off into the thick of the trees.

Millie is already up to her knees in the shallow water, her hips dipping from side to side as she eases herself into the cool waves with each step.

I can't keep my eyes off of her, and I'm done trying.

If I've only got a limited time left on this earth, then I'm going to spend every minute of it looking at her, making up for the lost time before we knew each other.

The black two-piece she's wearing is in a completely different league from anything I've seen her in before. There's so much more skin – the soft folds along the back of her waist, the plump curves of her chest. I've spent a lot of time imagining her body recently, but every time I see a little bit more of her, it's so much better than any picture I could ever have painted in my head.

I've been dying to get out here all day, to let the water take off the heat of the day. But now that we're out here, and Millie's looking every bit the fucking dream, I'm stalling.

"Do you plan on joining me? Or are you just gonna stand there like a lamppost all day?" She's lying back in the water, her legs splayed out like starfish as she floats with the gentle ripples.

I'm already hard under my shorts, my mind instantly flitting to fantasy. I want her in my bed, spread just like that, with my tongue all over the parts of her I crave the most.

I pull off my shirt, throwing it into the truck bed.

Sharp rocks bite at the soles of my feet as I stumble across the shallows towards the deeper water.

Millie looks like she learned to swim in a bathtub.

I bite down on my laughter as she moves through the water in some sort of makeshift stroke, halfway between breaststroke and a doggy paddle.

She looks ridiculous, but she looks free, like she's found a little bit of the peace she's been looking for.

This would be the perfect time to say the right thing, to let her know what I see in her. I should tell her that she's all of the things I never knew I wanted, that I need her like I've never needed anything in my life.

"Millie." I choke on her name as I move closer, hoping she'll keep swimming, and the words won't make it far enough.

"Yeah?" She turns with a little flip, treading water as her amber flecked eyes catch mine.

"Uh, I..." My mouth dries as I take her in, losing my nerve.

"What is it, Caden?" She's inches from me now, slow waves pushing her body towards mine.

"Just... uh." The words are on the tip of my tongue, but I can't bring myself to say them. *Fucking pussy.* I dunk my head under the water, cursing myself for chickening out. Confusion dappling Millie's face as I resurface. "Just watch out for the eels."

CHAPTER 37

Millie

Did he just say eels?

The world around me seems to stop spinning and become the eye of the tornado all at once. Visions of thick, gunky bodies wrapping around my ankles and pulling me underwater flood my brain. Before I can think about what I'm doing, I'm leaping in Caden's direction, throwing my arms around his neck and clinging to his hips with my thighs.

Anything to keep my feet as far away from the bottom of the lake as possible.

"Get me out!" I scream, kicking at the water, hoping to ward off any vicious beasts lurking below. "Get me out of this lake right now, Caden!"

He throws his head back in laughter, stumbling a little as he takes the full weight of my body against his, my boobs pushing awkwardly against his chest, just above the surface of the water.

"Settle down, I'm joking." He gasps between bursts of laughter. "There aren't any eels in this lake."

"Are you fucking joking me?" I try to land a hard slap on his bicep, but he barely flinches at the contact. "We're supposed to be friends."

He doesn't respond to that.

Instead, his gaze trails down my body, taking in the unfortunate position we've found ourselves in, and all of the places our bodies are connecting where they shouldn't be.

My breath hitches as he moves his hands lower, pulling my legs tighter around his waist.

"Friends?" He runs a calloused thumb across the scalloped edge of my bikini bottoms. "This doesn't feel like friends to me, Millie."

Heat rushes to my core as my eyes desperately try to avoid his. The icy water bites against my skin. We're so close to each other and yet my body is screaming at me to close the gap between us.

"You're right," I choke, taking in his broad chest. I run my fingers through the wet hair, allowing myself to believe he wants this – if even just for a second. "This doesn't feel very friendly at all."

He moves his mouth over my collarbone, lips brushing over my skin.

"Tell me you want this, Millie." His voice is a low rasp as he nips my ear lobe between his teeth. "I need to know you want this as much as I do."

Pulling back, he locks his eyes on mine in challenge.

I do want this.

I want it more than I could ever have imagined.

I dip my lips towards his, giving him what he's asked for.

"I want you, Caden."

At that, he loses all composure, pulling me into him, tasting me for the first time. The kiss is hungry, filled with want, like we've been starved of each other for far too long.

It's not enough.

I rock my hips over his, needing to feel more of him.

Without breaking away from my lips, Caden tightens his grip under my butt, moving through the water in slow, deliberate steps towards the shore.

The warmth of the sun dapples our skin as the lake water runs off our bodies.

My legs fall over his thick thighs, feet dangling above the ground, as he presses his weight into me, propping me up against the nearest tree.

Breaking the kiss, he pulls back, taking me in now that we're out of the water. I'm suddenly conscious of my body, aware that all of my flaws are on show for him to see. Releasing my hold from around his neck, I let my arm fall across my front, hoping to hide the way my stomach folds in this position.

"No." Caden grabs both of my wrists in one hand, holding them above my head against the tree bark. "Don't you dare hide from me, Millie. I've been dreaming of this moment, I want to see all of you."

He bites his lip as his eyes fill with dark heat. With his free hand, he traces the contours of my body in soft, gentle strokes. So slight that I can barely feel the movements, a contrast to the tight binding he has around my arms.

His index finger runs along my collar bone, then down further until he reaches my chest. He labours over my breasts, moving in slow, rough circles before pinching each peaked nipple between his fingers.

"I like the way your body puts on a show for me, Millie."

He dips his head forward, running his tongue over the thin material of my bathing suit. My head falls back, a tiny moan escaping my lips as he feasts on me.

"Fuck." My words don't come easy. "You're... killing me."

"I'm just getting to know all the parts of your body that I've been missing out on. Now that we've agreed that this—" he gestures between us, "—could never have been 'just friends.'"

My back scrapes against the rough bark as he continues to tease my body, but I don't care. Everything about this moment feels right, the perfect blend of pleasure and pain.

Caden's palm moves across my belly, his fingers trailing over each silvery stretch mark one by one. Finally, he moves his attention to the place where our bodies meet, his thumb rubbing against me with intentional, steady pressure just at the right spot.

"Perfect, Millie." He drops my arms, bringing one hand up to cup my chin as his eyes lock on mine. "You are perfect."

He closes the space between us, encapsulating me in the fevered pull of his kiss. I don't ever want to know a world where I can't remember what it feels like to have his lips on mine.

He drives his hips upwards, letting me know he's as turned on as I am as his hard cock rocks against my clit.

I try to hold it, but a small laugh escapes me, killing the moment like only I could.

"What's so funny, Adams?" he whispers the words over my swollen lips.

"Um, respectfully…" I move my hand over his shorts, attempting to measure his length against my fingers. "I don't think that's going to fit."

He pulls back, his breathing laboured as his jaw tenses.

"Respectfully," he mirrors my words back to me, "you were made for me, Millie. I can already feel how wet you are, even with all of this material between us." He lets a finger slip under my bikini bottoms, dragging it through my arousal. "Believe me, we'll make it fit."

Suddenly, I'm not laughing anymore.

The humour is gone, leaving behind pure desire. I curse the layers between us. I want to feel him against my skin, rough and raw.

I pull him back towards me, biting his lip as I draw him into my kiss.

He's no longer taking his time, his hands moving over my swollen breasts with insatiable need as he tugs them free.

I'm aching for him, grinding my hips over his cock when Doug's bark interrupts us.

Caden's glare is pained as he drags his head away from my chest. "Shut it, Doug," he snarks, digging his hands into my ass.

"Hey, don't speak to him like that!" I've come to be as protective of Doug as Caden is.

"Sorry, baby," he replies on a deep exhale. "Doug, if you wouldn't mind – a little peace, we're trying to fuck over here."

I tilt my head to the side, refusing to laugh at Caden's attitude. *Oh, fuck.* My attention is quickly snatched away from anything Caden is doing, slamming right back to reality with a thud.

"Umm... Caden." My breathing is stilted as I push him away from me, and it's no longer anything to do with how turned on he's got me. "Look."

His gaze follows mine, eyes landing on the same four-hundred-pound grizzly bear that caught Doug's attention.

"Fuck."

"What do we do?" I whimper, nerves causing me to shake in Caden's grasp.

"Just stay calm," he replies, taking a deep breath as he shakes his head.

Stay calm?! I'm about to be eaten alive.

Caden moves slowly, keeping me tight against his waist as he retreats from the tree towards the truck.

I fold myself back into my bathing suit, not thrilled by a wild animal of that size seeing so much of me on display.

"Hey bear," Caden says with more assertion than I could ever muster in this situation. "Sorry to bother you. We're leaving right now. You just stay where you are."

He doesn't drop his line of sight as he moves on an angle towards the tailgate, untying Doug's makeshift leash with one hand.

The bear seems to settle, satisfied that we're on our way out, and goes back to scuffling around in the leaves and broken branches.

Caden places me down softly on the passenger seat, prompting Doug to climb up beside me.

"We're not done." He fastens my seatbelt across my hips. "This doesn't end here. That's a promise."

CHAPTER 38

Caden

I can't believe I just got cock blocked by a fucking grizzly bear. This world really does have it in for me.

Millie has pulled on an oversized tee, leaving her legs exposed against the seat. I rest my hand on the spot where the cotton meets her skin, running my pinky finger across the soft skin on her inner thigh.

"I'm going to have to call in the Parks Ranger." Some dumb fuck left open garbage by the dumpster, which is now strewn over the main parking lot and is probably attracting wildlife down into the public spaces. "I'll probably have to come back to show him the spot we were at. Once I'm done, we're finishing what we just started."

Her cheeks flare as we pull up onto the grass in front of the staff house. Doug follows me out the driver's side door, running off in the direction of the main house – clearly unphased by how close he just came to certain death.

Millie tries to slide out of the truck, but I block her exit with my knee, stealing another searing kiss from her before I let her jump down.

"Caden!" She gasps. "We're not at the lake anymore. Someone might see us."

"The fuck do I care?" I press her against the side of the truck as I take one last kiss for good measure. "I'm more than happy to make it known that you're mine."

"I don't remember the part where I agreed to that."

"Don't you agree?" I ask, slapping my hand down on her ass as she walks off towards the staff house.

"We'll see." She winks, twirling round to face me as she goes.

By the time I made it back to the parking lot, more trash had been piled up by the dumpster, ravens diving and squawking all around it.

I directed the ranger back to the spot where we'd run into the grizzly, shuddering at the thought of what might have happened if Doug had gotten any closer. That big beast had nothing but rage in its eyes for a second.

This is why I hate people.

No matter how many signs there are, or how many bear bins Parks scatter through the outdoors, there's always one person who thinks they're above the rules. They leave shit at their ass, thinking someone else will clean it up, but all that ends up happening is a bear spends too much time in the same places tourists frequent and ends up getting moved on far away from its original territory or worse, being killed for the safety of humans.

You can't blame a bear for being a bear. But you can blame humans for being dumb as fuck.

The ranger said they'd be on the lookout and take care of things. I can only hope that by 'taking care of it' another bear doesn't end up dead.

I could barely get my words out when I was recounting a more appropriate version of events to the ranger. All I could think about was how good it felt to have Millie in my arms, her legs splayed over my hips, and my hands wherever I wanted them.

There's still a few miles of asphalt between here and the lodge, and I'm already hard again thinking about her sinking down on my cock.

My fantasy has no sooner started playing out when I'm interrupted by my phone buzzing on the passenger seat. UNKNOWN flashes across the screen. I reach over, keeping my eyes on the road as I try to grab it.

The next vibration sends it flying off the seat onto the foot well before I can catch it.

"Fuck it." I keep driving, hoping it's just spam or if it's important that whoever it is will leave a voicemail. I'm not interested in having to stop this truck once more. I want to make it back to Millie.

The vibrations start up again, louder this time as the phone rattles against the door frame. Someone really is fucking with me today, trying to keep me from the one thing I want.

I pull up on the shoulder, throwing my door open and rounding the truck in a blind rage.

"What do you want?!" I seethe.

"Hello, I'm looking for Mr Caden Thompson."

"Speaking." I'm already back in the cab, attempting to hook my phone up to the Bluetooth setup I've never used so I can keep on with the drive.

"My name is Ella, I'm one of the Nurses at St James Hospital in Aspen Ridge. We have you noted as an emergency contact for Josephine Thompson."

My world stops.

I'm only able to catch the words I don't want to hear.

Accident... emergency... head injury... alone.

My phone drops with a thud, shock rooting me in place and stealing precious seconds I can't afford to lose. Forcing my hands back to the wheel, I switch to autopilot, turning off the backroads and onto the highway towards Aspen Ridge.

I try to think rationally, but all of the worst-case scenarios start running through my head. I bite back tears as my mind starts throwing up images of Josie lying limp and lifeless at the side of the road, or crushed under the weight of warped metal.

I can barely breathe as zaps of hot electricity pierce through my skull at my temples.

I make it to the hospital in twenty minutes, jumping more red lights than I could ever come up with enough excuses for and yet, it still feels like the longest drive of my life.

I burst out of my truck, paying no mind to where I've left it. *No Parking* zones are none of my business right now. Forcing the automatic doors to part much faster than they were ever designed to, I barge past anyone in my way. I don't have it in me to care for the rest of the world when I don't know what's going on with Josie right now.

I slam my palms down on the reception desk. "Josie Thompson." I don't know what else to say, I don't have any more information, my brain shut down the minute I heard her name in the same sentence as 'hospital.' "I need to see Josie Thompson."

"Okay, sir." A plump, grey-haired woman in floral scrubs shakes her mouse, prompting a computer screen to bring up the wheel of death. "Which ward is Josie in?"

"I don't know."

"What brings her in here?" she asks, raising a concerned brow.

"I don't *know*." I feel my anger unfolding into fear as tears sting the corners of my eyes. I drop to my knees by the counter, holding my head in my hands as deep sobs threaten to rack through my hollow chest.

"I can't lose her," I cry out. "I can't lose her too."

A group of onlookers gather round me before an older man shoos them away, crouching in a squat beside me.

"Hello, I'm Dr Barnett." He rests his hand on my back as he continues. "I can see you're having a hard time—" *understatement of the year,* "—let's get you a glass of water. What's your name?"

"Caden. Don't need water. Need to see Josie."

It takes Dr Barnett far too long to extract Josie's details out of Floral Scrubs, but once he does, I follow his lead towards the Emergency ward.

I hold my breath as I walk alongside him, his steps a little too leisurely for my liking. The hallway walls continue to spin around me, as I prop myself up against them with each step. The smell of bleach coats my lungs until I feel like I'm drowning in it, unable to make my way up for air.

Dr Barnett places his hands beneath the sanitiser dispenser, nodding for me to follow suit as he punches a code into the keypad beside a set of heavy double doors.

"Evening, Gladys." Barnett nods to an older nurse as we move towards the nurses' station. "This is Caden, Josephine's brother."

"Oh lovely, let me just grab her chart." She waddles towards a filing cabinet, flicking through files one by one.

Everyone around here seems to be so calm, so unbothered by everything, not a single ounce of urgency as if the whole world isn't seconds from falling apart.

CHAPTER 39
Millie

CADEN

Phone's going to die.

Won't be back tonight, something's come up.

Explain later.

Hot tears prick at my throat as I read the text over and over.

I know this story too well. I've never known a man to continue to want me after he's known my body. I just naively never thought it'd be like this with Caden.

I waited for hours, thinking he'd eventually come back. Slowly falling into embarrassment, my hopefulness was replaced with the realization that I'd fooled myself into thinking that Caden could actually want me as much as I want him.

Stupid, stupid Millie.

I pull the armchair up towards the window, angling it away from the kitchen just in case anyone does happen to come in here this late. I don't want to have to explain that I'm sad over somebody who never really wanted me in the first place.

For a reasonably smart girl, I sure do let all of my brains go the minute my heart gets involved.

I pull a blanket up over my chin, hoping I'll fall into sleep to let the hours wash away into nothingness. Instead, I feel my lip tremble as full tears spill out of my eyes and roll down my cheeks.

I think about his hands moving over me, the feel of his fingers on my skin. I made the mistake of taking that for tenderness, when all it was momentary lust.

I wanted him to be different.

I read the texts again, cringing at the telltale shift in tone, the short sentences, the casual pull back that I'm so used to.

I'm always good enough to be the girl they fuck around with, but I'm never the one they want to stay, the one they want to come back to.

And I wanted him to come back to me.

CHAPTER 40
Caden

Josie is sat upright in the hospital bed, her swollen ankle elevated on a stack of pillows. Her hand is deep in a packet of chips as she mumbles through her words, her attention fixed on some reality show on the box TV in the corner of the bay.

"What do you *mean* you fell off the kitchen counter?"

"Well..." She licks the crumbs off her fingers before wiping her hand over the bed linen. Clearly, I didn't spend enough time teaching her not to be gross in childhood. "Garrett and I were experimenting. A little tipsy after an afternoon drink, you know? And I was crawling towards him and—"

"Enough." I hate that manchild with every fibre of my being. "And where is fuckhead Garrett now?"

"He had to open the bar."

"Right, because opening up The Ridge to gormless drunks is more important than making sure your girlfriend isn't suffering a head injury?"

"I'd rather you didn't make my boyfriend sound like such a piece of shit."

"He *is* a piece of shit." I seethe. "If he had even the tiniest bit of substance as a man, he'd be here right now."

Dr Rogers clears her throat behind me. I'm sick of this place and I've only been here two hours. There's far too many people, far too many buzzers and loud noises, and important conversations around me. I just want to get Josie out of here and as far away from Garrett Fernwood as possible.

"Josephine." She smiles warmly as she pulls back the curtain shut and moves round the bed to Josie's side. "I have your X-rays here. The good news is there's no break. Judging by the swelling, there's some soft tissue damage, but everything should heal in time. I'd suggest lots of rest over the next few weeks. We will give you some crutches to take home, and a prescription for painkillers, should you need them."

"Great," I puff, "so we're good to leave?"

"Not quite, Mr Thompson." She holds her clipboard taut against her chest, adjusting her glasses on her nose. "Josephine came down quite hard on her head, I'd like to keep her in overnight for observation. We want to rule out concussion. Just as a precaution."

A night in Aspen Ridge, *just* what I need.

"Thanks, Doc. You're the best." Josie's voice is a contented hum. "You can leave if you want, Cade. Seems like you're itching to get out of here. Garrett can pick me up tomorrow."

"Like hell he will. You're coming back to the lodge with me until you're healed. He couldn't even stick around here for five minutes to make sure you were okay. You think I'm not going to trust him to look after you now? Not a chance."

I was only planning on coming here to grab a couple of bags to get Josie through the next few weeks while she rests up, but that plan quickly evaporated. Seeing all of Garrett's junk in this apartment – the empty bottles and cigarettes, porn mags strewn all over the coffee table – sent me into hot rage.

Josie deserves a better man than this, so I'm packing everything she owns into bin liners and leaving the rest of his crap here to rot.

Heavy weight falls against the front door, announcing Garrett's arrival before he stumbles into the entryway.

"Oh if it isn't his lord and saviour himself." His drunken voice grates on me. "Caden Thompson, come to save the day once again."

I take him in, disgust oozing out of me.

His greasy hair falls in a centre parting, sticking to the corners of his forehead. The buttons on his creased shirt are misaligned, his gut pulling at the fabric. I don't think I could ever try to understand what Josie sees in this man, even if he were the last man on earth.

I keep packing up Josie's belongings, trying to ignore him as his stench permeates the air, begging me to open the window or vomit on the spot.

I scan my eyes around the living space, hoping I've

managed to grab everything that matters. Josie's leaving this jerk for good this time.

"You know, you're wasting your time packing up all of those things." Garrett smirks as he twists the lid off a bottle of Bourbon, letting it fall to the floor. "She'll be back."

"Over my dead body."

"You can't protect your little Josie from everything, you know? There's some decisions she has to make for herself." He takes another swig, slouching over the counter towards me. "And she'll decide on me. That little slut will come crawling back to me the minute she realizes she misses my cock, and I'll be back to fucking her any time I w—"

My hands are wrapped around his throat, pushing him up against the fridge and breaking his sentence in half, before I even have time to think about what I'm doing.

"You keep her name out of your mouth." His cheeks are turning purple as he splutters in my grip. I loosen my hold, letting him gasp for a single breath before tightening my hands once more. "If you so much as breathe in Josie's direction again, I'll make sure it's the last thing you do, Fernwood. You got me?"

He falls to the floor as I release him, the bottle of bourbon still clasped in his fist.

Pathetic.

I toss Josie's key to the ground and haul the last of her things to the truck, silently praying it's the last time I ever lay eyes on this washed-up stretch of road.

CHAPTER 41

Josie

Caden is driving well over the speed limit. It's not like him. Having to live in the aftermath of both of our parents being crushed to death by a truck has resulted in him driving at a snail's pace whenever I'm in the passenger seat. He treats me like I'm some sort of fragile package, seconds from disaster whenever there's any element of risk. That's how it's always been with us – he tries to wrap me up in cotton wool and I do whatever I can to shake free of his hold, rebelling at every turn.

He's not worried about driving slow today though, which makes me think there's something at the end of this drive making him throw caution to the wind and put his foot down.

"Try the lodge again," he demands, pointing at the phone in my hand.

We've found ourselves in a tricky situation. He's from the eighteen hundreds and the type of person who doesn't carry a phone charger with him, and I'm the type of person who lives in chaos and has never saved a contact to my phone in my life.

Which is why I'm now being ordered to call the lodge using the number posted on the website, for what feels like the 700th time.

Nobody is picking up.

If yesterday's fall didn't give me a headache, this shrill ongoing ringing definitely will.

Dr Rogers gave me the all clear to go home an hour ago, which is when I found out that going 'home' meant returning to Braggan Valley for the first time in two years.

Turns out my psychotic big brother packed up all of my belongings for me *and* decided to dump my boyfriend on my behalf.

I should thank him really. I was starting to get tired of cleaning up after Garrett and pretending to believe all of his dumb ass excuses.

"Try again!" Caden barks, interrupting my thoughts.

I do as I'm told.

I know better than anyone that trying to reason with Caden when he has his mind set on something is a bad idea.

The line rings out once more.

"Leave a voicemail," Caden grunts. I hold the phone up towards him. "Whichever one of you shitheads doesn't know how to answer the damn phone is getting fired as soon as I make it back to the lodge." He hits the red phone icon to end the call.

"You know only Maura can fire people, right?" I laugh.

"I'll do what I want." He taps his thumbs against the steering wheel.

"Who's the girl?"

"What are you talking about?" He pulls at his collar, a telltale sign that he's nervous.

This is new.

"I've not seen you this wound up since Daisy Felter dumped you for Chad Vickson in eleventh grade." I chuckle at the memory. It was the talk of the town in Aspen Ridge for at least a week and Caden faked sick the entire time.

"Were you put on this earth just to mock me?"

"Yes." I take pride in the role. "So, who is she?"

He chews at the corner of his lip. "Millie." He sighs. "Her name is Millie."

I'm taken aback by the ease of his admission. I've not known Caden to admit to having feelings for a girl in almost twenty years. I've heard enough around town to know that my brother hasn't ever been the type to stick around when feelings get involved, let alone admit to his feelings so easily.

"Sorry, hold up..." I clear my throat for dramatic effect. "Are you telling me you *like* someone?"

"I..." he pauses on the word, "yeah, I like her."

We pull into Braggan Valley and it's like I've never left. There's something comforting about coming back to the place you grew up where nothing ever changes. Even when there's so much going on in your own world, there's a place in the background that stays your constant.

I wince as Caden helps me down from the truck, pulling me into a bear hug and planting a kiss on my forehead.

"I'm so glad you're okay, Jose." He ruffles my hair before jogging into the house.

I hobble behind him, noting that he makes no effort to wait for his invalid sister who he *insisted* come home to Braggan Valley.

He's inside, cranking up the heat on the shower, before I even make it across the threshold.

"Thanks for helping me in, some nurse you are!"

"Make yourself at home," he shouts back at me, grabbing a towel from the linen cupboard. "I can't stick around right now, I've got to get washed and then I'm off to grovel. I left Millie halfway to fucked yesterday to come to your rescue. She's no doubt tied herself in knots overthinking what that means."

"This *is* still my home, dipshit," I point out, limping towards the back bedroom. "And I don't need to know anything about where you're sticking your micro dick."

I drop onto the single bed in my childhood bedroom, wrapping myself up in the comfort of my old quilted blanket.

Staring at the popcorn ceiling, I trail my eyes over the intricate patterns, wondering how many phases of my life have wound up just like this one. Lying here, not knowing what comes next. I didn't think this is where I would be at this age, back here in Braggan Valley – no further forward with my life, making worse decisions than I ever have before.

Yet, here I am.

Dating Garret Fernwood might have been way closer to hell than I realized, and it's about time I dig myself up and out of it.

"*Motherfucker!*" The words come from just outside my window.

I inch open the curtains, hoping to catch some guest drama.

I've missed spectating on the quarrels of married men and their mistresses, or rich families who've realized that a weekend without the nanny is too much of a burden to carry. People come to Braggan Valley for the fantasy of the wilderness, but more often than not, their realities follow them here with a vengeance.

It's not a guest though, it's Millie.

I don't even have to ask. Her pear-shaped figure is an exact match for the half-naked models Caden plastered his walls with in his early teens. He must have instantly known he was fucked when he first laid eyes on her.

She's adjusting the watch on her wrist, smashing her finger into the screen with pure frustration. There's a sass radiating through her, and I like it. Caden needs a girl with that sort of fire in her.

She starts off jogging again, her high pony swooshing in perfect rhythm with each jiggle of her ass.

Fuck me.

I hate to pre-empt the downfall of my brother's love life, but if things don't work out with Caden, then I'm definitely putting myself next on the list.

CHAPTER 42
Millie

I don't run. But I couldn't think of anything else that would take my mind off the way I'm feeling right now. If I have to turn my lungs into a heaving, deflated mess just for a fraction of peace in my mind, then so be it.

I keep retracing my morning, wishing that I'd just taken a little longer in the shower, or that my toast had burnt and kept me from looking out the window at that exact moment.

The tenderness in his embrace, the kiss on the forehead, the familiarity as she walked into the main house after him.

Realizing that the 'something' that had come up with Caden was another girl nearly broke me in two. I wish I'd never had to see her face, to know how beautiful she is. I'm already lost in the comparison of all of the things she is that I'm not.

I've fallen way too deep, hurt myself in ways I promised myself I wouldn't.

"*Motherfucker*!" I check my fit watch, realizing it hasn't captured the last two hundred metres between here and the staff house. I'm not putting myself through the torture of exercise without at least getting the victory of hitting my step goal.

I start to feel the burn in my calves as I pick up a steady pace, my feet thundering against the asphalt as I make my way towards the trail. Heat sears through my chest. I beg for more of it, figuring that the physical pain will at least do a good job of pushing down the poisonous mixture of emotions tangled up in my gut.

The terrain changes to tree roots and dusty earth as I round the corner and slow to a walking pace, pressing my right hand down into my abdomen, holding back the stitch that's formed.

"Uch!" I let out a scream, hitting my fist off a tree just off the trail. "Why did I have to be so fucking stupid?"

The first tear falls, and I can't hold back the ones that follow.

"All I wanted was to be chosen." I let the broken words fall out into the open air, not knowing who they are for or if anyone is listening. "Why am I never the one that gets to be chosen?"

CHAPTER 43
Caden

"Where's Millie?" I pull Elodie's headphones from her ears, spinning her office chair towards me, forcing her to pay attention. "And why aren't you picking up the reception phone?"

"Oh." She spins the chair back towards the computer, returning to the game she's been playing. Not what we pay her for, but whatever. "I had to mute it earlier, some moron kept calling over and over again while I was working on invoices."

"That *moron* was me."

I turn up the volume on the handset, hitting play on the new voicemails. *"Whichever one of you shitheads doesn't know how to answer the damn phone is getting fired as soon as I make it back to the lodge."*

She shrugs. "You're not going to fire me, Caden. I'm your favourite."

"Not right now, you're not." I sigh, this girl is exasperating. "Just tell me where Millie is."

She pulls up a map on her phone, a flashing blue dot outlining Millie's whereabouts halfway along Pika Trail.

"Do some work, Elodie!" I call, jogging back towards the truck. "And watch my dog!" I point towards the office, prompting Doug to hobble towards the front desk. I need my full attention to be on Millie. I can't afford to have Doug hounding wildlife again and making this situation even more of a mess than it already is.

I hate that I had to leave her yesterday. It was the worst possible timing giving how much she'd let me in, the trust she'd given me with her body, and her heart. I promised her I'd be back, and then I let her down.

Letting Millie down is the last thing I ever wanted to do.

I'm not even two minutes out from the lodge when I find myself lined up behind several cars and a swarm of tourists gawking at a herd of bighorn sheep.

Those sheep are the bane of my existence.

I honk my horn, hoping it'll prompt the cars in front of me to at least pull over. Instead, the humans ignore me, and the sheep mock me. One of them looks me straight in the eye, getting down on its hunkers in the middle of the road as though it's on a personal mission to ruin my chances with Millie.

Fucking wildlife.

I slam my truck into park on the shoulder, abandoning it there for the time being as I make my way towards the trail on foot.

I haven't exerted this much energy since I was fighting fires back in BC and I'm still no closer to finding Millie. No matter how much my lungs beg me to stop, I won't until I've got her in my arms.

My eyes finally snag on her figure up ahead, crouched down with her head in her hands. I'm sick of how many times I've had to see Millie hurt in the short time we've known each other.

I'm even more sick that this time it's my doing.

"*Millie,*" I call out, desperate to make this right.

"Go home, Caden," she pants between sobs, getting to her feet as I approach her.

"Millie, look at me." I reach out towards her.

"Just leave me be." She pushes me away, stepping back onto the trail. "I can't do this... don't make it harder than it already is. I don't want to be the other woman, or your bit on the side."

"*What?*" I grab her wrist, pulling her body back towards mine. "Millie, what are you talking about?"

"I saw you with that girl. You held her like she meant the world to you – I can't compete with that. I *won't* compete with someone else for your attention. I don't want to embarrass myself waiting around for you to pick me when I know I'm not the one you want."

"You're making no sense!"

"The girl!" she shouts, I can't tell whether her words are coated in anger or pure agony. "With the tattoos, the barely-there waist, the black hair. She's beautiful and she's nothing like me. I'm not going to pit myself against her."

I take the pieces of her fragmented sentences and slot them into place.

"*Josie?*" I choke out. "You mean my sister Josie?!"

Confusion dapples her face.

"*Fuck,* I'm sorry, Millie." I try to cup her chin in my hands, but she jerks away from me, skittish, like she can't trust my touch. "I should have straightened this all out last night, but my head was fried. The hospital called me, told me Josie was there, and I freaked out. Everything else fell to the wayside until I knew she was okay. And then my phone died, and Elodie wouldn't answer the lodge landline. It's all been a big fucking mess, I'm so sorry."

"That was your *sister*?" Relief washes over her, but it's quickly replaced with shame. "What happened? Is she okay?"

"It's a long story, but she's fine." I finally let out a breath, the tension releasing from my chest. "Now will you please let me hold you? I can't stand seeing you like this."

I expect her to soften but instead she crosses her arms as she backs away from me, her walls higher than I've ever seen them before.

"I..." Her voice cracks. "I don't think I can do this, Caden. We're hurting ourselves for no good reason. This—" she throws her hands up in the air, gesturing between us, "— it's all temporary, I have to go back to the city at the end of the summer. And you've got all of this here. It'll never work. We have to end this before it goes too far."

I know that's not what she wants.

"What!? Millie, no!" My legs are weak beneath me. "Don't do this, don't take the easy way out because you're scared."

"You think this is easy, Caden?" Her eyes are brimming with tears. "I didn't come here for this. I came here to feel something good – to find myself. I *wanted* easy. But now I feel like I'm falling for you, and I don't think I'm strong enough. I can't afford to give my heart to you, knowing how much it'll hurt when it ends."

She can't be calling this off right now, not when we've barely even scratched the surface of what we could be.

She's everything I want, everything I need.

I'm not ready to lose her before I've even had the chance to call her mine.

"You've come to think that love is just something that's going to hurt you, but that's not what this is, Millie."

"I know this isn't love!" She seethes, getting the completely wrong end of the stick and running with it. "You don't have to spell it out for me."

"No, *fuck*. That's not what I meant." I pause, dragging my palm over my stubble, knowing that whatever I say next has to hold the truth of everything I feel for her. "What I meant was... I love you, Millie." I tilt her chin up towards me, wiping the tears from her cheeks. "And I'm not going to hurt you."

Her face pales, eyes begging me to promise her that I'm telling the truth.

"You *love me*?" Her bottom lip trembles.

"I love you," I reply, knowing I'll never get tired of saying those three words out loud. "Desperately... with everything I've got."

CHAPTER 44
Millie

He loves me, he loves me not...

I pull another daisy from the grass, asking it the same question that I've asked the last twenty-odd that lie discarded by my side. They've all come back with the same consensus: he loves me, just like he said.

I just have to decide if I'm brave enough to believe him.

I look down at the note in my lap, the one I found pinned to my dorm door this morning, complete with a fresh bear claw from Stella's.

Millie,
Let me show you.
Dinner, Friday. I'll pick you up at 7.
Love, Caden. x

CHAPTER 45
Millie

"What underwear have you got on?"

"No comment." I twirl my hair around the curling wand, trying to keep an air of nonchalance about me as Elodie continues her inquisition.

"Oh, you are soooo doing the nasty tonight." Her laugh comes out more like a squeal.

"Enough." I groan, grabbing my purse from her hands. "It's our first proper date, I'm sure Caden's going to be nothing but a gentleman."

"With you looking this hot?" She fans the tiered skirt of my dress. "I should hope the fuck not."

Say what you like about Elodie Anderson, she's my forever wingwoman & biggest cheerleader – a true girl's girl through and through.

"Don't do anything I wouldn't do." She smirks, knowing full well that leaves plenty on the table. "I won't wait up."

The heels of my cowboy boots click as I walk towards

the front door, smoothing my hands over the lace bodice of my dress. There's a nervousness in me as I throw my denim jacket over my shoulders, reaching for the door handle.

I want Caden to like what he sees.

I want him to take one look at me and forget everything he knows about being a gentleman.

I step out into the warm haze of the early evening, as the soft breeze loosens my curls. Either I'm on heat, or Caden looks ten times hotter than usual. He's waiting for me with a bouquet of wildflowers in one arm, the other hand raking through his hair as he leans against... *the golf cart?*

"What's with the golf cart?" My face screws up with confusion.

"Oh, that?" He smirks, as if he's aware of some joke I'm not in on. "To get us to our date."

"I thought we were going for dinner?" I'd be happy with any sort of date, but if this is some sort of elaborate prank, Caden might not live to see tomorrow – especially given the extensive grooming regimen I committed to ahead of this date.

"We are." He leans in towards me, leaving behind a tender kiss on my neck as he hands me the flowers. "You look beautiful."

"Thank you." A blush heats my cheeks, distracting me from the issue of our transportation momentarily. I run my hand down his chest, taking him in slowly as I notice every detail, from his black button-down to the perfectly fitted Wranglers, and the rich scent of sandalwood that lingers after his kiss, drawing me in.

"And by beautiful," his voice is a mere whisper against my ear, "I mean I'm this close—" he holds his thumb and index finger half an inch apart, "—from tearing this pretty little dress off with my teeth and fucking you right here for everyone to see."

"Caden!" I try to push him away, but he's already pulling me into him.

"Judging by the fire in those amber eyes of yours, you'd like that. Wouldn't you?"

I can't deny that the thought of Caden claiming me as his own in plain sight, without a care for who's watching, turns me on.

"Are you taking me on this date or what?" I roll my eyes, accepting whatever fate I'm in for as I hop up onto the bench of the golf cart.

"Yes, ma'am." Caden seats himself beside me, resting one hand on the steering wheel, the other on my bare thigh.

We cross the main road and wind through the guest lodges, pulling up at the fence line where Caden jumps out and unties a wooden gate. I've never been this far down the riverside, but I think I can confidently say that there are no restaurants around here.

"I'm starting to suspect that you might be leading me to my death," I huff. "Care to tell me where we're going?"

"A wise soul once told me that patience is a virtue," Caden replies. "You'll see."

I've got no choice but to be patient, given that we're making our way to the date on a vehicle with what I presume is a max speed of 10km per hour – and even that feels generous.

"I am being p—" The words stop dead on my tongue as we finally make it through the dense thicket to a small clearing right on the riverbank.

The trees form a crescent moon backdrop to the open space, warm fairy lights hanging in soft loops between them. There's a picnic table covered with a plaid rug, the benches adorned with plush cushions and thick faux fur blankets. Caden carries an insulated picnic basket to the table, setting out stemmed glasses, dinnerware, and a single taper candle secured in a rustic wine bottle.

"How did you…" My sentence falls off as I catch Parker walking towards us, a campfire burning behind him. There are two Adirondack chairs facing out toward the river, the mirror image of Mount Braid reflected on the still water.

"I can't take all the credit." He drops a couple of notes in Parker's hand, pulling him into a hug before throwing him the golf cart keys. "I paid Parker a small sum to help me out and keep watch on the fire while I was gone. Chef Raph took a bit more convincing, but the Bison Lasagne is all thanks to him. I was merely the project manager for this date."

"Lasagne?" My jaw drops, belly rumbling. "That's my favourite."

"You think I don't pay attention?" He snakes his arms around my back, peppering kisses along the nape of my neck. "I've been taking notes for longer than I care to admit."

"Caden, this is too much. You didn't have to do all of this, I'd have been happy with a burger in town."

"No, Millie. It's not too much, it's not even close to enough." His next inhale is deep, breathing me in. "You deserve the whole damn world."

I gulp, struggling to believe that someone would do something this thoughtful for me. I've gone through life without even a dusting of romance in my encounters with men. Being treated like this feels foreign.

"Here's to our first date, Millie." Caden pours me a glass of red before raising his own glass in my direction. "To us."

"To us," I repeat, clinking his glass and taking a long swig as I turn over my shoulder to look out on the water. There's something vulnerable in this moment, a nervous excitement in my gut telling me that if I let myself fall, this could be it.

I want to fall.

To give in to whatever this is.

Us.

We float through conversation, time irrelevant as he takes me from laughing until I can't breathe, into deep conversations about what we want out of life, then back to pure flirtation as the dirtier corners of my mind take over.

"I love the way you see the world, Adams," Caden muses.

"Hmm?"

"Just hearing you talk, understanding the way you think about things, it makes me fall for you a little bit more every time." He starts clearing the table, packing up our dishes and leftovers. "You're beautiful, there's no doubt about that. And your body is incredible. But your mind? *Fuck*, that's what turns me on the most."

I hang on his every word.

We've barely touched the wine, but being around him is just as intoxicating. I feel different somehow, more free, like there's a version of myself that was reserved only for him, and I get to give into it now.

Rolling back my shoulders, I sit myself on top of the

picnic table, my legs hanging over the edge as I take in the ever-changing view. It's so quiet out here, save for the hushed sway of the pines as the wind moves through them, evening falling over the mountains.

"Isn't it beautiful?" I let out a calm sigh, contentment warming my cheeks.

"So fucking beautiful," Caden replies, closing the distance between us in deliberate strides. He cups my face in his palm, tilting my chin up towards him as his eyes bore into mine, wild with their own storm. "You have no idea."

CHAPTER 46

Caden

I slide my knee in between hers, spreading her legs as I pull her towards the edge of the table. The soft skin of her thighs glistens under the moonlight, sending fire coursing through me.

She's patient, waiting for me to take the lead, but her eyes tell a different story.

"Do you want this, Millie?" I wait for her answer.

She bites at her thumb nail. The apples of her cheeks flush pink as she nods, pulling my hips forward with her ankles until they're perfectly aligned.

I'm confident that's a yes, but I need to hear it.

"Say it." I tap her swollen lips. "Use your words."

"I want this." She swallows, there's no hesitation, but her words are too quiet for my liking.

"Louder."

"I want this!" she cries out, rocking against me in frustration.

I laugh, running my thumb along her jawline before folding a strand of hair behind her ear.

"No need to shout, darling."

She rolls her eyes, falling back on her elbows with a wanting moan.

"Rolling your eyes like that already?" I let my hands roam her body. "I've barely even got started on my list of the things I want to do to you."

She sucks in her bottom lip, her pupils dilating as she hears the words. "I'd appreciate it if you stop talking and start doing, Caden."

"So demanding." I remove her cowboy boots one by one, placing a light kiss on each ankle. "Maybe I want to take my time with you."

I strain against my jeans as I make good on my promise to take it slow.

I want to give every inch of her body the attention it deserves.

With each savoured kiss, I move closer to her core, knowing I'll be able to taste how ready she is for me by the time I make it to her panties. My cock throbs as I push her skirt above her waist, exposing a thin line of black lace barely covering her slit. I push the material to the side, eager to feel her melt beneath my touch.

"You're so wet for me, Millie." I bring my soaked fingers up to her lips. "Open."

She doesn't hesitate, letting out a soft moan as she sucks the taste of herself off my fingers.

Fuck.

I steady myself with one hand against the bench as I

return my mouth to her thong, running my tongue along the scalloped lace hem.

Moving over her curves, kissing and sucking every inch of her, I feel my own need rising. It takes everything in me not to lose control.

"Off," I demand, sitting her up to help her remove her dress.

Seeing her exposed like this – just two strips of lace and the necklace I bought her for her birthday left on her body – threatens to send me over the edge before we've even got started.

I dig into my jean pocket, pulling out a velvet box and popping it open. Millie shivers as I loosen the silver links of her necklace, feeding a second charm over the cool chain.

"What's this?" she asks, squinting to look at the tiny 'C.'

"A gift." I throb as I take her in, my initial hanging around her neck. "To mark our first date."

"Or to mark your territory?" She laughs, but there's a new rasp to her voice – like knowing she belongs to me turns on something primal within her.

I can't help thinking about all of the other ways I want to mark her as mine.

Over, and over, and over again.

"You know," she rubs her thumb over the pendant, "there's lots of names that begin with the letter 'C.' I could belong to anyone."

Not a fucking chance.

I spank her core.

She lets out a squeal, but it's coated in desire, confirming that that was anything but a punishment to her.

Her eyes are hooded and filled with need as I yank at my

belt with one hand, freeing my cock from the tight hold of my jeans.

I return to her body, mapping every freckle, line, and scar with my tongue, falling in love with each one as I do.

Running two fingers along the underside of her bra straps, I let each one drop from its shoulder, before releasing the back clasp with one hand.

However good she looked in the lace, she looks infinitely better without it.

I'm desperate for her.

My restrained kisses become more frantic, moving up her arm, across her collar bone, and over the prickled skin at her neck.

Millie grabs a fist full of my shirt, pulling me closer as her shaking hands unfasten each button.

"Caden," she moans, tension thick in her voice as a new side of her comes out, asking for what she wants. "Are you going to fuck me, or what?"

"Good things come to those who wait, Princess." I return my mouth to her body, hoping to tease her a little more, but she pushes me off, getting to her feet in front of me.

"I'm done waiting."

CHAPTER 47
Millie

Caden's jeans fall to the ground as I push his boxers down, letting his cock spring free.

Fuck.

It's bigger than I thought.

But I want it.

I want *him*.

I wrap my fist around the base as I sink to my knees, paying no mind to the dirt or branches below.

A glistening bead of arousal rests on his tip. I take a single teasing lick, relishing in the taste of him as torture paints his features.

"Can I?" I ask, looking up at him from my knees, his thick head resting on my bottom lip.

"Yes," he grunts. "*Fuck*, yes. You never have to ask."

I flatten my tongue against his shaft, letting it roll around him. Moving my head back and forth, I moan, taking more of him with each stroke.

Our eyes lock as I pull back and spit on his cock, letting

it run down his length. My cheeks hollow out as I continue to suck, both hands moving over his shaft in perfect rhythm with my mouth.

"Deeper," he groans, stroking his hand through my hair, holding it away from my face. "Give me more, Millie."

I do as I'm told, placing my hands on either side of his thighs as I pull his hips forward, leaving him to take the lead.

My core tightens as he hits the back of my throat, the pressure building in me as I let his tentative thrusts become more fevered, leaving me gasping for air in the best way.

"*Fuck.*" He pauses, pulling out of me as he holds my mouth open with his thumb. "Good. Fucking. Girl."

His eyes fall shut, teeth gritting back and forth as he holds me still.

"You still want to take it slow?" I tease, sensing he's seconds from boiling over.

"Absolutely fucking not! Get up here."

I'm no sooner on my feet than I am off them again, my body falling back against the picnic table as Caden tears the remaining lace off my body.

He pulls my thigh up to his hip, lining his thick head up with my slit as he drags himself through my wetness.

I gasp, sharp heat prickling at my walls as he slides the tip in, stretching me open. I'm ready for him but it still hurts. Regardless, I can't help but want so much more.

"Deep breaths, pretty girl." His thumb finds my cheek, rubbing against it with a tenderness that reminds me just why I want to give everything to this man. "Just like that."

I nod, hanging on his every word.

Each thrust brings a mixture of pain and pleasure with it, adding to my mounting ache for release.

"You're taking me so well." He leans forward, pulling me into a fiery kiss, his tongue commanding mine, reminding me that he's in charge. "Just like I knew you would. You were made for me."

He's attentive, taking it slow, letting my body adjust to the size of him, until he's fully seated in me.

"Fuck," I cry out. "You feel so good."

I want all of him, but he's still holding back.

I push up to my elbows, cocking my head as I watch him move in and out of me with careful, restrained thrusts. I don't want him to treat me like I was built to break.

I want him to let go.

I want the dark, depraved, hungry version of him.

I want it all.

"Don't be gentle with me, Caden." I shift my hips towards his, angling them up slightly, forcing him deeper. "I want you to fuck me like I belong to you."

His jaw tightens, pupils dilating until his irises are inked in black.

He steps back, pulling out as he scoops his hand under my hips and flips me onto my stomach. I feel his cock resting against my ass cheeks. His fist wraps around my hair, tugging me up towards him, his mouth close against my ear.

"You are mine, Millie. You've been mine since the first day I laid eyes on you." His breathing is laboured. "But I need you to be ready, I need to hear it from you. Tell me you're mine and I'll show you just how good it feels to belong to me."

"I'm yours," I reply without hesitation, trusting him now with my body, but knowing it goes way deeper than that. I'm ready to give myself to him in every way, in every corner of my life.

I want to be his.

Without question.

"Good," he replies, leaving a tender kiss on my temple before he drives into me in rough, desperate movements, giving me exactly what I asked for.

His cock fills me completely.

I am at his mercy, pinned beneath him as he thrusts deeper with each stilted breath, but I've never felt more safe in my life.

His free hand grips my hip, fingers digging into my skin as he pauses, holding me in place.

"I'm close, Millie." His voice is a mere rasp. "I want you to come for me."

"Then make me," I reply, knowing that I'm closer than I've ever been, but not sure if my mind will let me fall over the edge.

He reaches his hand round my hips, rubbing my clit with steady, even pressure.

"Tell me what you need."

"I... I don't know." Embarrassment threatens to kill the moment we've created. "I've never... finished."

Caden steps back, pulling my body up until I'm standing, my skin flush against his. His hard cock is warm against the small of my back, calloused hands roaming my curves as his teeth nip at my shoulder.

"Are you telling me you've never had an orgasm, Adams?"

I nod, grateful that I'm facing away from him so he can't see the shame spreading over my face.

"Fuck, how lucky am I?" He turns me towards him, lifting my ass up to rest on the edge of the table. "Getting to explore your body, taking my time to find out what you like." His hot lips brush my forehead. "Now, lie back for me."

He doesn't give my embarrassment an ounce of air time, refusing to let me beat myself up over my stubborn body. That kindness sends a jolt of heat through me, reminding me how turned on I am simply by the man that he is.

Lifting my legs, he spins my body so I'm stretched out over the width of the table, my head hanging back over the edge.

I feel his fingers first, moving in and out of me with slow, intentional pressure, curling against my walls.

"That's it, Princess." He rests his free hand on my lower abdomen, pressing down slightly. "Close your eyes, try to relax if you can."

He lets his mouth follow, pecking softly against my clit before adding his tongue, licking and sucking, coaxing sensation to my core.

"You taste so fucking good, Millie."

Blood rushes to my head, as a black haze starts to move through my mind, taking the place of my thoughts one by one, begging me to let myself go.

A knot forms in my core, tightening with each stroke of Caden's tongue, tighter and tighter until my legs are trembling, my walls clamping down on his fingers.

"You're so close." Caden's voice is brazen. "You feel that? You're gonna come for me, aren't you?"

He drops his head again, feasting on me until I'm feeling everything, all at once. I'm teetering on the edge, seconds from falling in, when he pulls back, drawing his fingers out of me.

I instantly feel the void.

"Please, Caden," I cry, desperate to feel release. "I need this."

"I'm sorry ," he replies, notching his head at my entrance. "I'm being selfish, but I've got to feel this too."

He pushes his length into me, one hand pulling my hips up towards him, the other rolling my clit between his thumb and forefinger.

His thrusts are deliberate at first, and then rabid, as I fall deeper and deeper into my own building pleasure.

His mouth finds mine, biting at my puckered skin.

"Come for me, Millie." He drives into me, hard and deep. "I want to feel you throbbing on my cock."

An involuntary moan tears through the quiet of the night, Caden's name on my lips as I clench tightly, only to fall apart completely, ripples of pleasure moving through me.

He stalls, holding my hips in place as his body jerks in mine.

"Holy fuck," I laugh, all other words wiped from my vocabulary as my body starts to come down from its high.

Caden slumps down next to me – our breathing ragged, both of us bare, satiated and spent under the star dappled night sky.

"You okay?" he asks, moving a wet wipe over my skin as he cleans up the evidence of his release. "Things got a little rough there."

"I'm the furthest thing from *okay*. I think I might have entered another dimension for a minute there... I can't believe I've gone this long without becoming acquainted with the wizardry of your cock."

He lies back against the table, pulling a blanket up to cover us and placing a cushion under my head.

"That good, huh?" He laughs, slotting his body in behind mine and looping an arm over my stomach. "I was prepared to go all night to get it right for you, but it seems I nailed it right off the bat."

"Oh, well..." His gentle kisses along my neck send a new wave of need through me. "I certainly wouldn't be opposed to another round, just to make sure the first wasn't a fluke."

"I don't do flukes, Adams." He drags his fingers through my hair, massaging my scalp. "But rest assured, if you need me to prove that to you, I will. I'll do it again, and again, and again. Until you realize that I look after what's mine, I won't fuck around when it comes to giving you what you deserve, and that includes making sure you come, every time. Got it?"

"Got it," I gulp, pushing his hand down my body towards the apex of my thighs.

Greedy.

Hungry for more.

CHAPTER 48

Caden

We've been lying here, wrapped up in each other's bodies, for hours. Millie quickly fell into a deep sleep after I made good on my word, but I couldn't tear my eyes away from her for long enough to close them.

Watching the gentle rise and fall of her faint breaths as she rests in my arms, her perfectly freckled cheek on my chest, feels like a heaven all of my own.

I've been so absorbed in her, remiss to take myself away for a single moment, that I almost missed the pinks and greens reflected on the meandering river beyond us.

Disoriented, I gently move her body a fraction, propping myself up on my elbow as I follow the path of the neon hues.

The sky is dancing with colour, fluid lines moving romantically across the darkness in animated paint strokes. The two tones weave in and out of each other, merging together until they are almost one.

Two distinctly different colours, coming back to each other again and again, like they were always meant to be, inseparable once they meet.

"Millie," my voice is a whisper, careful not to scare the Aurora away. "Millie, wake up."

"Mmmm." She opens one eye, letting out a sleepy moan as she does.

"Look up." I nod towards the water, pulling her body up to rest against mine.

She groans, nuzzling into my chest and pinching her eyes closed again.

"Millie." I steal another kiss, certain that I'll never get enough in this lifetime. "Bucket list number seven, see the Northern Lights." I've memorized that list top to bottom, adding in some of my own that I hope she'll be onboard with.

"*What*!?" She gasps, jumping down from our makeshift picnic-table-come-bed, pulling the blanket off me as she goes. "You're joking!"

"Thanks for that," I laugh, pulling my boxers back on and wrapping my flannel around my shoulders to replace the warmth she's taken with her.

She runs towards the water's edge, wrapped up in the blanket like it's a robe. I hold myself back, letting her take in this moment – experiencing it for the first time in her own way.

She always looks beautiful, but in this light, she is spell-binding. I could watch her for hours, not just because of how she looks, but because of everything she is beneath the surface, and the way that it can't help but shine through.

I've never been one for art, but now I understand the galleries filled with paintings of lovers. If I could capture this moment right now, it'd be a masterpiece, a permanent imprint reminding me that life could never be better than it is with her.

The campfire has burned down to embers. I work on bringing it back to a steady burn, throwing fresh logs into the centre of the ring, stoking the flames until they're ready to take care of themselves.

Millie holds her hands out over the heat.

"It's beautiful." She sighs, moving closer to me and resting her head against my arm. "That's been the highlight of my night."

"What?" I fake balk. "Better than dinner? And the shift I put in after?!"

"Way better," she laughs. "You'll need to up your game for next time."

"Listen, I ordered in the Northern Lights especially for you – it was all part of my master plan to woo you."

"Consider me suitably wooed, Mr Thompson."

I pull forward a chair, angling it out towards the river, the roar of the fire close enough to keep us warm.

Leaning back against the cool wooden slats, I pat my knee, signaling for Millie to come sit. She settles against me, her skin on my skin, head in the crook of my neck.

We fit so perfectly, her body and my body, her heart and my heart. I spent a lifetime thinking fate was just a romanticised version of coincidence, I didn't believe that things were ever truly meant to be, or that they happened for a reason.

But Millie *is* my reason, and she *was* meant for me. Our

paths would always have crossed, every road would have brought us back to each other. Because our souls were made for each other, long before this lifetime. And I think they've been waiting patiently ever since, for a moment just like this.

CHAPTER 49
Millie

Between the banging, barking, and clanging outside my bedroom window this morning, and Elodie's deep, quaking snores inside, any hopes I had of a long lie quickly evaporated not long after 7 a.m. Maura's been on some sort of mission ever since, much like the day of the Barnhoff wedding, and we've all been slapped with a job to help ensure things run smoothly.

It's the annual Braggan Valley Community Fundraiser, and this year, Braggan Valley Lodge is in charge of the event. Each fall, the town gets together to part with some cash for good causes and enjoy the last of the sun before winter sets in. Maura's got her sights set on this being the fundraiser to beat all fundraisers, but I've seen the pictures from last year's Fire Station car wash, and I think it might be a hard act to follow.

The open space between the lodge and the staff house has been transformed, with a small stage set up by the creek, several trestle tables lined with homemade salads, pastas, and appetizers, and three industrial BBQs manned by Chef Raph and his culinary team. The lawn is strewn with mismatched tables, chairs, and picnic benches for the guests and drinks are aplenty, with an old bathtub filled to the brim with ice and a mixture of local beers and soda's from Braggan Brews.

For the kids, an entire section of grass has been cordoned off with celebratory bunting – inside, there's a life-size chess board, a timber climbing frame and what seems like hundreds of multi-coloured space hoppers. It's magical, but most of the children seem to be more interested in the *Soak The Teacher* stand, where poor Principal Bates has just taken yet another sponge to the face.

We've been lucky with the weather, the sun beaming through the trees making it feel like the perfect summer's day even though the larches are already well on their way to their fall oranges and yellows. It's the final touch on an already perfect set-up. This could never have been a half-assed fundraiser with Maura at the helm, but it's even more filled with life than I'd imagined it would be.

I pluck a pamphlet from one of the empty tables, glancing over the entertainment order of the day, it's mostly smaller artists or bands, with the exception of the final act, Weston Hayes. He's an up-and-coming country artist from Calgary, no doubt used to bigger, and more equipped, venues than this one. Lord only knows what kind of strings Maura pulled to make that happen, but I'm sure it'll bring in the crowds to top up donations later in the evening.

"Miss Adams!" I hear the rattling of coins in the base of a bucket as Elodie takes long strides in my direction. "Care to donate to the cause today?"

I've already donated, but I know Elodie is on a mission

to beat her donation target before the first hour of the event is through, so I pull another ten-dollar note from my pocket and slide it through the slot in the top of the bucket.

"Thanks, babe," she beams, her green eyes glistening in the hazy sun. "Your donation will make a big difference to the library's Early Years Literacy Program."

Choosing Elodie to be the donation bucket bearer was another of Maura's smart ideas, I have no doubt she'll be able to get additional donations out of some of the most tight-fisted guests here today.

And she'll do it with a smile.

"I don't know how you look so full of life right now," I groan. "I heard you giggling at what I can only assume was 3 a.m."

"Listen..." She fakes a sigh. "I had every intention of going to bed at a reasonable hour, but just as I was about to close my book, Ronan and Elira finally made it to the village... after a five-hour trek through the forest... and there was only one bed at the inn. How do you expect a girl to stop reading at that point?"

"You're obsessed."

"Guilty as charged." She shrugs. "Anyhoo, gotta dash – this bucket won't fill itself."

She trots in the direction of the next table, animated and vibrating with energy as she encourages more guests to pull out their wallets.

I slide onto the nearest picnic bench, taking in everything going on, all of the mingling and laughter. I know everyone at the lodge, and a fair few locals from town, but there's still an overwhelming number of new faces. I need a minute to psych myself up before I throw myself into the introductions and small talk that come with still being relatively new around here.

"Maura, darling!" Stella's shrill voice comes from the make-shift parking lot as she throws open the passenger door of Frank's beaten-up truck and jumps to the ground.

"Stell!" Maura's voice is bright, almost childlike, as she jogs towards her. "You're here!"

I watch as the pair reconnect like they haven't seen each other in years, dancing around the lawn in each other's embrace with an infectious energy that screams girlhood.

Frank follows behind, his arms laden with bags, and two small humans hot on his heels – their grandchildren, Reuben and Daisie.

"Hi Cade!" Reuben squeals, noticing him before I do. It's the first time I've seen Caden all day, he's been busy setting up and making sure everything's done right. "Put me on your shoulders! Put me on your shoulders!"

Caden wastes no time swinging Reuben's body in the air like he's weightless, letting little legs fall around his shoulders as he runs the perimeter of the main house.

They disappear out of view, but I can still hear Reuben's hearty chuckles as they round the corner.

Daisie stays glued to Frank's side, pulling on his trouser leg to get his attention. He bends at the hip, pointing her in the direction of the kids' area, but she just shakes her head, clasping her arms tighter around his shin, as though she can't bear to be away from him.

"Daisie's turn!" Caden calls as he pulls Reuben off his shoulders with one arm & plonks him down on his feet. "Get up here."

She shakes her head again, her eyes fixed on the ground as she pulls Frank's hand over her face.

Caden doesn't push, just nods and slumps down on the ground a few feet from her. He sticks his fingers in his mouth, letting out a wolf whistle meant for Doug. On command, seventy pounds of thick black fur careers through the crowd, licking Caden's face excitedly on arrival.

"Look who's come to see you." Caden scratches Doug's belly as he rolls around like a puppy. "Daisie and Reuben came all the way from Calgary, just to give you a hug."

Caden keeps talking, directing his words at Doug, though they're really meant for Daisie. She peeps out from behind Frank's hand, slowly uncoiling herself as the corner of her lip tips up at the sight of Doug.

With careful, hesitant steps she pushes off from the safety of Frank's side. Her hands are clenched in front of her, body swaying from side to side, as she asks Caden a question without meeting his eyes.

Dropping to her knees, she lets Caden guide her tiny fingers as she moves them across Doug's coat in tentative strokes.

My heart melts.

Watching Caden be so *good* is healing something deep within me. He's gruff, and stand-offish, and blunt on the outside, but underneath all of that he's everything a man should be – kind, protective, caring beyond measure.

He's shown me that good men do exist, and he keeps proving it with his actions, not just his words.

To see him being unashamedly playful with Reuben and then taking his time with Daisie, has just made me fall for him that little bit more. Something that I didn't even know was possible.

I push up from my spot, making my way in his direction, lingering a little and hoping not to spoil the sweet moment he's absorbed in. He catches sight of me in the corner of his eye, before whispering something in Daisie's ear, and jumping to his feet.

Watching him jog towards me, I'm not sure where I played my cards right to bag a man this *hot*. But I'm counting my lucky stars that I've found him.

"My girl." He pulls me into him as his lips find mine, devouring me like they've been starved of me. "I've missed you today."

"I've missed you too." I blush, feeling eyes falling on us. "But you're going to need to stop kissing me like that in public, people are looking."

"And?" He laughs. "I'm in love with you, Millie. And I'm not afraid to let the world see that."

"Say that again," I say, my lips hovering over his. "I like how it sounds."

"I'm in love with you," he whispers, stealing another kiss as he does. "I'm—" another kiss, "—in love—" and another, "—with you."

I laugh into the crook of his neck, as he scatters kisses up and down mine, loving me out loud without an ounce of shame.

Maura was right, Braggan Valley does have a way of giving people exactly what they need.

And I needed a man like this.

I needed Caden Thompson.

CHAPTER 50
Caden

"Ewwww," Reuben's high-pitched voice breaks through the bubble I've found myself wrapped up in. "Cade just kissed Millie... on the *lips*!"

Daisie brings her hands up to his ear, whispering, "I think he's got a crush, Reubie."

Kids.

They're objectively cooler than adults, but still a pain in the fucking ass. It's a good thing I love those two so much.

Millie's cheeks are scarlett, but I don't have any regrets.

I meant what I said – I'll make it known how much I love her. Anywhere, anytime, and I don't care who's watching.

"Okay, you two love birds." Maura's bony finger taps my shoulder. "Enough traumatizing the children, there's plenty of work to go around."

"Yes, boss," I mock, reluctantly letting my arms slip from Millie's waist as I follow Maura to the salad table. "What can I do for you?"

I'm barely taking in her instructions, her words mere background noise as my mind wanders somewhere else entirely.

To my bed.

With significantly less clothing.

And the girl I miss the second we're apart.

"Caden!" Maura reprimands me, shoving an apron into my chest and throwing a pair of tongs down in front of me. "Get rid of those heart eyes and focus on the task at hand. The meat is almost ready, and I don't want the guests to have to serve themselves."

It appears I have very little interest in the task at hand.

The line up starts to trickle past the BBQ and towards my station. I dutifully hover over the fancy lettuce, heaping generous servings onto paper plates as I steal secret glances in Millie's direction.

"Ummm, daydreamer." A soft Scottish accent pulls me from my reverie. "Care to throw some salad on my plate?"

"Hey, Brenna." I smile. "Sorry, I was... *distracted*."

"We can tell," Evan butts in. "And I'm not surprised. How'd you manage to lock that one down?" He tilts his head towards the table where Millie's helping Elodie with raffles.

"Fucked if I know," I answer truthfully, rubbing my palm across my jaw. "Chance, or luck... or fate, maybe. All I do know is that I feel like the luckiest man alive."

They share a knowing look between themselves that I can't quite decode.

"What's that look for?" I ask.

"It's just... Josie told us you were down bad." Evan

laughs. "But this—" he gestures towards me extravagantly, looking me up and down, "—this is truly something else."

Maura bumps my hip, shunting me to the side, as she swaps out my salad bowl for a fresh one.

"All thanks to me," she gloats, slotting herself into the conversation with ease. "Did you know that when Millie arrived Caden wanted to send her packing?"

Brenna and Evan both shake their heads, jaws agape with horror as they lap up Maura's tale.

"Had the cheek to come sit at my kitchen table demanding I book her the next bus home... But I knew she was supposed to be here. I believe that everything happens for a reason. I had this feeling in my bones – a *good* feeling."

I can't help but feel like I'm going to be hearing this story on repeat for the rest of my life.

"And well—" she shrugs her shoulders, faking nonchalance, as if proving me wrong doesn't bring her infinite joy, "—looks like I was right."

"Yup," I agree, accepting defeat and giving her the win. "Looks like you were right."

And for once in my life, I'm not even remotely mad about it.

The sun has dipped behind the mountains, leaving behind candyfloss clouds dipped in orange and pink. The crowd seems to double, filling the empty spaces on the lawn with camping chairs and blankets as the band performs their final sound check.

As Weston Hayes takes to the stage to close out the evening, cheers, wolf whistles, and the odd *'Fuck Me Weston'* float through the air.

His songs are the perfect blend of rock and country, all raspy vocals and heavy drums, belting out stories of heartbreak, hot sex, and undeniable chemistry.

And, for whatever reason, whether it's the few beers I've thrown back throughout the day, or the love I have for the girl twirling around in front of me, I find myself dancing.

Two left feet, be damned.

Millie's arms fall around my neck, and I pull her into my chest, desperate to be closer.

"Millie?" I whisper her name, a distinct quiver to my voice.

"Mhmm?" My hands rest on her hips as they dip from side to side in effortless loops.

"I've got one more for your bucket list."

"Is it skydiving?" she asks. "Because I really think that's a step too far."

"No," I tut, raising an eyebrow.

"Some sort of unorthodox sex position you've seen on Reddit?"

"Still no." I laugh. "But I do like that idea."

She opens her mouth to speak, but I stop her, pressing my index finger down on her top lip, cherry flavoured lip balm coating my skin.

"Number fourteen," I say, steady breathing suddenly harder to come by. "Fall in love with me, Millie. It doesn't have to be right now, but when you're ready, whenever it feels right. Please... try to fall in love with me."

She stops swaying, pushing her hand against my chest to create some distance.

"Caden..." She pauses, looking at me like I've lost my damn mind. "I'm not adding falling in love with you to my bucket list."

I can't tell whether my heart is beating out of my chest or not at all.

"Why not?" I beg.

"Because I don't need to." She laughs, as if what she's about to say next is the most obvious thing in the world. "Because I've already fallen, dumbass. Deeply, completely, without question. I've fallen for you, Caden Thompson – so fucking hard."

It's not until I hear her say the words that I realize just how much I needed them.

"You have?"

"I have." She smiles, clasping her hands around my flannel as she pulls my body back towards hers. "I can't believe you even have to ask. You've seen all of my broken parts, the ugly ones, the unfinished, and you haven't forced me to put them back together, haven't asked me to be anything other than myself. I'm still healing from my past, and probably always will be, yet you've chosen to love me as I am. You walked right into the heart of my chaos, met me in the mess, and still decided to stay. How could I not be in love with you?"

I draw her mouth towards mine, desperate to taste her now that I know she loves me too.

"Not finished," she mumbles over my lips. "I came to

Braggan Valley looking for something, and I'm not sure I ever really knew what that was. A chance to start over, maybe. A place that my heart didn't need to run from. A little bit of peace. What I didn't expect to find was... well... you. But I did. And in our laughter and adventure, our shared quiet and untamed tears, I found my tiny something to live for. I found it here—" she breaks her sentence with the kiss I've been waiting for, pausing only to give me her final words, "—I found it with you."

Epilogue - Millie

One Year Later

I lean back in my chair, running my hand over my swollen belly, cursing myself for wearing jeans instead of leggings. I wonder if it would really be *that* unacceptable for me to undo my zipper right now.

Caden reaches over me, one hand kneading my shoulder while the other grabs a forkful of stuffing.

"You might want to reconsider your hand positioning." He laughs. "We don't want to give Stella any more fuel to add to her fire."

I choke.

He's right.

Stella has been bugging us about marriage and babies ever since we officially started dating last fall. You'd think laying the groundwork on our first home would've stopped her and Maura from plotting for a while, but no such luck.

They're adamant that we paint the cabin's spare bedroom yellow, 'just in case.'

But I like being Caden's girlfriend. One day I'll be his wife, and with any luck, the mother of his children. But for now, I like where we are, and I want to keep him to myself a little bit longer.

Doug is more than enough of a handful, and Caden still treats him like a baby.

"You're right," I say. "Let's not give her any ideas."

Hunching over the table, I push my forearm into my gut, hoping it'll help make some room for the homemade pumpkin pie Maddie and Stella have made for dessert.

"I'm so full I could die right now," I groan.

"I'd rather you didn't," Caden laughs, "but isn't that the whole point of Thanksgiving? Eat until you're eighty percent carbs and molded to your chair?"

"No, dipshit," I roll my eyes, "the point of Thanksgiving is to be *thankful.*"

He dives his hand back into the serving dish in the middle of the table.

"Well, I'm thankful for this stuffing." He kisses my cheek, the scent of sage thick on this breath. *Delightful.* "What are you grateful for this year, my girl?"

I look around the lodge dining room, at all of my favourite people together in one place. I take in everything that's changed since this time last year – the things I have now that I could never have imagined for myself, the love I've found that I didn't think was meant for me.

"This," I answer, gesturing around the room.

Holidays like these used to just be me, Mom & Maddie, but now we're surrounded by all of the friends I've made here in Braggan Valley, the people who've looked out for me no matter what I've needed, the family I've found.

There's laughter, there's joy, and there's five different kinds of potatoes. It's so simple, and yet it's everything I could ever have wanted.

"Me too..." He smiles, and it's a genuine smile, the kind we've been seeing more of lately, ever since he got back to doing something he loves.

As much as I'd rather his work didn't involve him putting his own life on the line, firefighting is who he is. It matters to him that he's making a difference, and I can't help but love that about him.

Plus, I'm not at all mad about the uniform either.

"*Noooooo!*" Elodie calls out, slamming her hands down on the coffee table and rising from her spot by the fire. "You can't win like that."

Parker leans back in his chair, trying to conceal the smirk rolling over his face.

"What have you done now, Dickweed?" Josie sighs, falling into the leather couch by his side, with a fresh glass of red filled to the brim.

"I won the game." He shrugs. "And Elodie's mad about it."

"He won with an 'S,'" she protests, "on the end of my word!"

Picking up the Scrabble board, she spins it around in her arms, imploring us all to take a look at what she deems to be Parker's greatest sin.

"That's ironic," Caden whispers in my ear with a chuckle. "You see that? He won with the very same word that plagues him."

I squint my eyes, scanning over the neatly organized wooden tiles.

F-R-I-E-N-D-S.

"Oh, Parker." I sigh, ruffling his curly brown hair as I perch myself on the arm of his chair. "You should've just let her win."

He crosses his arms across his chest, screwing up his face as if he's just realized that even when he's winning, he's still on the backfoot.

"Hey, Elodie," Josie cuts in, "you should play against Caden, he doesn't know how to spell."

"That's enough from you, Jo," Caden warns, his big brother voice coming out in full force. "Unless you want me to tell everyone about that time you shit yourself at Disney World."

"I'll tell them myself," she retorts. "You've got nothing on me."

I kiss Caden's cheek, leaving the two of them to squabble as I return to the dinner table and pull out a chair between Mom and Maddie. I need to soak up the time we have left together before they head back to Rowenbridge.

One of the hardest things about choosing to stay in Braggan Valley for good was knowing I'd get to see less of my two favourite people, that I'd have to save up all of my hugs for a couple of visits a year, and that I'd be swapping sofa chats for long phone calls across the miles. But somehow, whenever we're together, the time in between seems to slip away.

Mind you, I barely see Maddie when she's here. You'd think after spending so much time away from her big sister, she'd want to hang out a little, but instead she spends all of her free time at Stella's. She calls it work experience, Stella calls it free labour – but either way, I'm proud of her. Seeing her so passionate, listening to her explain different techniques, and watching her eyes light up as she fantasizes over owning her own bakery one day – it's everything and more.

"Mildo," she says, interrupting my thoughts and reminding me that even though she's growing up faster than I'd like, she's still young enough to find rhyming my name with dildo hilarious. "Is this your phone?"

"Not mine." I shake my head, taking in the black lace case and matching leather strap. "It must be Jo's."

"Well, she should answer it," she tuts, sliding it across the table in my direction. "Somebody won't stop calling, and I'm trying to have a conversation with Frank."

She's still got the teenage sass too, it seems.

The vibrations start again, sending the phone flying off the edge of the table. I bend to retrieve it, catching a glimpse of a man I'm sure I've met before as I turn the phone face up. His name moves across the screen in bold white letters as the call rings out.

"Uhhh." I turn over my shoulder towards Josie, immediately rethinking calling her name when I see Caden sprawled out next to her.

I might be three glasses of wine in, but I've still got enough sense to realize that there are some things better kept between the girls.

I flick the phone into silent mode – making a mental note to add a new discussion topic to next week's book club agenda... *Wyatt Holden.*

Acknowledgments

I have been writing this book for months, planning to publish for years, and dreaming of being an author for a lifetime. Along the way, I've stumbled across so many people who have shaped my life, encouraged my creativity, and stood firmly in my corner. I am so grateful for every moment that has led to Found With You being published, and the start of a beautiful new chapter in my life.

It's hard to know where to start with my acknowledgments, but there has been one person for sure who's been my number one cheerleader throughout everything. Mama, I owe you endless thanks for the unconditional love and support you have provided me. I am so grateful for how you've shown up for me throughout this writing process – the constant FaceTimes about cover design, reading my drafts, being my sounding board for new ideas, and just being *there* when this journey hasn't been easy. This book would not exist without your love, so thank you. I'll give you a small break before enlisting you as my PA for book 2.

Kirsty-Jo, the one I can trust wholeheartedly. My biggest fear was writing a lack-lustre dumpster fire, but I knew you'd be the one to tell me the truth. Knowing you have read & loved Found With You inspired me to keep going and get this book over the finish line. Thank you for walking through life alongside me, dragging me up when I'm down, and always being someone I can turn to. And thank you for convincing all of your friends to read my book, I should probably cut you a percentage.

My baby brother, Gregs. Thank-you for supporting me, even though you will never read my books (a decision I totally respect by the way, I am equally in favour of you never reading my smut.) I know I can always turn to you for advice, a fresh perspective, or a witty pick-me-up. Aside from championing my creativity, thanks for always making me laugh – I am so proud to have such a funny, kind, empathetic little bro. You're the best.

Granny, thank you for always believing in me and my writing. We're both big lovers of words, which is why it just felt *right* to use Harper as my pen-name. I hope you survived this unredacted version of my story, and that you enjoyed reading about Doug, whose character was definitely inspired by Grandad in parts.

Gemma, my best friend. You are my Elodie, the person who just gets it. I'll love you forever and a day, in every phase of this life. Thanks for putting down your true crime for a day to step into the land of romance.

Francesca, there is not one person who has made more of a material contribution to this novel than you! I am so glad that work brought us together. Thank you for beta-reading the shit out of my draft, giving me the best feedback, and always being my hype-girl. Life would suck without you.

Lyle, thanks for calling me an imbecile when I've needed it.

To my primary 7 teacher, Vanessa, and my head-teacher,

Jenny. Thank you for igniting a spark in me and making me believe that my writing was special. I wouldn't be where I am today without you both believing in a little blonde girl who liked to tell stories.

I'd love to list the names of everyone who has supported me, but truly there are too many to fit in one book – so to my family, friends, beta readers, arc readers and followers on Instagram and Tiktok, thank you for believing in Found With You before you had any reason to. Every shared post, edit, passing conversation, or question about my book has encouraged me to keep going. I never expected the love I have received and the way you have all believed in my little dream, but I am so grateful for it.

As a hopeless romantic, it doesn't feel right to finish my first ever acknowledgement section without a shout-out to my future husband. We haven't met yet, but thank you for choosing to love me when the time comes, and thank you for being hot as fuck.

Acacia & Kristina at Ever After Cover Design, thank you for making the prettiest cover and putting up with all of my demands and tiny edits.

Ramona, thanks for proof-reading Found With You and catching my silly mistakes.

And finally, thank YOU, the reader. It is my dream to have people reading my books, and I hope you'll stick around for book two.

Until next time,

Lynsey x

About the Author

Lynsey Harper is a Scottish romance author living in the heart of the Canadian Rockies. Her special interests? Grumpy men, foul-mouthed cowboys, and daddies with big... hearts. When she's not reading or writing, you'll find her in her hammock, on her paddleboard, or warming up with a hot choccy and a cinnamon bun.

Found With You is Lynsey's debut novel, and the first in what promises to be a tension-filled backlist written especially for the lover girls.

📷 instagram.com/authorlynseyharper

🎵 tiktok.com/@authorlynseyharper

100 Other Romance Authors

Supporting indie authors is very fucking cool. So, here's a list of 100 other romance authors you might like. Most are indie, or started out that way, and came highly recommended by my amazing readers. I'm so excited to get stuck into this list & to discover my next instant-buy author.

Happy reading!

A.C. Wonderland

A.R. Rose

Afton Seeser

Aj Wilding

Allison Speka

Alyssa-Ray Bouman

Ambar Cordova

Anastasia Wright

Anastasjia White

Ashtyn Kiana

Aurora Steinhart

Ava Hunter

Bailey Hannah

Blake Gallows

C.L. Close

C.N. Rudy

Carly Robyn

Cassandra Moll

Cassidy Hudspeth

Clarissa Mae

Cleo White

Clio Evans

E. Salvador

E.L. Stevens

Elena H. Covens

Elle Mariah

Elliana Rose

Elliott Rose

Ellory Douglas

Em Hardy

Emilia Rossi

Emily Blackwood

Emily Louise

Emma Lucy

Erin Cornia

Erin Graves

Erin Page

Fanny Lee Savage

Harlow James

Holly Renee

Ivy Dawes

J.K. Maclaren

Jada West

JC Hawke

Jen Morris

Jenn McMahon

Jenn Plummer

Jessica Ann

Jessica Peterson

Julia Jarrett

Julie Olivia

Kat Singleton

Katherine Elle

Kathryn Moore

Katya Summer

Kayla Grosse

Kaymie Wuerfel

Kelli Cooke

Kyra Parsi

L.A. Shaw

L.D. Pack

Landyn Hill

Layla Frost

Lily Miller

Lindsay Saenz

Liss Montoya

Lo Everett

Lora Nox

Lottie Moore

Luna Day

Lyla Andrews

Lyla Sage

M. Hartley

Madison Myers

Madison Myers

Maggie Gates

Marren Moore

Megan McSpadden

Melissa Dymond

Michelle Naomi Mosley

Morgan Elizabeth

Nicci Harris

Nylah Monroe

Paisley Hope

Paisley Nash

Penelope Black

Piper Rayne

Rachel Kaye

Riley Winters

Ronnie Matthews

Sarah Bailey

Shann McPherson

Sophie Snow

Stephanie Rose

T.R. Hill

Tierra Stockham

Tina Spencer

Vanessa Stock

Victoria Lum

Yinn Quiros

Printed in Dunstable, United Kingdom

63674463R00184